PROLOGUE

Her mother was smiling.

Chloe paused at the entrance to the ballroom. Her small fingers lifted to curl against the edge of the wooden doorframe as she watched her mother. Her parents liked to hold big parties on the weekends. They'd invite so many people over to the estate. Women who wore pretty dresses. Men in dark suits. They'd drink and they'd dance, and she'd hear their laughter and voices drifting to her bedroom.

The music would fill the air. Everything would seem...happy.

Her mother liked to dance. She'd been a dancer, a ballerina, back in her younger days. She often told Chloe about how wonderful she'd been. How she'd owned the stage when she'd danced upon it.

Chloe was supposed to dance, too. But she wasn't very good at it. When she tried, she tripped and fell.

No music played now. No one else was in the cavernous ballroom. Just her mother. Spinning round and round as she lifted up her hands. Each time she spun, Chloe could see the smile on her mother's face. She liked it when her mother smiled. She liked it when her mother was happy.

There were too many days when she wasn't happy. Not really. Her mother faked being happy. Why didn't anyone else seem to notice that?

Her mother started to hum. The spins slowed down as she turned to gliding back and forth, from her left foot to her right. Over and over.

That was when Chloe noticed something was on her mother's white dress.

A gasp slid from her lips. Her mother was hurt. That was blood on her shirt. Bright, red drops. Chloe let go of the doorframe and took a quick step forward.

Her mother lifted one hand and beckoned to her. "Come dance with me, Chloe."

She took another step. Not quick this time. But slow. Something was... "You're bleeding."

"Dance with me." Her hand stayed extended. Her mother's voice had turned harder.

Chloe looked at her mother's hand. She looked at her mother's broad smile. At her mother's gleaming eyes. "I—"

"*No.*" A hard hand clamped over Chloe's shoulder and spun her around.

Chloe sucked in a sharp breath and found herself staring up into her brother's eyes. "R-Reese?" His thin frame seemed to shake with tension, and his lips were pressed into a tight line.

"Don't dance with her, Chloe," he barked. "Do you hear me? *Don't dance with her*. I don't care what she tells you, don't you—"

Why was he so angry? What was wrong with dancing? She didn't want Reese angry with her.

Save Me from the Dark

A DEATH & MOONLIGHT MYSTERY

CYNTHIA EDEN

Her shoulders stooped, and her head lowered. "She's bleeding," Chloe whispered.

"It's not her blood."

Her head whipped up.

"It's not," he gritted out. "Go back to your room, Chloe. I'll deal with her."

But...

He pushed her away from the door. She looked back and saw him straighten his spine. His hands were clenched at his sides as he marched into the ballroom. "Mother..." His voice was low, but Chloe could still hear him. She could hear him because she wasn't going back to her room. She was staying there to find out who was bleeding. If someone was hurt...

"Mother, what have you done?" Reese demanded.

CHAPTER ONE

Blood covered the dancer's body.

Chloe Hastings stared at the ballerina, and for one dark moment, past and present merged for her. She could hear her mother humming. Could see her spinning round and round...

Mother, what have you done?

"Uh, Chloe?" Detective Cedric Coleman cleared his throat and squinted at her. "Are you with me?"

She blinked. Once. Twice. Her head cocked as she stared at the body. "Of course, I'm with you." Where else would she be? "I'm right beside you." Surely the man saw her. Normally, he was highly observant.

"Yeah, but, you..." His throat cleared again.

Was he having an allergy attack? Getting choked on something?

"You have been staring at the body for about five minutes now, and you haven't said a word."

Five minutes? Her gaze slid off the body. Darted to Cedric. Then she glanced toward her partner, Dr. Joel Landry.

Joel shrugged his broad shoulders. "I wasn't watching the clock." His handsome face was expressionless, but his dark eyes gleamed with curiosity.

She didn't usually go so quiet at a crime scene. It wasn't as if death was something new to her. No, she and death were well acquainted. A very long and turbulent history. The more violent the crime, the more at home she normally felt, but this time...

Something is different. The problem was that Chloe didn't quite know what was different. Not yet. Her gaze trekked away from Joel. She didn't look back at the victim. Instead, her attention shifted to the wall of mirrors that waited just a few feet away. Her own reflection stared back at her. Joel edged closer, a tall, muscled form that came in protectively. He knew something was wrong. He just wasn't going to push her in front of the cops who were at the scene.

A crime scene tech eased around them and snapped a few photos of the victim.

"Why the hell do her feet look that way?" The question came from one of the young, uniformed cops who was waiting nearby.

Chloe knew him. Tommy Avarett. He'd found the body. Someone had called in a tip about a break-in at the dance studio, and Tommy had come to investigate. Instead of a break-in, he'd found a body.

"Did the bastard smash her toes? Look at all of those bruises. There is no way she could walk on them—" Tommy began.

"That's what a dancer's feet generally look like." Chloe's voice was quiet. Considering. "Usually, the toes are wrapped up. Especially for the dancers who are doing pointe technique. The toes have to support the weight of a dancer's entire body." She wasn't bothered at all by the bruising or the condition of the ballerina's toes. No, she was wondering... "Did anyone retrieve her shoes from the scene?"

"No," Cedric replied. "We got her bag, but no ballet shoes were inside."

"Then the killer took them. She wouldn't be here without her shoes." She'd been dressed to dance, and she would have brought her shoes.

Lucia Rossi. Cedric had given her brief stats on the victim when Chloe arrived. The vic was twenty-two. An up-and-coming dancer who'd been discovered dead in the building. No signs of forced entry. No witnesses.

Lucia had been beautiful in life. Her dark hair was in a loose bun, and faint tendrils had escaped to tease her oval face. She had a slight, delicate build. Her long, thick lashes were still against her cheeks, and even in death, a faint hue of color still stained her cheeks and lips.

Joel knelt but made sure not to touch the body. "The slice in her throat starts on the left and goes to the right. You can tell based on the depth of the wound. The spray pattern of the blood indicates that she was standing and probably staring at her own reflection when it happened."

Joel knew his wounds. He was a former surgeon, after all. But in addition to his skills with a scalpel, he'd gotten plenty of his own up-close and intense experience with slices on the human body.

A low whistle came from the young cop. "The perp made her watch him kill her?" Tommy asked. He winced. "That is cold."

Chloe stared at the mirror. At the blood that had dripped down the glass. Joel was correct. Lucia had been facing the glass when the assailant sliced her throat. *From ear to ear.* The blood spatter had flown forward and hit the mirror before it dripped down in those long, red streaks. "I've seen enough." A brisk nod. "Let's go outside." Without another word, she turned on her heel and marched for the door.

The scent of blood was bothering her. Too strong. The ballerina's body needed to be moved. Covered up.

Come dance with me, Chloe.

Her steps were fast as she hurried for the exit. A cop beat her to the door and shoved it open. Chloe yanked off her gloves—and the little booties that had been over her shoes—and tossed them aside. She sucked in several deep gulps of air and—

"Are you going to tell me what the hell is happening or am I supposed to guess?" Joel's voice was mild.

Slowly, her head turned toward him. She'd been aware of him following behind her, even though he hadn't made a sound. That was one of Joel's skills. He could move ever so quietly when he wanted. But as to what was happening... "Cedric had a crime scene he wanted us to see." That had been apparent. Why was Joel—

He shook his head. Stalked toward her. "No, sweetheart." He'd ditched his gloves and the shoe booties, too. His hands curled around her shoulders as he brought her closer to him. "I'm talking about what is happening with you. I swear, Chloe, if I didn't know better, I'd think you'd just seen a ghost."

Ghosts aren't real. Or, if they were, she'd certainly never encountered one. But then again, you didn't always have to see something in order to believe in it. She'd learned that truth long ago.

"You can trust me," he murmured. "Chloe, let me in."

She was *trying*. Didn't he get that? She stared into his eyes and saw the flecks of gold buried in the darkness of his gaze. *Joel.* He'd agreed to start working as her partner. Her job wasn't typical. Far from it. Chloe spent her days and nights tracking killers, and she'd decided that she wanted someone around to watch her back.

Enter Joel Landry.

He wasn't just physically strong, though, of course, that was certainly a lovely bonus. He had a very unusual skill set that she quite admired. Because he was a former surgeon, he was intimately familiar with the human body. He had a vast knowledge of medicine and health care, and, in a pinch, the man was absolutely great at patching up a knife wound or a bullet hole.

He also was well trained in a variety of marital arts. He could, quite honestly, kill a man in a hundred different ways. He was skilled with knives. Guns. He was a perfect predator.

Mostly because...he'd once been a victim. And he was determined to never be one again.

Her stare swept slowly over his rugged features and lingered just for a moment on the faint scar that cut across his upper lip. There were more scars on Joel. On his neck. His arms. His chest. He didn't talk about them. As a rule, he didn't talk about the nightmare attack he'd survived. Joel liked to keep his secrets close. She could understand that. She did the same thing.

"Talk to me," Joel urged her. His voice deepened, turning into that rough growl that Chloe had discovered—much to her surprise—caused a dark, primitive response within her.

Her lips parted.

"Chloe!" And Cedric was there. Rushing from the building and adjusting his blue tie as he hurried toward her. Wind blew against his body and sent his coat billowing back to reveal the holster strapped beneath his left arm.

She found herself stiffening as he approached her. "Why am I here, Cedric?"

"Uh, because you usually love jumping into a killer's head?" His answer was immediate.

He wasn't wrong. Usually, she did quite enjoy that endeavor. "You can handle this case. I know you saw everything that I did." Cedric was the best homicide detective on the NOPD force. If he wasn't the best, he wouldn't have been one of her closest friends.

He straightened his coat. "You were requested. If you must know."

Joel finally let her go, but he didn't move far away. He stayed at her side, and his broad shoulder brushed against her. Protective. That was Joel. But, then, he *had* been hired to be her muscle. And for other reasons...

At the beginning of their partnership, she'd been the profiler, the brains who got into the heads of killers. He'd been the brawn. The man there to kick ass if things got out of hand.

Though, truth be told, Chloe was pretty good at kicking ass. *I'd just needed Joel close. I'd needed the chance to get to know him better.*

She had gotten to know him better. Intimately so.

"Who made the request?" Joel asked.

Cedric glanced over his shoulder, then back at them. "You know you make the papers a lot, Chloe."

Not like she tried to be in the Press. In fact, she worked hard to avoid any interaction with reporters. They often misconstrued statements, and, in her experience, they were too hungry for blood. Much like many of the killers she tracked.

"Lucia's stepdad is Glenn Towers," Cedric revealed with a wiggle of his dark brows. "As in Towers Casino. He has money to burn, and he's a frequent contributor to our dear mayor's political fund. Before I could even get my ass in the car to come to the scene, I was being told that you *would* be a consult on this. The mayor wants the case closed yesterday."

So Cedric was already getting political pressure and the body was barely cold. "The mayor should trust you to do the job." In fact, as far as Chloe was concerned... "You should be in charge of the entire police force."

"Thanks." He flashed her a grin. "Working on that."

She knew he was. She also knew that a faint headache was pounding behind her eyes. "Lucia was acquainted with her attacker."

Cedric inclined his head.

"But that was obvious to us all." She knew that was why he'd inclined his head. "There were no signs of a struggle. No marks at all her arms or hands. She didn't fight. Because of the mirrors, there would have been no way for her *not* to see him closing in on her." She considered the scene in her mind. The way it must have unfolded. "They were close. Friends or lovers. Probably lovers."

"Why probably?" Joel asked.

He was still new to profiling so she explained, "Because she had on lipstick. Blush. Mascara." The color hue that had survived past Lucia's death had been due to the careful application of cosmetics. "If you're coming to the studio to sweat for hours while you perfect your dance routine, you won't really care about how you look...unless someone else is going to be there. Someone you want to look good for." The killer. "He was right behind her. They were staring at each other in the mirror." She could see it so clearly. Chloe found herself moving. Going behind Joel. "He's bigger than me, so it's not quite the same but..." She put her left hand around Joel, curling it around his chest. "One arm would be here... and the other would have come up with the knife..." She lifted her right hand and put her fingers to Joel's throat. She pulled her hand across his throat to mimic the movement of the knife. "Before Lucia even realized what was happening, her lover had killed her. She probably saw the blood even as she felt the pain." By then, it had been too late.

Her hand lingered on Joel's throat. She'd risen onto her tip toes behind him, but he was still so big that she had trouble reaching—

"Did you just kill me?" Joel asked softly.

She stiffened. Pulled back her hands. She hurried back to his side. "We're searching for a male assailant. Someone who plays a major role in Lucia's life. I'd look at the dance studio. See if a male instructor had a lot of contact with Lucia. Ask her friends to learn about her romantic involvements." This was all stuff that Cedric would know. "You truly don't need me. You have this." She turned away. Oddly eager, once more, to leave the scene—

"So you don't think we're looking at a serial?" Cedric's voice stopped her.

Her heart thudded into her chest. "A serial killer, by definition, has to kill more than one person. The FBI, in particular, likes to say that you must have three victims before you can start talking about a serial murderer." She looked over her shoulder. "Is there another body that I didn't see?"

"Not that I've found."

"Then you ask because...?" She knew he'd have a reason.

"The shoes were gone. Seems odd, right? And serials like to take trophies. You're the one who told me that. If you're going to kill a ballerina and you want something to remember her by, seems like the shoes are the thing you'd take."

She stared at him.

His brows pulled together. "What?"

"Maybe there was something about the shoes that could tie him to her. Perhaps they were a gift that he gave to her."

Cedric nodded and seemed relieved. "So it *wasn't* a trophy…"

"No, it very well could have been." She exhaled a low breath. "I just didn't want to say that because if this perp is a serial…" Her words trailed away.

Come dance with me, Chloe.

"Chloe?" Joel prompted.

She shook her head and focused on Cedric once more. "I was requested for this case."

He nodded. Kind of side-eyed her. "Uh, yeah. I mentioned that to you before. Chloe, are you feeling okay?"

She was perfectly fit physically. "I want to know who told the stepfather to contact me."

"Your name was in the paper. I'm sure that's—"

Chloe came to a decision. "I'm going to talk to the stepfather. Now."

Alarm flashed on Cedric's face. "The man is probably grieving! We both know you do not handle grieving family members well. You don't want to rush over there now. Work the case. There's a bonus in it for you if we close before—"

"I'm going to talk to the stepfather. Call me if you need me for anything else." Urgency rode her.

Chloe didn't like it when puzzle pieces didn't slide into place.

The pieces weren't sliding into place for her.

She hurried back to the SUV, but Joel beat her to the door. When she reached for the door handle, his fingers closed around hers. "Stop." He was behind her. Seemed to surround her.

Chloe whirled to face him. He was so close that he seemed to cage her. Dammit, he *was* caging her.

"Explain," Joel ordered. "Just take a breath and bring me up to speed."

"I want to interview the stepfather. I thought I had explained that."

His lips quirked as Joel slowly shook his head. "More is at play. With you, there always is. Tell me what I'm missing."

That was the thing. Chloe felt as if she was missing something, too. So how could she tell him what she didn't know? "It feels personal."

"Murder usually is personal. Especially if you're right and the perp was the vic's lover."

"No." She lifted her chin. "This feels personal...to me."

His eyes narrowed as he studied her. "I don't get it. You've literally had sick fucks sending you notes asking you to 'Come and get me' and that didn't seem too personal for you."

That had felt like a challenge. This was different. This was her past. Rising up to try and bite her in the ass. Or...

Slice her throat. From ear to ear.

"Take two minutes and explain to me," he urged, "just how the hell this is different."

They were on the edge of the street in the French Quarter. It was early evening, and a few cars ambled down the road. People were strolling along the sidewalk. The road glistened slickly from the afternoon rain that had rolled through the city.

"I'm not psychic," Joel rumbled. "Despite my best efforts, I can still not manage to read that mind of yours."

She didn't want him to read her mind. "It was staged."

"The scene? You didn't tell that to Cedric."

No, she hadn't. "The blood on the mirror...when I looked straight into the mirror, it was like I had blood on me." *Blood is on your hands*. That had been the message she received from her reflection.

"Chloe, that was a blood spatter pattern. You know that. You—"

"The building wasn't always a dance studio. At one point, a long time ago, it was a dress shop." She didn't look away from him. "Your mother used to work in that shop."

His broad shoulders stiffened. "Do I even want to know how you learned that?"

"When I was doing my research on you, I came across this place," Chloe whispered. Joel had lived in New Orleans a lifetime ago. His return to the Big Easy had been a fairly recent occurrence, as in...he'd come back when his world in Dallas had turned to ashes around him. He'd come back to New Orleans for a shot at a different life. "I remembered the address. I don't...it *could* be a coincidence."

"Fuck that." He reached around her and yanked open the SUV's door. "You said it was staged. Staged at a place that has a link to me. Staged and *you* were specifically called to the scene?"

Yes, all of those things were setting off red flags in her mind. She was glad that he could appreciate her unease.

"Hell, yeah." Joel gently pushed her into the passenger seat. "We're going to talk to the stepfather."

Hmm. Interesting. She hadn't even needed the full two minutes in order to convince him.

***

The stepfather didn't live far away. Chloe got his address from—well, hell Joel didn't honestly know how she'd gotten it. While he'd started the vehicle, she'd fired off a quick text to someone, and then started giving him driving directions. Her voice was calm and cool—quintessential Chloe with just the faintest hint of her British accent sliding beneath the words—but something was off with her. He should know. He was her lover. He knew her, inside and out, and when something rattled her, he was one of the few people who could see her small shakes.

But she wasn't telling him enough about what was happening and that fact pissed him off. He didn't want Chloe keeping secrets from him. He wanted to be all-fucking-in with her.

He braked in front of the stepfather's sprawling house. Also in the Quarter, it reeked of old money. For a moment, Joel considered the location, and his stomach twisted. Hell... "This isn't too far from your place."

"No." Her eyes were on the house that waited behind the iron gate. An *open* iron gate. "It isn't."

"Do you know the man, Chloe?" He knew *of* the guy. The man owned a chain of casinos in New Orleans, but Joel had never personally met Glenn Towers. Chloe had a way of knowing folks, though. Her friend—or maybe acquaintance list—was surprisingly large.

"We've never met." She was still looking out the window. "A Porsche is in the driveway, so it looks like someone is home." Her hand reached for the door.

He leaned across the seat and touched her cheek.

Her head whipped toward him.

Finally. He could see her actually focusing on him. When he'd been at the crime scene, Joel could have sworn that Chloe had gone a million miles away from him. Cedric had noticed her distance, too. "It's okay to talk about it."

"It?" Her delicate eyebrows rose.

"Yeah, you know, 'it'—the fact that you just left a dance studio that was soaked in blood and a poor twenty-two-year-old victim had her throat sliced wide open. It's okay to talk about it. To be upset about what happened." He knew Chloe didn't like the bloody scenes. They reminded her too much of her own past.

"I'm not upset."

Baby, maybe you should be.

"I really need to get inside that house, Joel."

"Fine. Just—shit, Chloe, his stepdaughter is dead. Let's try to use a light hand with the man, all right?" Cedric hadn't been wrong when he said that Chloe wasn't exactly the best with families.

Her eyes—the most incredible blue he'd ever seen—widened. "What are you talking about?"

"You have a tendency to..." He was stroking her cheek. A cheek that felt like absolute silk beneath his hand. "To be a little cold."

She stiffened. "You think I'm cold?"

Oh, fuck. Hello, disaster. "No! Hell, no." He pressed a quick, hard kiss to her slick, red lips. "Baby, you are hell hot in my hands." The woman could wreck a bed and leave him begging for more. "You think about death differently from other people, that's all." He was so screwing this up. "When you're dealing with families, you have to remember that they are grieving."

"Grieving." Her tongue swiped over her lower lip. "I'm not so sure that's what he's doing." She shoved open the door.

"Wait, dammit, Chloe—"

She was already out of the vehicle and leaving his ass. He double-timed it to catch up to her. Dammit to hell and back. Joel knew he'd hurt her feelings. He hadn't meant to say she was cold. Chloe was as far from cold as it was possible to be. She just...she didn't show her emotions. Other people didn't understand her like he did. When they'd first met, *he* hadn't even understood her.

They walked right through the open gate. Up the steps. He saw that the stepfather had one of those video doorbells installed. Chloe leaned forward to push the button in the middle of the doorbell, then she hesitated.

Joel realized he needed to ask her an important question. "If he's not grieving, just what is the man doing?"

"The door is open," Chloe whispered instead of answering him. "We need to go in." She pushed her hand against the door, and yes, it was open. Beneath her touch, it slid in a few more inches.

He grabbed her wrist. "What in the hell are you doing?" His voice was low, just for her ears. He knew she'd seen the video doorbell. The video option meant...*Smile, baby. We are on camera.* He brought his mouth close to her ear and said, voice barely above a breath of sound, "You can't just waltz into his house. You don't have an invitation." Or a warrant—*because they were not cops!*

"I don't think he's going to give me one."

That still didn't mean that she got to just—

Her head turned toward him. "Don't you smell the blood, Joel?"

Smell the—His eyes widened. No, he damn well didn't smell blood. Was this something she was just doing for the camera? Because he didn't think she smelled blood, either. The woman was incredible, but she didn't have freaking super senses.

"We have to get inside," Chloe added as her tone turned urgent. *"Now."*

Breaking and entering. Sure. That was his life now. Life with Chloe. Though the door was unlocked, so technically, he figured they were not breaking anything. Just doing the entering part of the equation.

Chloe shot through the door before he could try to convince her that this wasn't the best idea ever. Swearing, Joel surged after her. *"Chloe!"* She wasn't supposed to race into danger—or whatever she was racing into. They'd talked about this. He'd been hired originally as a bodyguard/partner, so she should freaking let him guard that gorgeous body of hers.

The house was eerily quiet. Still. And Chloe was hurrying down a narrow hallway like she knew exactly where she was going. As if she'd been in the house dozens of times and—

Joel stiffened. *Fuck me.* Now he smelled the blood, too. Maybe Chloe hadn't been lying about that. He grabbed her shoulder and hauled Chloe to a halt just before she'd been about to shove open yet another door. "Stop," he rasped. He pulled Chloe back against him.

"You smell it, too."

Yes, he did. Not like you could mistake that scent.

"He may need our help." She jerked against Joel's hold. "We can't just stand out here."

No, they couldn't. But it didn't mean she had to run into danger. "Stay here."

"What?"

Instead of replying, he pushed her behind him, and then Joel opened the door. *A study.* Home office. Whatever. There was a big, massive desk. Bookshelves that lined the walls. And a dead man on the floor. Blood covered him, probably because he'd been stabbed over and over again.

Fucking hell. One look, and Joel recognized Glenn Towers. He looked just like the photos that were often in the news. Except he was covered in blood and stiff as a board on the floor of his study.

Joel couldn't even count the number of stab wounds on the victim. There were deep punctures on this chest and stomach. Small, shallow wounds on his neck, his arms, even his face. There was one slice that went right across the man's lip…

Joel flinched. *Just like me…*

"Move back, Joel." Chloe's voice. Soft. Firm. Her hand curled around his arm.

He couldn't look away. He stared at the body. At the wounds. So many. Wounds that reminded him of his own attack. Only this poor bastard hadn't survived.

I did.

And in the middle of the blood that soaked the expensive rug beneath the victim, Joel saw a pair of ballerina slippers. Half-white, half-blood-stained red with long ties that dangled in the congealed pool of blood. There were streaks of red nearby on the floor, as if the bloody shoes had been dragged around the area. "Chloe," Joel breathed. "What the hell is going on?"

"He's been dead a while," she said. Her hand tugged on Joel. "Based on the lividity, I'd say he died before Lucia did."

His head turned toward her as a chill covered his skin. If Glenn Towers had been dead that long… "Then how the fuck did he request that you work on the case?"

She shook her head. "He didn't request me. A killer did."

CHAPTER TWO

"Does it bother you that killers want to fuck with you?" Joel's voice was low and rough. They were back at his place, and the tension pulsing inside of Joel made him feel as if he were about to explode.

But Chloe just sat—all calm and composed—on his couch. Not a hair was out of place. Her clothes weren't wrinkled. She looked as if she didn't have a care in the world.

"I supposed I'd be more bothered if they wanted to *fuck* me," she told him with a small roll of her shoulders, as if the matter was not that important.

Joel stopped his pacing to frown at her. Had she just made a joke? In her deadpan voice? When he was trying to keep his shit together? "Chloe..."

She rose. Strolled toward him. Stopped when they were a foot away. "Why don't we talk about why *you* are bothered?"

That was easy. "I'm bothered because some freak with a knife thinks he's going to play a game with the woman I love!" There. Hell, yes, he'd said it. Dropped the l-word and hadn't hesitated. He'd been damn well drowning until Chloe burst into his life with the force of a hurricane. He'd given up practicing medicine. He'd left his friends and his home back in Texas. The attack he'd survived had changed him, and Joel hadn't known what to do with the darkness inside of himself.

He'd been afraid the darkness would erupt. That he would be dangerous to the people around him.

Enter Chloe. She hadn't cared about his darkness. Some days, he thought the darkness might have been what attracted her to him in the first place.

"Death is never a game." Her head tilted back as she stared up at him. Her dark hair slid over her shoulders.

"To some psychos, it is. And you know it." Because she knew so much about killers. "Baby…" He tried to calm down, but it was hard. That scene with Glenn Towers had hit far too close for him. "I couldn't even count the number of the stab wounds on him."

"Normally, that many wounds would indicate that the attacker was experiencing a great deal of rage."

Normally. His hold tightened on her. "Not always. The bastard who carved me up was ice cold." He didn't like to go back to that time and place. Why should he? There was no need. Joel had taken care of the sonofabitch who'd attacked him. The freak who'd tortured him before finally burying Joel in the ground.

Chloe's gaze was tender as it held his. "Sometimes, scenes can be staged for deliberate effect."

"That's the second time you've used the word 'staged' to describe this shit today. First you did it at the dance studio, and now you're saying the scene with Towers was arranged, too?" Just to make sure he was following along.

"I think both were set, yes."

"Why?"

Her bright gaze slowly swept over his face. "I don't know yet."

He almost didn't believe her. Almost. But why on earth would Chloe lie to him? "I don't want you hurt." The words pulled from him. He knew this whole case was going to get worse before it got better. Day one, and there were two bodies. *Two*. His heart thudded hard and fast in his chest as his hands smoothed over her arms. "You matter too much to me."

"Then it's a good thing you're here to protect me, isn't it?"

Damn straight.

"And I'm here to protect you," she added, the words so soft that he almost didn't catch them.

He would do anything to protect her. The fact that some mystery killer was trying to fuck with her? It enraged him. A large part of Joel wanted to grab Chloe and run away. Take her someplace safe so that she could never be threatened.

But...that wasn't Chloe. Chloe didn't run and hide. She ran *to* danger. Not away. An issue he was trying to work out with her.

Her hand rose and pressed lightly to his cheek. "It reminded you of your past."

Of course, she'd noticed the similarities. Even someone who wasn't as hyperaware as Chloe would have made the connection. But he wasn't going to talk about his past. Not then. "Why were the shoes there, Chloe? Did the killer want Towers to know that he was going after his stepdaughter next? More torture for the guy before he died?"

Her eyelids flickered.

He caught the small movement. "Chloe..."

"I want to talk to Ruben first."

Ruben Minote. The medical examiner.

"I don't want to be wrong," she continued and her determined tone almost made him smile. No, Chloe didn't like to be wrong. Ever.

But he still had to push and say, "We're looking at the same killer for Glenn Towers and Lucia."

She gave a small, negative shake of her head.

"What?" No, she couldn't know that. Not yet. And the odds of those two people being attacked by two different perps...

"I need to visit with Ruben. See the bodies again." She exhaled on a long sigh as her hand dropped away from Joel's cheek. "But I can't get inside his lab until tomorrow morning."

His hands slid to her waist. Tightened. "Don't even think of cutting me out on this one. Where you go, I go. We're partners, remember?"

"How could I forget?" She smiled at him.

His gaze lingered on her mouth. Chloe had a beautiful mouth. Plump lips. Sensual. When he was with Chloe, the darkness around him didn't seem to matter as much. His head lowered toward her. "I don't want you fucking hurt."

"I won't fucking be," she said right back.

His mouth took hers. Joel tried to be gentle. With Chloe, he wanted his control to stay in place. Lately, he'd found himself worrying that he might do something to scare her. The more time he spent with her, the more he wanted her. He'd had nothing—no one—of his own for so long. A fear was growing within him. Things with Chloe were so good. Nothing good lasted, did it? What if something happened? What if someone took Chloe away?

Like the freak with the knife who'd carved up Glenn Towers...

"You're not doing it right," she chided.

His head jerked back. "What?"

"You're kissing me, but you're not thinking about me. That won't do." She pulled from his arms. Backed away. "I want all of you, Joel. I won't settle for less. You know that."

He swallowed. "Chloe..."

She kicked off her shoes. The small flats that she'd been wearing. Then she curled her hands under the hem of her loose, black top and pulled it over her head. She dropped the shirt on the floor.

His throat went dry. His eyes dropped to her body.

Her hands slid to her waist. A waist he'd held so many times. She unhooked the button on her pants and let the zipper slide down. The pants hit the floor with a soft rustle of sound.

Black panties and a black bra. That was all she wore as she stood before him. So beautiful that she made him ache. So perfect. But...

Delicate. Fragile.

I can't lose her. No one can hurt Chloe.

Lately, he'd started to have dreams. Nightmares that showed him—

"You're doing it again. Don't you want me, Joel?"

He wanted nothing—no one—more. "Hell, yes." He wanted to rip those panties away and sink into her as deeply as he could go.

"Then what are you waiting for? Come and take me."

Like he had to hear that twice. He hauled her into his arms and his mouth took hers with a rush of need. He didn't think about anything else as his tongue thrust past her lips, and he tasted her. Only Chloe. She moaned and arched into him, and his cock shoved hard against the front of his jeans. He wanted in her. Wanted her surrounding him. Wanted them both to get lost in the white-hot pleasure that they gave each other.

His hands curled around her hips, and he lifted her up against him. Chloe's legs wrapped around him and he began to walk toward the bedroom. He pulled his mouth away from her, but only so he could turn his head and watch where the hell he was going. When he lifted his head, Chloe began to press a trail of kisses along his neck. A hot path that made him growl.

She licked his skin. Nipped.

His cock was so hard he felt like he'd explode right then and there. When it came to distracting him, Chloe was a master. He wasn't thinking about the case. He could only focus on her.

He lowered her onto the bed and his hands immediately went to her panties. He hauled them down and Chloe kicked them away. For a moment, he stood by the bed, staring at her. She was so gorgeous to him. He wanted to touch and caress every single inch of her.

His hands pushed her thighs apart as he crawled onto the bed. His fingers slid into the hot haven of her sex. Stroked her clit. Enjoyed the way she arched eagerly up toward him and hissed out his name. But he wanted more than a hiss of his name from her.

He spread her legs apart even more and put his mouth on her.

"Joel!"

That was better. Still, he'd take more. He worked her with his tongue and his lips. Tasting and taking and trying to drive her wild. He liked it when Chloe went wild. When her careful control was gone, and she was demanding in her need. Her hands grabbed his shoulders, and her nails raked him even as she pushed her sex eagerly against his mouth.

So hot.

He could feel her body tensing as the first orgasm surged closer. He didn't ease up, but used his fingers and mouth to push her even harder, even higher. When she jerked against him and her body shuddered, he let her ride out the climax. He freaking loved her taste.

Another lick, and he lifted his head. He knew he wasn't even going to be able to strip off all his clothes before he took her. The need was too strong. Her scent and taste consumed him, and he wanted to drive deep into her.

"What are you waiting for?" Her sensual whisper.

He yanked open his jeans. Wasn't wearing underwear so his dick sprang forward. He put the head of his cock at the entrance of her body then caught her hands with his. He pushed her hands back against the bed and thrust into her.

Her breath sucked in on a gasp. His erupted on a guttural groan. Her sex clamped around him like a greedy, tight glove. Joel thought he might lose his mind because she felt so insanely good.

Perfect.

Even before he withdrew, Joel knew he wasn't going to be able to hold back. Knew that he would be too rough and uncontrolled. A dangerous intensity seemed to be riding him. Maybe because of the day...maybe because of the new nightmares that plagued him...Joel just wanted her. Needed her to wipe everything else away. He wanted to imprint himself on Chloe. Bind her to him.

Never let go.

He drove into her over and over again even as his fingers threaded with hers. He stared into her eyes as she surged up and met him thrust for thrust. They were racing toward a release that would crash over them both. Harder. Deeper. The bed heaved beneath them, and he didn't ease up. Joel kept driving into her. When he felt her delicate, inner muscles start to tremble, he knew she was close.

"Come on, sweetheart..." He kissed her. Thrust his tongue past those lush lips of hers. "Let me feel everything."

She did. Her sex squeezed him tight and her body shuddered as the release ripped through her. Her hands tightened around his, and he was gone. He drove into her one more time, sinking as deep as he could go, and Joel came with a release that obliterated everything else. Pleasure blasted through his whole body, and the world seemed to fade around him. She was his focus. The only thing that mattered. He emptied into her and never, ever wanted to let her go.

***

"Stay," he growled.

Sometimes, she left him. Went back up to the main house. He lived on the massive estate that she owned—an estate that had been some mysterious gift to her. Joel had never gotten the full details on that deal. The place had once been known as the "Mob Murder House"...now it was Chloe's home. His home, too.

He lived in the guest house. A hold-over from when he'd first started working with her. She stayed at the main home, along with her brother and one of Chloe's friends, Marie Kim. The mysterious Marie had just as many secrets as Chloe did.

Chloe had a habit of collecting friends with secrets. Part of her charm.

Friends with secrets and friends who were very, very dangerous.

At his growled command, Chloe turned toward him. Joel had ditched the rest of his clothes earlier and she'd been cuddled against him, completely naked, in bed. He'd felt at peace with her beside him. She was the only person who ever did give him peace.

Then he'd felt her careful movements.

"I thought you were asleep," she murmured.

"That why you were slipping away?" She'd thought she could get out without him noticing?

Chloe settled back down against him. "I'm not in any rush."

His arms slid around her. She felt good against him. Right. Darkness filled the room, but when he looked up, he could see the night sky. A thousand glittering stars. A huge section of the bedroom ceiling was made of glass. To the side, massive glass doors let him look out to the pool area. Chloe had done that—put in all of the glass. Even before he'd moved in, she'd had the updates made to the place.

Because even then, she knew I couldn't stand to feel confined. Before we even met, she'd learned so many secrets about me.

Despite the fact that he hadn't been thrilled to discover Chloe knew about his confinement issues *before* he met her...Joel still loved the damn view. Before he'd moved in, there had been too many nights when he'd felt trapped. The walls and ceiling of his old place had closed in on him.

And he'd felt like he was back in the grave again.

But with Chloe curled at his side and his arm wrapped around her, it was easy to let go and slide into sleep. So very easy...

Until the nightmares came.

***

"Why the fuck are you doing this?" Joel demanded. Blood covered his body. He'd been stabbed. Over and over. The sonofabitch had started with light slices, but then he'd begun to drive the knife deep into Joel's body. He'd been careful—he knew what he was doing. He'd avoided all major organs, so far. No way had that been by luck.

A mask was on his face—a surgical damn mask—and a bright light was strapped to his forehead. Sometimes, he hummed while he cut into Joel. Didn't seem worried or rushed.

They were in the hospital. Someone should come to help him. Someone should—

"I want to see what you'll become," the bastard whispered. He always whispered. Whispered and laughed and—

The knife sank into Joel's abdomen.

***

Joel grunted, and Chloe froze. She'd been tip-toeing her way out of his bedroom because there was work she needed to handle. Calls to make. Favors to call in. Yet at that rough sound, she looked back.

His eyes were still closed. Definitely still sleeping. But his head was jerking against the pillow.

She bit her lip. Took a step back toward him...

***

He couldn't move. Every part of him hurt. The pain consumed him. It was all he knew. His body was covered in blood. Slick with it. And...

Something fell on top of him. It took him a moment to realize that he wasn't in the hospital any longer. He was somewhere else. His eyes strained to see. The bright light was gone. That stupid light that his tormentor had worn. Now there was only darkness.

Something hit him again. Right in the face. It got in his mouth and it—

Joel spat it out. Dirt. Dirt was falling on him.

He tried to call out, but more dirt hit him. It came down, faster and harder, and Joel realized that he was surrounded by the dirt. On all sides. Even beneath him. The dirt kept raining down, and understanding dawned.

He was in a hole. And someone was pouring dirt on top of him. He was being buried.

But he wasn't dead. There was a mistake. He was still breathing. Joel opened his mouth to call out once more...

And he choked on dirt.

***

"Joel?" Chloe frowned at him. He was gasping. That wasn't good. She knew a nightmare held him in its grasp, and she hated that those terrible dreams wouldn't stop.

But they weren't just dreams, and she knew it.

They were memories. And after what he'd seen that day, she'd been afraid this would happen. He'd looked at the body of Glenn Towers, and Joel had seen his own torment.

She sat on the bed and lifted her hand toward him. She didn't want to scare Joel, but she wasn't leaving him trapped in that pain.

He made another rough, choking sound.

Chloe wrapped her fingers around his shoulder and shook him. Hard. "Joel, wake up. *Wake up.*"

***

He clenched the dirt beneath his hands and dragged himself out of the hole. Dirt dripped from his mouth and stung his eyes.

Buried alive. The horror filled him, but it was distant, second to the rage that had given him the strength to get out of that hole. The spot that would have been his grave. His breath heaved in and out, and he looked around blindly. He was on his hands and knees. Didn't have the strength to rise. Not yet. Not...

A man was nearby. Standing near a pickup truck. He was loading a shovel into the back. The man started humming.

"H-help..." It was the only thing Joel could manage. Barely a gasp. Desperate. Weak. He was still on his hands and knees.

The man spun to face him. His eyes widened in shock. "You're supposed to be dead. You should be in the ground!"

The shovel. He was running toward Joel with the shovel in his hand. Before Joel could react, the man heaved the shovel against him.

The edge of the shovel's blade tore across Joel's lip and sent him careening back.

Into the hole.

For a moment, he froze. His first instinct had been to call for help. He'd ignored what was around him. What he could see.

The fucking shovel.

That sonofabitch had buried him. That man—he'd done it all. Tortured Joel. Sliced into him. Stabbed him. Left him for dead in a grave he'd created...

An inhuman roar tore from Joel's ragged throat. The rage that had helped him to climb from the dirt poured through him even hotter, even stronger than before. He surged forward. Surged up. Joel slammed his body into the bastard's. They hit hard, and the shovel clattered to the ground. The man was fighting him, but Joel knew what he had to do.

Kill or be killed.

His fist swung at the bastard's face.

***

His fist swung out.

"Joel!"

He froze. His hand hung in the air. It was inches away from Chloe's face.

Horror filled him.

What the fuck? *Chloe?*

He looked around, frantic, and realized he was in his bedroom. The covers were twisted around him, and Chloe hovered nearby. She'd put on one of his shirts, and she was staring at him with concern clear to see in her eyes.

The lights were on. And he had almost hit her with his fucking fist. His breath shuddered out. "I'm sorry."

She shook her head. "You were having a nightmare. You don't need to apologize to—"

He grabbed the sheets. "I almost hit you, Chloe." Each word was bitten off. "You know you're not supposed to wake me up when I have a nightmare!" His voice was angry and rough, but the anger wasn't directed at her. It was all for him.

I almost hurt her.

He'd seen a few shrinks after the hell he'd survived, and the news from them hadn't exactly been good. One jerk in particular had pretty much told Joel that he was screwed for life. That he'd be a danger to those around him.

Just like I am dangerous to her now.

Sweat covered his body. "We've been over this," he growled. "Baby, it's dangerous. *I'm dangerous.* I get disoriented from the nightmares, and I don't know what's happening because I—"

"You relive it. I know it. I can see it." While his voice had been rough, hers was soft. Soothing. She reached for his fingers and stroked the back of his hand. The hand that was still clenched into a fist. "I wasn't going to leave you to face that alone."

He uncurled his fingers. Turned his hand. Caught hers. His hand was so much bigger and rougher than hers. Calluses lined his fingers from the workouts that he did. All the therapy that had been recommended hadn't done jack for him, so he'd come up with his own coping mechanisms. And the best way he'd learned? Channel the rage. "Never, Chloe," he warned.

"Never what?"

"Never come near me when I can hurt you." He looked up at her face. If he'd hit her...a shudder worked over him.

She smiled. *Smiled.* "Joel, I could have stopped the blow long before it landed." She leaned forward and pressed a kiss to his lips. "I could have twisted your wrist. Dodged. Done a dozen other things. I know how to protect myself. But you are quite precious when you worry."

Precious? He didn't feel fucking precious. He felt out of control. Violent. Dangerous. Like he damn well shouldn't be close to Chloe.

"You'll never be normal again." The words from Dr. Gordon Jennings blasted through his mind. Old Gordo had been convinced that Joel was a threat to the world around him.

He can't be right. Joel swallowed. "I can't hurt you, Chloe."

Her head tilted. She studied him in silence. Processing the way Chloe did. He could feel the wheels spinning in her head, and he wished that he could read her thoughts.

"We protect each other, don't we?" Chloe finally said. "That's part of our arrangement."

He tucked a lock of dark hair behind her ear and tried to pretend that his fingers weren't shaking. "I think the arrangement actually was for me to protect you." His hand lingered against her cheek. Her soft, silken skin. "You know, for me to watch that gorgeous ass of yours and all."

Her hand rose and curled around his wrist. "It's only fair for me to protect you, too." She held his gaze. "Don't you think so? Isn't that what real partners do? They look out for each other."

His head moved in a slow nod. Where was she going with this?

"Good." Her smile flashed, and it was brilliant. Only...it didn't meet her eyes. "Remember that, would you? You protect me, I protect you, and, other than that, I don't think we need to worry about any additional rules."

"Chloe..."

"Do you want to tell me about the memories?" Her smile was gone. Just that fast.

Joel sucked in a deep breath.

"I don't like to push you." Now she was halting. Odd for Chloe. She didn't seem to normally worry about pushing anyone.

But she does with me.

Because he knew that Chloe was different with him. Just as he was different with her. No one understood him the way Chloe did. No one made him burn and ache and need the way Chloe did.

She'd brought him back to life. Become his obsession and his dream all at the same time.

But when it came to his past, to the darkness that lurked there...

Joel shook his head. "There is no point in letting it touch you."

She brought his hand to her lips. Kissed his knuckles. "But you touch me. All the time. And your past is part of you. If we follow that line of reasoning, it already has touched me. Over and over again."

"Chloe..."

"There is nothing you could tell me that I would not understand."

"I fucking beat a man to death." The words erupted from him. He tried to pull his hand back. *Can't touch her. Can't—*

She tightened her hold on him.

"He'd buried me alive, Chloe." Joel swallowed and swore he could still taste the dirt. It had filled his throat. Coated his tongue. He'd tried to open his mouth and scream when it rained down on him, and the dirt had choked him. He'd been spitting it out of his mouth when he climbed from that hole. "He was still there. He had the shovel. He swung at me with it and I..." But his words trailed away.

His gaze had landed on his hand. On the hand that Chloe still held. The hand she'd kissed.

When the authorities had finally found Joel, his fingers had been stained with dirt and blood.

Once more, he tried to pull away from her.

Once more, Chloe just tightened her grip. "You did what you needed to do." Her voice was certain. Firm. "You survived, Joel."

For a long time, he hadn't been so sure he had survived. He'd felt like a freaking shell of a man. He hadn't been able to go back to surgery. Every time he looked at a scalpel, every single time he thought about cutting into a patient...

I remembered him cutting me.

"I'm glad you did," she said into the heavy silence that followed. "Survived, I mean. Though I am also glad you killed that man. I think he probably needed a good killing."

Typical Chloe.

She pushed him back on the bed. Came down beside him. Snuggled her body against his. Her fingers pressed to his chest, sliding over some of the scars that marked him. "I imagine my life would have been entirely *less* interesting if I had not met you."

A laugh sputtered from him. "Uh, thanks?" Was that her way of making him feel better?

"You are welcome." Again, her fingers slid lightly over his chest. "You can tell me anything, I hope you know that. And...if you are not comfortable talking to me, you can always go and see—"

"No." He stopped her right there as his whole body stiffened. "Not going to see another shrink, baby. Especially not after that last asshat." Dr. Gordon Jennings had been utterly useless. And the fact that he'd basically said Joel was a ticking timebomb waiting to explode? Yeah, no thanks.

He felt her body tense against him. The movement lasted only a second before she relaxed. But he was so attuned to her, so focused on Chloe that he felt it. Alarm flared through him. He immediately rolled to face her. "What?"

"About the asshat in question..." She sounded ever-so-proper even as she said the word "asshat" in that faint accent of hers.

"Gordo? You want to talk about Gordo?"

Her lips pursed. "Want is a strong word. I don't actually want to discuss him, but there has been a development that you should know about."

"Why do I need to know anything about that jerk? He's gone back to Texas, and I—"

Her head moved in a small, negative shake.

His heart squeezed. Oh, no. "He has *not* gone back to Texas."

"He had gone back to Texas. He now has a new home, according to my sources…"

Because she had a million sources. He still hadn't quite figured out how she had so many connections. She just did. Most of the connections were on the shady side. Chloe seemed to like that side of the world.

"Dr. Jennings developed quite the chummy relationship with the local FBI branch. He moved down here. Rented a house. Even got a small office space in the Quarter."

"You are shitting me."

"No. I wish that I was."

"Why didn't you tell me this *sooner*?"

"Because I was distracted by other things and I only learned of his presence within the last twenty-four hours. I should have monitored him better. This was my mistake."

Hell, no, it wasn't her mistake. Gordo was just a jackass. "He thinks I'm a monster. That I'm dangerous."

She stared at him. "You are dangerous," Chloe told him.

She didn't pull her punches.

"But you're hardly a monster." Her hand stroked his cheek. "And I should know. I've met plenty of them."

"Chloe..."

"Forewarned is forearmed. He's invading our city. We need to see what his real motivations are. Don't worry. I have complete confidence that we can handle whatever he throws at us."

About that... "I don't want him near you."

"Why? Are you afraid he'll tell me that I'm a monster?" Her hand reached out. Turned off the light. As the darkness covered them, she snuggled back against him. "Silly, Joel. I've known that for years."

***

He went back to sleep. It took a while, but Joel's body finally relaxed as sleep claimed him. Chloe didn't try slipping from the bed this time. She stayed where she was and enjoyed the feel of Joel's body against her.

He'd been so sweet. After Chloe had confessed about being a monster, he'd instantly told her she was wrong. He'd proclaimed that she wasn't a monster. She hunted killers. She helped people.

Adorable.

He still didn't understand her. Not completely. Oh, he was certainly close. Closer than most people had ever been. But...

He didn't know the truth. She was hiding it from him. As she hid so many secrets. Secrets were dangerous. Secrets could hurt.

She was Joel's partner, and her job was to protect him. She'd *told* him that. Been as clear as it was possible to be.

From the den, she heard the quick beep that told her a text had come through on her phone. Part of her thought of ignoring the text but...

It was one a.m. A text at this time had to be important. She slipped from Joel's arms. Avoided the part of the floor that would squeak.

Her phone's screen was still glowing when she picked it up. It was a note from her friend Ruben...Ruben who happened to be the chief medical examiner. His text was simple. Short. Just...

104.

Her hold tightened on the phone even as an unfamiliar emotion seemed to rise and cover her. Ice filled her blood, and for the first time in longer than she could remember...

Chloe was truly terrified.

CHAPTER THREE

"I brought you beignets," Chloe said as she lifted the small, white paper bag in her hand. "They are still warm."

Dr. Ruben Minote glanced at her with his eyebrows raised. "If you really loved me, you would have also come with my favorite iced latte. If you *really* love me, and weren't just, oh, trying to bribe your way inside my lab to see the bodies."

Chloe slanted a glance over her right shoulder.

Joel lifted the iced latte he carried.

"You love me," Ruben sighed. "I suspected it. So nice to have the suspicion confirmed."

But he still didn't move from his position at the door. The man was blocking access to the facility and currently burning up time that Chloe didn't have to lose. When he reached for the beignet bag, Chloe pulled it out of reach. "I think these would be enjoyed more if you had them *inside*."

"You're not supposed to be here." His gaze stayed on the bag. "I haven't gotten permission from anyone in authority for you to enter the facility."

She nodded. "Of course, but has anyone in authority told you that I could *not* be here?"

His mouth opened. Closed. "No?" He made the one word sound like a question.

"Excellent." Her shoulders squared. "Then you have plausible deniability. You can say that since you were not informed I could not be here, then how could you know that I didn't have access to view the bodies?"

"That's not how plausible deniability works."

"Certainly, it is." Chloe got tired of waiting for him to move. She advanced. Dangled the bag. When he grabbed it, she darted past him. "We'll only be here a moment. I just need to check a few things."

"They *are* warm." He opened the bag. "Look at all of that powdered sugar."

"I told them to put extra on for you." She was already heading to her destination. It was barely past seven a.m., so the place was deserted, except for Ruben. Just as she'd intended. She hurried to his lab and was aware of him and Joel following quickly behind her. When she entered the lab, the temp immediately dropped, but Chloe didn't shiver. She was too intent on her goal. She ignored the smell of bleach and antiseptic and got to work.

"Here." Joel pushed the drink at Ruben. "It's your iced whatever."

The files were on Ruben's desk. As they always were. She went for the files, but Joel stopped to don a pair of gloves.

"I'm still working on the report and waiting for results," Ruben told them as he sat in his swivel chair and went to town on the beignets. His eyes closed as he savored a bite. "Heaven." Powdered sugar dotted his lips. "Just what I needed after an all-nighter. You would not believe the stress I am under. Cops want the results yesterday, of course. Already getting pressured because certain people in the old chain of command think we're dealing with another serial. Like the mayor wants that to happen. The Big Easy does not need to be known as the serial killer capital of the world." He paused to sip his latte. "Sweet, precious caffeine. God, I needed you."

Chloe slanted him a quick glance. "There is no serial killer capital of the world. Serials don't congregate together. They are—by their very natures—solitary. It is extremely rare to find a serial killing duo, and in those instances, you have one who is the dominant leading the other. A group of serial killers would never—" She stopped because Ruben was staring at her.

"He was joking, Chloe," Joel said as he stood by a covered body.

Of course. "I knew that."

"She just likes talking about her killers." Ruben took another bite. Powdered sugar danced in the air around him. "Want one?"

"I already had one." She thumbed through his files. As he'd told her in his one a.m. text, there had been exactly one hundred and four—

"Why did you want to know how many slices there were on the body?" Ruben asked her. His voice seemed overly loud, and she immediately winced. Could the man have not just satisfied himself with the beignets for a few moments longer?

But no, Joel had heard his words. Joel's head whipped toward them. "How many slices were there?"

"One hundred and four," Ruben announced cheerily. He pulled out another beignet. "Deepest ones were to the chest. One went straight in the heart."

"Not like he could fight after that," Chloe said.

"Nope. That's why—in my report—I said that based on my analysis, it was the deeper wounds that were administered first. Obviously, the man was not just going to sit there while he's sliced all over. I mean, he'd need to be restrained in some way. Hands and feet tied. Or he'd need to be drugged. Now, note, I don't have the tox reports back yet, so everything I'm saying is preliminary, just between us friends, but to be sliced all over that way—deliberate slices that weren't meant to do anything but maim, I don't think—"

She shook her head.

He didn't get the message because the man kept talking. "You do those kinds of marks if you want to torture the vic. The poor bastard was already so far gone he wouldn't have felt them. Hell, with that wound to the heart, he wasn't even alive for—"

Another shake of her head. Harder this time.

Ruben paused with a beignet poised toward his mouth. "What? Why do you keep shaking your head? You think I'm wrong?"

Silence. But, no, she didn't think he was wrong.

Her head turned toward Joel.

Swearing, Ruben seemed to finally *get it*. His head swiveled toward Joel, too. "Oh, man. I am sorry." He jumped to his feet and shoved the half-eaten beignet back in the bag. "I did not mean to stir up old memories for you. Shit. Again, sorry, I—"

"There were one hundred and four wounds on him?" Joel's voice was flat. No emotion.

"That's what I counted, yes." He hurried close to the body. "I texted Chloe that number last night after she asked me to give her a count ASAP. Didn't see why it was important, still don't," he muttered as he glanced back at her. "Obviously, the perp was in a rage or just freaking crazy so the exact number probably didn't matter for—"

"It matters," Joel cut in. His gaze rose to pin Chloe. "You didn't tell me."

"I asked Ruben to check the body again. There was no point in telling you something that could have been a mistake. With that high of a number, it would be easy to miscount." She shut the file. Rose and headed toward the exam table. The body on that table was that of Glenn Towers. His eyes were closed. His skin had turned the chalky color that came with death. She studied him for a moment. Looked at the stab wounds and all the slices. Chloe was aware that Joel and Ruben were both doing the same thing. The wounds in the chest were the deepest, anyone could see that. The slices on the rest of Glenn's body were much lighter. Intended to torture—*if* he'd been alive when they'd been delivered.

She wasn't so sure that he had been.

"He has one on his lip, Chloe," Joel stated flatly. "But you saw that last night, didn't you?"

Yes, she had. And that slice had set off alarm bells for her. "No defensive wounds," she noted, instead of answering him. "Just like the stepdaughter. No bruising at all that I see." Some bruising could still show up much later. She doubted it, though. "The killer walked right up to him. Stabbed him in the heart."

"Uh, Chloe..." Ruben began.

"It was the first stab that disabled him. Glenn was a big man. Six-foot-three. Much taller than she was. That's why she had to jab up with the first attack." She didn't touch the body. Just waved her fingers very carefully toward the wound over Glenn's heart. "The point of entry is different. He was still standing when this wound occurred. But with this one..." She moved her hand a bit to the right. "The entry angle has changed." She indicated another deep wound. "Here, too. I think she was crouched above him at this point. The wounds are harder. It was easier for her to drive deep when she was above him instead of when he was standing up and he was taller than she was." Her hand came back to her side. Fisted. "Then the shallow slices occurred either as he struggled to live or when he'd already died." Her gaze flickered to Ruben. "I'll let you determine that."

"You know who the killer is?" His eyes had gone wide. "Already?"

She lifted a brow. Why did he sound so surprised?

"No." Ruben shook his head.

"Yes. You suspect it, too. That's why you made a notation in the file about the attacker being of smaller statue than Glenn Towers—"

His gaze darted to the right. To the covered body that waited on the nearby exam table.

"It's why her shoes were left in his blood." This part made her uncomfortable. "I think she danced in his blood, and she left that message there for everyone to find. She enjoyed his death." The part that puzzled Chloe...

After Lucia killed Glenn, why had the dancer then wound up dead herself?

"That is messed up," Ruben noted. "Dancing in someone's blood is twisted shit."

"You have powdered sugar on your cheek." She turned back to Joel. Found him staring at her.

Her hands wanted to flutter in the air. A strange, useless gesture that she didn't need to make. Chloe kept her hands at her sides as she faced him.

"Is it a coincidence?" Joel finally asked.

She knew exactly what he meant. "It could be." Though she'd rarely found a true coincidence in her line of work. So she would not lie. Not about this. "But I doubt it. Given the number of wounds and the fact that Lucia was killed where your mother once worked...I'd say we need to be very cautious with this one."

She could feel Ruben's stare darting between them. "What am I missing? 'Cause I'm missing something. I can feel it. I don't like the feeling. I want to be in the know. I'm part of the gang, too."

"One hundred and four," Joel growled.

Chloe nodded.

"Yes, that's how many wounds he had," Ruben agreed. "But what does—"

"That's how many times the bastard sliced *me*," Joel returned in a voice that was dark and gritty. "Exactly one hundred and four times. I know because I laid on that table—strapped down and unable to move—and I counted every single time that he cut me."

***

"What in the hell is going on?" Joel caught Chloe's arm as soon as they left the lab. He spun her around to face him. "And why didn't you tell me about Ruben's text?"

"Because he could have been wrong. I needed him to be thorough, so I asked him to count again." Her chin notched up. Her voice remained perfectly calm as she added, "You were already having a difficult night. Why should I burden you more if it turned out to be nothing?"

"Burden me. Burden me any fucking time. Especially if it's about a psycho murderer, okay? Put that down as a rule for me or something. I want to be burdened." His heart was jackhammering in his chest. When he'd looked at the body of Glenn Towers—seen him with all the blood cleaned away and Joel had studied all of those cuts on his body...

Like I was looking into a twisted mirror.

"All of the wounds weren't in the same positions." He sucked in one breath. Another. Pulled her scent in to him—strawberries when the rest of the place reeked of antiseptic—and tried to get his focus back. "I got the scar on my lip from the shovel. Not the knife. So that was wrong. I mean, shit, technically, I guess that would make mark one hundred and five for me so—"

Chloe's gaze slid from his. "I don't think the lip wound counts for you. It was from a different—a different weapon. We're looking specifically at wounds from a knife. You had one hundred and four knife wounds. Glenn also had one hundred and four. Only for him, one of those wounds was the slice to his lip."

He shook his head. This was so messed up. "The slices on his arms were all in roughly the same place as mine. But the ones on the chest—they..." He broke off.

"Close, but not quite the same." She nodded. Watched him carefully. "Almost as if someone was following a model. A guide. Trying to put the marks in the same spot, but it's hard to stay controlled enough to do that when your victim is bleeding out and you're riding a high from taking him down. You want to dance and twirl, but you aren't supposed to do that. You are just supposed to follow the map."

His lips pressed together. *Bam. Bam. Bam.* His heartbeat was too fast. "Who the hell sent the text requesting you? Do you already know?"

She shook her head. "I only know the text was sent to the mayor from the phone of Glenn Towers. Cedric updated me on that."

"Why?" he rumbled. "Why is this happening? Stabbed and sliced like I was, then *you're* called in to investigate. Is this some other fucker who wants his fifteen minutes of fame by deliberately trying to mimic the shit that happened to me? A copycat?"

"Copycat," she repeated consideringly. "That's certainly what the police will think. But we can't overlook the fact that someone else killed Lucia. And her method of death certainly wasn't a copy of what happened to you." She cocked her head and studied him. "If you want someone to—literally—stop a person from talking, do you know what you need to do?"

Yeah, he had an idea. "Cutting her throat works wonders." You couldn't talk when someone had sliced through your vocal cords.

A door opened down the hallway. A woman in a white lab coat stared at Joel with wide eyes.

Wonderful. Of course, she would have heard that throat cutting line from him. "I'm not...I'm not threatening to cut her throat." He motioned toward Chloe.

The woman backed up a step.

"We should leave," Chloe advised. "A new shift starts soon. More people will be coming in."

"I didn't threaten her," Joel muttered to the woman who was still gaping at him.

The woman—with dark red hair and pale skin—didn't look reassured.

Chloe began hurrying down the hallway. Joel followed right behind her. When they stepped outside, the bright sun glinted off their parked ride.

"We should go to Lucia's house." He was trying to work through angles. Options. "Search there and see what could possibly have led her to kill her stepfather." *And slice the bastard so many times.*

Chloe stopped next to the SUV. She slowly turned to face him. "We could," she agreed. "But I suspect her home is being searched by the cops, and though I do have a warm and positive relationship with Cedric, the rest of the PD doesn't always share his enthusiasm for me. So it's doubtful they will let us inside. We'll have to wait and break in later."

Right. Like breaking into a dead woman's house was a done deal. In Chloe's mind, though, it obviously was. "I'm guessing you have a better option?"

"Joel, we don't guess, remember?"

She didn't. He did. All the fucking time.

"But, yes, I do have a better option."

"Then do not keep me in suspense."

She smiled. "Wouldn't dream of it."

He wasn't so sure he believed her.

"I've seen Lucia dance before. She was amazingly talented, by the way. She could move her body in so many ways, always perfectly matching the beat of the music." Chloe sounded admiring. "She was quite something to see." With a nod, she headed for the driver's side of the vehicle.

Looked like he'd be shotgun this time. She *had* snagged the keys before they'd gone inside to see the body.

Joel hopped into the passenger seat. Turned to study her as suspicion churned. "Just *where* did you see her dance?"

"Now you're catching on." She cranked the engine. "She wasn't just into ballet, and when she wanted to make money, Lucia knew exactly where to go."

His eyes narrowed on her profile. "Just how much do you already know about Lucia?"

"Not enough. But I know someone who is going to be able to tell us a great deal more."

"I don't like this, Chloe." The bad feeling he had was getting worse with every single moment that passed.

"Yes, well…" Her fingers did a light tap around the wheel. "You'll like it even less when you realize where we are going."

"Spit it out already," he groused.

She slanted a quick glance at him. "I could always go to see him on my own. He'd probably talk more freely if it was just me."

His stomach knotted. "Not happening."

"Right. Then I guess we're heading to the Serpent. We'd better hurry. Kingston usually leaves by eight a.m. to go home and sleep."

The Serpent. Fuck. The bar that was a criminal front?

Perfect.

***

The snake wasn't dancing. Joel exited the vehicle and stared up at the image of the snake high on the side of the two-story building. At night, the snake was illuminated, and it seemed to sway back and forth as its long, forked tongue shot out. There was no other signage on the building. Just the snake.

And the snake wasn't dancing right then. Its tongue didn't flicker.

They were at one of *the* major hotspots in the city. The Serpent. A place Joel hadn't even known existed, not until he'd stepped into Chloe's world. The rich and overindulged headed into the club to party, and in the VIP rooms, games were played. Bets were waged. People traded jewelry. Homes. Probably drugs. Hell, Joel suspected they traded *everything* in those upstairs VIP rooms. Once upon a time, Chloe had gotten him in one of those private games. They'd been tracking a killer.

When they'd left, Joel had realized how very dangerous Kingston Broussard, the club's owner, truly was. Not only was he tied to all the major crimes in the city, but the SOB seemed far too personally interested in Chloe.

"We're in luck. Kingston just walked out of the club."

His head jerked to the left. Chloe was right. Kingston, "King," was ducking out of the club's front entrance. He was wearing a white dress shirt that he'd rolled up to his elbows, and the collar was undone. He had his black coat slung over one shoulder, and he still wore his matching black pants and some shiny-ass shoes. He was flanked by two big, hulking guys that Joel immediately pegged as bodyguards.

"Kingston!" Chloe called.

The bodyguards sprang into action. They immediately whirled toward Chloe and those sonsofbitches pulled their guns.

Joel grabbed Chloe and shoved her behind him. He put his body in front of her, and he got ready to—

"Fire a bullet, and I will end you," King's voice was low and lethal. As lethal as his threat. It was a threat Joel believed the other man was fully capable of carrying out. "That is my *personal* friend, and you will not ever point a weapon at her again, do you understand me?"

The men quickly lowered the weapons.

"Although..." Now King's voice was considering. "The man with her isn't my friend. So if you see him without her...do what you will to him."

Joel glared at the bastard.

King smiled back at him.

The bodyguards were edging back toward King—and the waiting, black limo that idled near the curb.

"We need to talk!" Chloe announced. She didn't seem even mildly upset about the fact that she'd almost been gunned down by two trigger-happy bodyguards.

Joel was upset. Fucking furious, in fact.

Chloe tried to hurry past him. Joel threw out one hand and chained her wrist. He tugged her back to his side. "No," he said simply. Because there wasn't anything else to say.

No, she wasn't going to run toward the men with guns.

No, she wasn't going to put herself at risk.

And, hell, no, he wasn't going to let those bastards get away with nearly shooting her. He studied them carefully, making sure he would never forget their faces.

"Chloe, as much fun as this odd encounter is," King was at the limo's open door, "it's been an incredibly long night, and I need to go crash. Be a sweetheart and come back tonight, would you? I'll get Wedge to let you right inside. You can come up to the VIP room and spend some quality time with me."

"In your freaking dreams," Joel snapped.

"Yes. Frequently."

Joel surged toward him.

"Stop it." Now Chloe was the one who blocked him. "You know he's just antagonizing you."

"I just want to kick his ass." Was that so wrong? The guy had rubbed him the wrong way from the very first moment.

King's laugh rang out. "He is adorable, Chloe. Now I see why you keep him around."

She whirled for King. "Lucia Rossi."

He stopped laughing.

"We need to talk," she repeated. "Now."

King's gaze darted around the street. "I'm not talking in public." He motioned to the limo. "Let's go for a ride."

"He sweeps his limo for listening devices," Chloe whispered. "He'll feel comfortable there. We need to get in."

"Oh, yes, sure. Because we want him to feel comfortable." *Let's let the criminal mastermind feel comfortable, by all means.* Chloe had once told Joel that King was actually working undercover, some bit about being more FBI, not NOPD. But every time Joel was around him, the man just seemed more and more like the worst kind of trouble.

Chloe inclined her head and offered Joel a quick smile. "I knew you would understand."

His sarcasm had gone right past her. As he watched, she hurried forward and just casually tossed the SUV's keys to one of the bodyguards. "I assume you'll tail us?" Chloe asked courteously, as if the man hadn't pointed his gun at her less than two minutes before.

The guard glanced at King. King nodded. The guard quickly rumbled, "Uh, yeah, yeah, I'll tail you."

"Thanks. Don't change my radio channel, okay?" She slid into the limo.

King kept waiting by the ride. His eyes were on Joel. "I'm guessing you will join our little party, too?"

"Wouldn't miss it for the world." But he did have one matter he needed to take care of first. Joel slowly advanced toward the limo. And when he was close to the guard who'd caught the car keys...

Joel's hand swung out and he punched the asshole in the jaw.

The man bellowed and surged at Joel but—

King stepped between them. "Was that nice?" he asked Joel. "Sometimes, I think you forget that you're supposed to be the *nice* one."

"Says who?" He stepped to the side—the better to glare at the fool who'd had his weapon aimed at Chloe. "Your finger was starting to tighten. I saw it. You ever point a gun at her, you ever think about pulling a trigger again...and it will be your last mistake."

A long sigh slipped from King. "I already warned them—"

Joel let his gaze sweep to the other guard. "Now I've warned them. But what they need to know is that you won't get a chance to carry out your promise. If they go for Chloe, I'll make sure nothing is left for you to handle."

The guards were sweating.

"Don't fucking so much as scratch the ride, either," Joel barked at them. "Drive it like the precious baby it is."

The men rushed away. One ran back into the Serpent while the other headed for the SUV.

"Precious baby?" King repeated.

Joel narrowed his eyes on the bastard.

"My, my. Someone spends a few weeks with Chloe and suddenly thinks he is all big and bad." King sidled a bit closer. "Don't make promises you can't keep."

"I don't." If some bastard came at Chloe with a gun, he would protect her. She was far too important to him. He couldn't lose Chloe.

"We'll see about that," King murmured. "Things haven't really been intense for you yet. Just wait."

Joel had to laugh. "If you think that, you're more of an idiot than I realized."

King stiffened.

Ignoring him, Joel climbed into the back of the limo. He made sure to sit right next to Chloe, putting his leg against hers. He wanted to be damn clear on this. He was with Chloe. To hurt her, anyone would have to go through him.

"You need to be more careful," Chloe chided softly. "Kingston isn't an easy enemy to have."

Neither am I.

King entered the limo and sprawled on the rear seat. The door slammed shut, and a few moments later, the vehicle pulled away from the curb. The privacy screen was up. The bar well stocked. And King's hard gaze was on Joel. "I have a reputation," King finally said. "I don't take insults. Remember that. If you ever insult me again in front of my crew, I will be forced to react." His gaze dipped to Chloe. "No matter what friends we may have in common."

Joel shrugged. "If you don't like being called an idiot, then don't be—"

"Stop." Chloe's voice. Calm. Smooth. "Whatever game you two want to play, do it later."

"Count on it." But King focused on Chloe. His expression subtly shifted. The rage disappeared— no, it was hidden—and he studied her tensely. "I assume you know. As you always seem to know secrets in that witchy way of yours."

Her nose scrunched. "Witchcraft isn't involved."

His lips twitched. "No, of course, not. My bad. Probably just got that idea from the time I spotted you in the St. Louis Cemetery with the group of chanting figures. A simple mistake to make."

Joel hadn't heard that particular story.

"Not really," Chloe returned without missing a beat. "Those were voodoo practitioners, and no witchcraft was involved at all. You should be careful making that mistake in this town."

King's eyes narrowed. "I can't tell if you are making a joke or being dead serious."

She stared back at him. "Interesting." She didn't sound like it was, though. "You know what I can tell? When you're lying and when you're speaking the truth."

He laughed. "Doubtful. Most people can't."

Chloe didn't smile. Her expression didn't alter even a little.

King's laughter slowly faded. "But you're not most people." He raked a hand over his face, and his shoulders sagged a little. "I was sleeping with her."

Chloe nodded. "Yes, I am aware."

She was aware? She could have enlightened Joel on that point. He'd just thought that Chloe had seen Lucia dancing at one of King's places in town—

"I saw the way you watched her. The way you touched her—and how she touched you."

King swallowed. "It didn't last long. Just a few weeks. Nothing lasts long in my world." A mocking smile tilted his lips. "She knew I was her stepfather's biggest competitor. It's no secret I want to take over his casinos. He's been in my way for a while now. She hated the guy, so screwing his enemy was an extra thrill for her."

This was certainly an enlightening conversation. Joel cleared his throat. "Sorry. I'm going to have to ask you to back up a minute for me."

King raked him with a hard glance.

"I thought you were FBI. Why the hell would you be someone's casino competition when you're just working undercover?"

King's face underwent a subtle shift. His jaw tightened. The faint lines near his eyes hardened. His nostrils flared. "You are mistaken."

"I don't believe I am." Especially since the information had come from Chloe. His gaze slid to her.

King swore. "You fucking know? Seriously?"

Chloe shrugged.

"How." A demand. Not a question. "I never told you jack about that. Never gave you any reason to suspect—"

"There were a few incidents that occurred when I was in your presence that tipped me off. Would you prefer for me to go into detail about them now or can we get back to discussing Lucia Rossi?"

His lips clamped together. His nostrils flared again on an angry exhale. Then his stare shot back to Joel. "Chloe doesn't know everything about me. I am *not* an acting FBI agent. Don't go spreading that shit around. You'll start a war in this town that will destroy far too many innocent lives."

Joel lifted his eyebrows. "I don't make it a habit to talk to others about you. I prefer to deny that we know each other."

King seemed to measure him. "Good. Keep going with that." Some of the tension slid from his shoulders as he pressed back against the seat once more. "I *am* interested in expanding my business in this area. Casinos are a natural fit for me. I wanted what Glenn had. But he didn't exactly like some up-and-coming stranger taking customers from him."

Well, how about that? Glenn Towers had been in King's way. Now the man had been eliminated.

Lucia had been involved with King. Chloe had already said she thought a friend or lover had killed the dancer. Someone who Lucia trusted. She would have trusted an ex. She would have let King come right up to her...

And cut her throat?

Joel knew that King had dug into his own past. King liked to know as much as possible about the people who entered his world. Had he learned how many slices Joel had received in his attack? Had he known that Joel's mother used to work in that—

"Say what you're thinking, doc," King invited. "Don't just glare." He snagged a glass from the bar. Poured amber liquid in it.

"Little early, isn't it?" Joel asked.

"More like late. Still celebrating from the night before." King saluted him.

"Celebrating." Joel absorbed that word. He was aware that Chloe was very still next to him. "You're celebrating Lucia's death?"

He was watching King closely, the way he'd learned to watch suspects since partnering with Chloe, so he saw the faint tightening of King's fingers around the glass.

"You knew," Chloe said. It wasn't a question. "I could see that when I said her name the first time." A pause. "Who told you?"

"Oh, Chloe..." He drained the glass in quick gulps and set it down with a clink on the mirrored surface of the small bar. "You know news travels fast in this town. And bad news? It goes at the speed of light."

"Fine. So someone reported her death to you." She nodded. "What about Glenn? Did you hear about his death already, too?"

King didn't so much as flicker an eyelash. "Might have caught a whisper or two about that. Not like I'll be mourning the bastard. He was the type to put on airs. To pretend to be so noble and good in public, but behind closed doors, he was a real sonofabitch." King's head turned a little so that he was looking at Joel. "And before you say it, doc, I like to be a sonofabitch in both public and private. Why pretend to be anything else?"

"Why indeed?" Joel muttered.

"We all wear masks, I suppose," King continued as the limo drove smoothly down the road. "I just find them tiresome most days, so I don't see the point in bothering."

"Did Lucia wear a mask?" Chloe asked.

King rubbed his neck. "It's been a long night. Why don't you just ask the real question that you want to know..."

Chloe blinked. "I did ask a real question. It was hardly make-believe."

King's lip thinned. He pointed at Joel. "You spit it out."

Fine. "Did you kill your ex-girlfriend?"

CHAPTER FOUR

King's lips parted to reply.

Chloe rolled her eyes. "Of course, he didn't kill her."

King fired a fast glance her way.

Chloe waved away the suggestion of his guilt. "If Kingston had killed her, we wouldn't have found the body. He would have made certain that both Lucia and Glenn Towers were not discovered." She paused and considered the matter. "Unless, of course, he wanted to send a message. But the only message I saw at the scene was for us."

Joel had turned his head to frown at her. "You have that much faith in this guy? You trust him without even questioning his guilt?"

Had that been an edge of jealousy in his voice? Sure sounded like it to her.

"Chloe." And Kingston...the man's voice was a little choked up. "I appreciate your faith in me. I knew the optics of this wouldn't look good for me, but—"

"It's not about faith," she explained quickly so that he wouldn't have the wrong idea. "It's about facts. As I said, you'd make sure the bodies weren't found, as you've done in the past."

His body stiffened.

"Oh, come on. You said this car was clear. If we can't be truthful here, we are wasting time." She wasn't going to touch the specifics of his past. Not yet. "Though I do suspect the cops will be looking at you—and very hard, too. From the outside, you do make a good suspect."

"Thanks?" he asked.

She shrugged. She wasn't looking for thanks. Chloe had something else in mind. "Even with your ties to authorities—and no, I won't get into those now—it would be in your best interest to hire us."

"Uh, excuse me?" He coughed. Maybe choked.

"You do want us to prove that you didn't slice your ex-lover's throat and let her bleed out on the floor of the dance studio, don't you?"

He flinched.

A telling movement. Interesting. He had cared for Lucia. It hadn't just been about screwing the daughter of his competitor. That was the thing with Kingston. He might say he didn't wear a mask, but Chloe knew those words were a lie. She'd warned him that she could see through his lies. She'd picked up his tells long ago.

The first night they'd met, when she'd caught him trying to dispose of a—

"How much?" Kingston demanded.

"I'm sure I can offer you a discount. A friend rate, if you will." That was kind, wasn't it? "With my help, you won't have to reveal those...associations you have with the FBI—or, the associations you once had." She was growing more convinced that he was *becoming* the persona he'd created so long ago. Maybe he'd signed on with the intent of helping people, but she feared he was in too far now to go back to the life he'd led before. "You need me," she told him softly. "And we both know it."

He shook his head but said, "Consider yourself hired."

"Wonderful."

Joel's body shifted next to her. "Chloe, are we sure King here isn't a killer?"

Why would she be sure of that? "He *is* a killer," she assured Joel. But, so he wouldn't fret, she added, "Just not the one we are after now."

She could tell by Joel's expression that he wasn't reassured.

"I want to know who killed her stepfather." Kingston's voice roughened. "I didn't like the SOB but I still want to know. Whoever killed him has to be the same person who—Chloe, why are you shaking your head at me?"

"Because the same person didn't kill Glenn and Lucia. Joel and I already know who killed Glenn. I can't take your money to figure out something we already know. That's hardly ethical." A friend wouldn't do that to a friend.

Kingston gaped at her.

"Let's get back to Lucia," she urged him. "You didn't answer my question before. Did she wear a mask? Was Lucia hiding secrets?"

"Who killed her stepfather? And why the hell do you think the same person didn't kill Lucia? What are the damn odds that they'd both be killed on the same night?"

Her gaze darted upward as she began to calculate.

"No." Joel's fingers curled around her wrist. "Not important."

Fair enough. Once more, she focused on Kingston. "I got in the limo so that you would answer my questions. So far, I feel like Joel and I have spent all of the time talking. If you want our help, *you* answer questions. Then I'll tell you what we know. Deal?" It was the only offer she was prepared to give him.

A jerky nod. "Lucia liked to take risks. She wanted to be her own person, but she was trapped under her stepfather's thumb. He controlled the money so that meant he controlled her."

"Money isn't everything."

His laugh was bitter. "You know who says shit like that? People who've always had money. People who grew up on fucking estates in England with servants at their beck and call."

Joel leaned forward. "Watch the tone."

"What?" Kingston just shrugged one shoulder. "You know I'm not wrong. Money *is* everything to people who haven't had it. When your mom died and you hadn't gotten placed with a foster family, weren't you scared out of your damn mind, doc? Didn't you wonder where you'd go? What you'd do?" Bitterness. Pain. Both twisted in his voice. "Or has that been so long ago for you that you forgot what it was like to do without?"

"I haven't forgotten anything," Joel assured him grimly. "But you don't know Chloe or what her life has been like. You don't know what—"

"Lucia wasn't like Chloe. She was scared. I told her I could help her out, but she was terrified her stepfather would cut her off. The man had something on her. I could tell. Sometimes, she'd flinch when she said his name. Most folks in this town idolized him, but Lucia seemed to hate him as much as she feared him."

Chloe filed all of this information away. "And you never wondered why she was so afraid?" Chloe asked.

His gaze cut away.

"You did wonder." A piece slid into place for her. "But when you pushed her, she left you."

"Told me it was none of my damn business." He scraped a hand across his jaw. "You think I didn't get it, Chloe? Shit, I might not have your skills at seeing into the heads of people, but I knew the signs." His voice roughened more. "I even tried to get her counseling. I wanted to help her. But..." He exhaled. "She said we were done. That I wanted to fix her, but you couldn't fix what was broken."

His words gave her pause. "I've always thought you could. If you just knew how to put the pieces back together even something broken can be rebuilt."

A furrow appeared between Kingston's dark eyebrows as he stared straight at her.

"How long ago was your break-up?" Chloe asked in a quick turn of topic.

"Four months. No, five."

"And had you talked to her since then?"

"When a woman tells me no, I move on. She cut all ties with me. The last thing I was gonna do was start stalking her. Not my style."

No, she didn't imagine it was. Not with what had happened to his sister so long ago.

"So I'm guessing you don't know if she was seeing someone else?" Joel pushed.

"No clue." He glanced away, staring out the window at the passing blur of scenery. "I'd hoped she was out there being happy. Dancing."

"I don't think she was happy at all," Chloe replied.

"Jesus, Chloe." Kingston closed his eyes. "Sometimes, you can just lie to me. White lies are supposed to make people feel better. Try giving me one of those next time, will you?"

"I'll remember to do that."

His eyes opened. For a moment, he glared at her. "Don't toy with me."

Joel stiffened.

"Easy, tiger," Kingston murmured with a sigh. "Don't have to bare your teeth at me. I'd never hurt Chloe, and she knows it."

"Just like you'd never hurt Lucia?" Joel returned silkily.

"Hurting women isn't my thing. Chloe knows that." He pointed toward the window. "We're getting close to our destination. If you have other questions, ask now."

She had plenty of other questions, but, unfortunately, it would seem she was also running out of time. "Was Lucia ever violent with you?"

His eyelids flickered. "What in the hell kind of question is that?"

"The kind that I just asked." He'd heard her. "Was she violent?" Chloe persisted.

"Lucia was like one hundred pounds lighter than me. She couldn't have been violent—couldn't have hurt me—if she tried."

"Hmmm."

"What the hell does that mean?"

"It means she tried to be violent with her stepfather. Tried and succeeded. She's the one who killed him."

He lunged out of his faux-lounging position. "Bullshit."

"No. Quite the opposite. She took revenge on her abusive stepfather. She walked right up to him and drove a knife into his heart. When he fell and started bleeding out, she sliced him over and over again. Then she left her ballet shoes in his blood."

He paled. "No."

Now she was almost offended. "Are you telling me that I'm wrong?"

"Proof. You need proof. You can't just accuse people of—"

Her head angled toward Joel. "He's saying I'm wrong. He'll stop lying to himself soon and ask who killed her."

"Who. Killed. Her?" Kingston snarled.

She slanted him a glance. "As I told you before, I don't have specifics on that. Joel and I are working on the situation." She paused. "I can tell you it was someone she trusted. Someone who was able to walk right up to her and slice her throat, from ear to ear."

He swallowed then pressed a button near his right hand. "Stop the car," he ordered hoarsely.

The limo immediately stopped.

"I'll pay whatever you ask. Find the bastard." His breath huffed out. "The cops will come for me. You prove to them that I'm innocent." Another huff of air. "And try to fucking be tactful will you, Chloe?"

"My apologies," she said. But even to her own ears, she didn't sound sorry. She wasn't. She'd wanted to know if Kingston had been emotionally involved with Lucia. Now she had her answer.

The driver opened the limo's side door for them. Joel exited first and turned to wait for her.

She started to slide toward him.

Kingston wrapped his fingers around her wrist. "She wasn't a monster."

"I never said she was."

"You think I didn't get it?" His voice was low. "She was broken like me. I wanted to help her, but she...God, she stabbed him?"

"Stabbed him and then danced in his blood."

He let her go. "Maybe the bastard deserved it."

She studied him in silence.

"How long until the cops figure out my connection to her?" Kingston asked.

"Cedric is leading the investigation. I'm sure he has a team at her house. If she had anything to tie her to you...I'd say you'd be hearing from him in just a few hours."

He swore.

"You're welcome. The heads up was free of charge." She exited. Didn't look back at him when the driver slammed the door.

The SUV pulled to a stop behind the limo. The guard killed the engine, hopped out, and hurried toward her as—

"Close enough," Joel snapped. "I'll take the keys."

The guard tossed the keys at Joel before he jumped into the front of the limo with the driver. Moments later, the limo was gone.

And they were left standing on Canal Street. The limo had been circling through the city. A streetcar ambled by them.

"Is it wrong that I want him to be guilty?" Joel finally wondered. "You know, so he could be tossed in jail for a while."

"He's been in jail before. Kingston always gets out. Then he goes after the people who put him there." She tilted her head. "Are you driving this time?"

He'd closed his fist around the keys. "You sure he's not guilty?"

"Of killing Lucia? Yes, I'm sure." As to the other deeds in his life...they weren't talking about them.

Joel stepped closer to her. The air was chilly, blowing in off the Mississippi River, and she could feel the heat of his body reaching out to her. "Would it have killed you to tell me that he was involved with her?" Joel rasped.

"You're in training. I was hoping you'd figure that out on your own."

"Chloe, you have to stop keeping secrets. We're a team, and teams don't keep secrets."

They did, if those secrets would only hurt the other team member. Before she could think of a way to distract him from this line of questioning, her phone rang. "Hold the thought," she said, but she really meant...*forget the thought*. "That's Cedric's ringtone." Had he already figured out that Kingston was connected? She'd given him a slight clue when she told him to look at romantic involvements in Lucia's life. But, because Kingston was also her friend—just like Cedric— she hadn't felt good just saying...

Take Kingston in for questioning.

She swiped her finger over her phone's screen. She put the phone to her ear. "Have you made any interesting discoveries at Lucia's?"

Silence.

"Cedric?" she prompted.

"Do you know where your brother is, Chloe?"

Her heart stuttered in her chest. Her brother...

"Because I'm staring at Reese right now. He reeks to hell and back of booze, and he's unconscious at Lucia's house."

"That...can't be right." But she hadn't seen Reese last night. She'd gone to Joel's place, not the main house. The last time she'd seen Reese had been...around breakfast the previous day.

"It's right, and I'm afraid we're taking him into custody. This shit doesn't look good, Chloe. He broke in through a window."

No, this was wrong. "Reese didn't do anything to Lucia."

"Maybe you need to open yourself to the possibility that your brother is a killer. Because from where I'm standing, he looks guilty as hell."

Her real brother was a killer. But Reese *wasn't* her real brother. Reese was kind. Good. And he'd given up booze. He hadn't drunk so much as a drop in the last two weeks. He'd been proud. At breakfast, he'd even showed her his sobriety chip.

"I'm assuming you can afford a good lawyer for him," Cedric continued gruffly. "Because he's going to need one."

"Test his blood alcohol level. Get a sample of his blood, too," she urged.

"Uh, Chloe..."

"He was drugged," her immediate reply because it was the only option that fit. "Run his blood work. Get him a doctor. Take care of him because—"

"You don't give orders in this situation. Jesus. He's in a dead woman's home. In her freaking bed and reeking of alcohol. Get him a lawyer."

Her hold tightened on the phone. She was staring straight into Joel's dark eyes. His gaze was intense. Worried. "Please," she whispered. She didn't usually beg anyone for anything. But this was different. This was Reese. Her only family.

Even if he wasn't really family.

"Run the tests on him. See what you find out. This isn't...there is more at play here, Cedric."

"More than your brother being guilty of murder?"

She swallowed. "Yes, more than that..."

Before she could say more, Cedric ended the call. The call had been against the rules. She'd owe him—so very much—for the tip.

"I caught enough of that conversation to be damn worried," Joel growled. "What the fuck, Chloe?"

What the fuck, indeed. Her heart felt heavy in her chest. She was oddly conscious of each hard thud. Her hand was slick around the phone as she shoved it back into her purse. "I have to think."

"*You* have to think? You're always thinking. That's what you do. Your mind works constantly and—"

"Reese." She whirled for the SUV. Grabbed the door. Realized she didn't have the keys. "Give them to me!"

He caught her hands in his, but didn't give her the keys. "What about Reese?"

"Cedric found him in Lucia's bed."

"What?" His eyebrows shot up.

"He's been drinking."

"Your brother drinks all the time, that's hardly—"

"He stopped. Two weeks sober. He didn't do this."

"Didn't do...what?" Then he whistled. "Cedric thinks he killed Lucia?"

"That is an option he is considering."

"Fuck me."

"Give me the keys."

"They aren't going to let you see him right now. You know that. You have to wait. They'll process him."

Her body jerked.

"Process him. Book him if they have enough evidence. You need to get him a lawyer. The way you seem to know everyone in this town, I'm sure you have someone on speed dial who can help your brother."

She knew plenty of someones. "I need to see him. I have to make sure Reese knows it's okay."

Sympathy filled his eyes. "Baby, I hate to break this to you, but things are far, *far* from okay."

CHAPTER FIVE

"I wasn't made for jail. I'm entirely too handsome to waste my days in a cell." Reese Hastings tried a broad smile for the police detective who just glowered back at him. "No? You disagree?"

"Cut the shit, Reese. I want to help you, so give me a story I can believe."

Reese rubbed his sweaty hands on the front of his jeans. "Don't I get a phone call? It's been..." He had no clue how long it had been. An hour. Two? An eternity? "A while. I need to call my sister. She'll be worried to death about me." Conspiratorially, he added, "She frets, you know."

"I already called your sister," Detective Cedric Coleman revealed. "She knows where you are."

His stomach clenched. "And Chloe left me here?"

"Chloe is the one who requested a tox screen for you. She's the one who wanted your blood taken. She insisted that you'd been sober so there was no way you should reek to high hell like you did."

He looked toward the door, wishing that Chloe would burst in and stop this madness. "You took my fingerprints."

"Um."

His heart was about to jump out of his chest. Was this what a heart attack felt like? Oh, God. This was so bad. Bad, bad, *bad.*

"Tell me again how you wound up in Lucia's bedroom."

"I'll tell you again...*I don't know* any Lucia. I have no idea how I wound up in that house. The last thing I remember..." His brows beetled. Hell, should he say this part or not? Would it make him look better or worse?

"Holding back doesn't help you."

Reese's gaze darted around the small interrogation room. "That's one of those see-through mirrors, isn't it? People are on the other side, watching me?"

"What is the last thing you remember?" The detective was determined.

"I was...at the Serpent. Getting a drink." Reese's head ached like a bitch. Pounded and pounded. "It's hot in here. You're hot, right?"

"I thought you were supposed to be sober."

"That's why I got a non-alcoholic drink at the place." Or so he'd thought.

"You go to clubs just to get virgin drinks?" The question was heavy on the doubt.

"There are plenty of reasons to go to the Serpent, and they don't have a thing to do with alcohol." Okay, he would like to take those words back. Huge mistake.

He was just off his game. He'd woken up to see cops all around him. Armed cops. They'd been pointing their guns at him and shouting and he'd barely been able to lift his hands up to show that he wasn't armed. Then he'd realized something wet and sticky was on his fingers. Something red.

"I really want to talk to my sister," he whispered. "And I think I might throw up."

"You already did throw up," Cedric reminded him with a disgusted twist of his lips. "Twice. Once on my shoes."

Reese winced. "Is that why you're extra pissed off?"

"I'm extra pissed off because I have two dead bodies on my hands."

With an effort, Reese pulled his eyes off his reflection in the mirror. Man, he looked like warm hell. "Two?"

"And you're tied to them. You were in the dead woman's home."

Reese shook his head. "No, I—"

"You don't remember how you got there. You took a virgin drink at a club, then woke up in that bed."

Now he nodded. "Absolutely. That is what happened. Thank you." He beamed at the detective. "See, I knew you could help me. Chloe is always raving about what a great detective you are and—why are you shaking your head?"

"Because I am not here to help you. My job is to help the victims."

"I'm...not a victim?" He felt like one.

"Right now, you look guilty as sin."

Oh, no. "Lawyer," Reese choked out. "I should get one of those. Talk to one, now."

"Should have done that shit hours ago," Cedric muttered.

"Then why didn't you tell—"

A knock rapped against the door.

Cedric's head turned toward the knock, and a frown pulled at his brows. Before he could call out, the door opened. A tall, ice-cold blonde strolled into the room on killer high heels. Her gaze was a glacial gray, and diamonds glinted in her ears. She was wearing a light-blue blouse and a pencil skirt to match and her hair was pulled back into a no-nonsense twist. "Detective Coleman..." She made a tut-tut sound. "Are you interviewing my client?"

"Your client?" His eyebrows jerked down. "Since when?"

Reese had no idea who the blonde was, but that shark-like smile of hers both reassured him and terrified him.

"Since..." She looked at her wrist. There was no watch there. "Four hours ago. And that means you've held my client for four hours too long."

"That's not what it means, Ella Grace."

Her mouth tightened. "You know I hate it when you use both of my names."

"Blame your mother. She gave you two, not me."

Her eyes narrowed on him.

"Ahem."

Reese strained his neck and realized that two people were behind his new lawyer, er, Ella Grace. When he caught sight of Chloe and Joel, Reese surged to his feet. "Finally!" Now he was reassured. Less terrified. Chloe was there. Things would be fine. "Get me out of here!" It sounded like a plea because it was.

Chloe hurried to him. He could have sworn that she looked worried. Chloe *never* looked worried, and when he caught what could have been fear in her eyes... "Oh, God." Reese gulped. "Am I going to prison?"

"Absolutely not," Chole assured him. She pulled him in for a fierce hug. That close, she whispered, "You know I would never let that happen to you."

He squeezed his eyes closed and just held her for a moment. Chloe was there. He should stop freaking out. He should, but he couldn't quite seem to manage that feat. "I don't know what—"

"Do not say another word!" This came from the blonde. "Nothing else."

He clamped his lips together. Held Chloe a bit longer, then slowly eased back. Reese glanced over at Joel. The guy was studying him with hooded eyes. Hell, did Joel believe he was guilty?

Am I guilty? He couldn't remember much about the night before. He'd gone to the Serpent. Thought he might get lucky at a few hands of cards. He'd known King would let him in because of Reese's connection to Chloe. But...

I don't remember playing cards.

The last thing he remembered was downing his drink.

"What evidence do you possibly have to hold my client?" Ella Grace was asking.

Cedric waved one hand in a slow roll. "Oh, the usual. He was found in the dead woman's bed. The window in her bedroom had been smashed. Got a strong B & E case right there."

"I think I was drugged," Reese said miserably.

The blonde immediately whipped around to glare at him. "What did I tell you?"

"Not to say another word."

"Then *why* are you talking?"

"She's frightening," he mumbled to Chloe. And he meant frightening not in a good, sexy way.

"Damn straight, I am," the blonde didn't miss a beat.

"EG," Chloe said. "Give me a moment."

A grudging nod from the lawyer. EG...Ella Grace.

Chloe closed in on Cedric. "Did you run the tests?"

"Yes, but you know how backed up the labs can be and—"

Another knock at the door. Reese wondered who'd be coming in this time. The little room wouldn't fit many more people.

A uniform cop popped his head inside. "Lab reports are back, detective. I was told it was a rush order and to bring them to you immediately."

Cedric took the file. Didn't open it. As the uniform hurried out, Cedric kept his gaze on Chloe. "How did the lab get the results so fast?"

She shrugged. "They must have been motivated."

Reese wanted to kiss her. Of course, Chloe had been involved. She had his back. They were family.

"You should look inside," Chloe advised in her cool and calm voice. "See if he'd been drinking. I'm curious about his blood alcohol level with the amount of booze you reported smelling..."

Cedric didn't look inside. "You know I did a breathalyzer analysis at the scene."

"Um, you did?"

"You know I did."

Joel was just watching, with his arms crossed and his shoulder propped up against the doorframe.

The lawyer frowned as she watched the byplay between Chloe and Cedric. Frowned, but didn't interrupt.

"He hadn't been drinking," Cedric finally said.

Reese's jaw dropped. Then he hurriedly snapped it shut. "Damn straight. Chloe told me to try going sober, so I—" She put her hand on his chest. He got the message. Reese stopped talking. Man, his heart was still beating so crazy hard. Too hard.

And the room was just getting hotter.

Once more, he wondered...was he having a heart attack? It sure felt that way.

"Why don't you open the file, Cedric?" Chloe prompted.

His stare didn't waver from her. "You already know what's inside."

"I do."

"'Cause you read the report?"

"Because I trust my brother and only one explanation makes sense here."

Despite feeling like absolute shit, Reese's shoulders straightened. Chloe trusted him. He was somebody. Not dirt to be tossed away and locked up. Forgotten. Chloe was his family. Thicker than blood. She would always come to help him.

He wrapped an arm around her shoulders and kept her at his side. "I love you," he told her and damn if he didn't get a little teary.

Cedric lifted his brows. "Would've bet money he was drunk," he muttered. He opened the file.

"You would have lost the bet," Chloe told him. "Joel? What do you think Cedric is discovering right now?"

Joel edged closer. Reese couldn't help but tense and pull Chloe a little closer. While he trusted Chloe with all of his being, he still wasn't sure how he felt about Joel. The doctor was...intense. Dangerous.

Chloe had always been drawn to danger.

"Do you have any memory of last night?" Joel asked.

"Seriously?" The lawyer tossed her hands into the air. "What part of *do not say another word* did everyone miss?"

Miserably, Reese shook his head. "I had my virgin drink, then I woke up in a weird bed with guns pointed at me."

"Rohypnol," Joel and Cedric both said at the same time.

Reese narrowed his eyes because he knew that term. "The date rape drug? I thought that shit was illegal."

"Setting a man up for murder is also illegal," Chloe confided in him. "I don't think the perpetrator that we are after cares a whole lot about legality issues." She pursed her lips. "Perpetrators," she corrected.

His stomach couldn't knot more.

"Drug and urine analyses confirms it." Cedric flipped the file closed. "Your brother had some of the highest concentrations of the drug in his system that I've ever seen."

He'd been drugged?

"Where were you when you got that beverage?" Chloe asked him.

The lawyer shook her head.

"The Serpent," Cedric replied before Reese could say anything. "He already told me that."

Because he was watching his sister so closely, Reese caught the faint narrowing of her eyes. Chloe didn't like that answer.

But her voice was still clear and cool as she said, "In light of this evidence, don't you think my brother should be released?"

Cedric hesitated. "There's a B and E charge..."

"He was incapacitated last night. That means someone had to carry him to Lucia's home. Someone else broke into the house and left him in her bed. We should ask around at the Serpent and see who remembers what happened there."

"Oh, we should." Cedric's mouth tightened. "We all know how cooperative King likes to be. I'm sure he'll welcome my team with open arms."

"I want my brother to come home." Now she focused on the lawyer. "What do we need to do in order to make this happen?"

EG nodded and straightened her shoulders. "My client is a victim. He was drugged and kidnapped. He needs to be released immediately..."

Ignoring the lawyer, Cedric asked Chloe, "Why the hell would someone drag Reese into this mess? Why leave him at Lucia's?"

"I do have a few ideas on that..." Chloe murmured.

***

"Chloe, stop!"

Chloe stilled at Cedric's booming voice. She and Joel had headed back into the station's bullpen while the lawyer hashed things out with the cops—and with the chief, who'd also been called in because obviously, the case was a nightmare.

Two bodies. A drugged—and kidnapped—victim. Plenty of blood and gore. The Press was going to become insane when they learned the full details of this story.

She and Joel both turned to face Cedric. Even though it was heading late into the evening, his shirt was still perfectly pressed. She wondered how he managed that. How did he always look so unruffled and controlled? Except...his shoes were wrong. Scruffy sneakers that looked too small when he normally favored his expensive loafers.

"I want to know what you aren't telling me," Cedric demanded.

Chloe dismissed the matter of his shoes. "What makes you think I'm not—"

"You think Ruben didn't tell me about your early morning visit? Come on, Chloe. He tells me everything."

She'd rather suspected that he did.

"The number of cuts on the vic was significant." He waved toward Joel. "Just like what happened to you, am I right?"

"Not exactly what happened." Joel's voice was grim. "But damn close."

"And now your brother is pulled into whatever the hell is happening." Cedric took a step closer to Chloe and lowered his voice. "How much danger are you in?" Cedric asked her.

She didn't know. That was one of the things that worried her. "Reese isn't some lightweight. It would have taken at least two people to move him. He didn't just disappear from the Serpent. Someone saw him leave." And she was...angry. Angry because she'd gone to Kingston, and he hadn't mentioned a word about her brother.

But maybe I'm supposed to be angry at him. Maybe that's why my brother was taken from the Serpent. Another nail in Kingston's coffin...

"I talked to Lucia's friends," he revealed. "They said she hated her stepfather. Never told them why. But when I dug deeper, I found out that she attempted suicide when she was fifteen years old. The year after her mom died. She was sent into a treatment facility, but I can't learn what the hell she talked about with her counselors. You know how that stuff is kept confidential."

Yes, she did.

"There have been whispers—never anything solid—that Towers liked the women young." Cedric's gaze was hard. "Abuse? Is that what we're dealing with here? Talk straight with me. I can't help if I don't know what's happening."

"It's hard to know for sure what happened to her," Chloe replied carefully. "Since Lucia is dead, she can't really tell us—directly—what might have been done to her."

"You think he abused her."

She held his gaze.

Cedric swore. "And she killed the stepfather."

A nod. "Looks that way."

Cedric pointed to Joel. "Why the hell did she mimic your attack? Don't say that she didn't. The fact that we found Chloe's brother in her bed means all of this mess is tied to you both. Did you know Lucia, Joel? Had you crossed paths with her? Dated her? What?"

"I'd never met her. Never seen her until we walked into that dance studio."

Cedric kept studying him, as if trying to weigh Joel's response for truth or deception. Finally, he grunted and glanced at Chloe. "And did you know her?"

Lying would serve no purpose, and she didn't enjoy lying to Cedric. "I'd seen her face before."

A muscle jerked along his jaw. "Where?"

"Dancing."

"Dancing...where? Jesus, it is like pulling teeth."

She wouldn't know. Chloe had never been a dentist. "At the Serpent."

He closed his eyes. She knew he was counting to ten. She counted along with him. When she reached nine, she paused a beat for him to get to ten, then said, "I know you're not a Kingston Broussard fan."

"I am not a fan of career criminals. Yep, you nailed it." He opened his eyes.

"Kingston wouldn't do this to Reese."

"Oh? Why not? Because he's such an upstanding member of society?"

"No. Because he knows that if he comes after my family, I can burn his house of cards to the ground and never hesitate." She felt Joel's stare on her. Was he trying to decide if she was telling the truth? She was. Completely. When it came to Kingston, she knew where he'd buried all of his dark secrets. She also knew how to dig them up. "It wouldn't be smart for him to hurt someone I care about."

"Maybe that's why Reese is still breathing. Maybe leaving him that way was a message—a threat—for you."

"No. It's more." She could feel it. "Someone told Lucia what to do to her father. Someone gave her instructions to follow, and when she was done, when she'd followed those orders, Lucia was killed."

"The dead don't talk." Cedric's hands flexed at his sides.

"Sure, they do. You just have to be very quiet so you can hear them."

He flinched. "You freak me out when you say shit like that."

Now who was lying? "I freak you out even when I don't say shit like that."

Cedric didn't reply.

"Going by the timeline I'm working," Chloe turned brisk, "my brother wasn't pulled in until *after* Lucia was dead. The killer eliminated her, then turned his attention to Reese."

"Why?"

Chloe did not like the answer that sprang to mind.

***

Cedric had stormed away. But before he'd rushed off, he'd told Chloe that he'd make sure Reese was taken care of. Her brother wasn't going to be released right away, but with the blood and urine analysis reports, she knew it was only going to be a matter of time. Especially with EG on the case.

And maybe the cops would get lucky. Everyone had security systems these days. Perhaps a neighbor had managed to catch a video of the perps hauling Reese into Lucia's home.

Doubtful, though. Nothing about this case seemed lucky.

From the corner of her eye, she slanted a glance at Joel. "You're being oddly quiet."

"Trying to figure things out. With you, I always feel like I'm running several steps behind."

She faced him. She was vaguely aware of the noise in the bullpen. The ringing phones. The voices. The slam of drawers. The jingle of keys.

"It's like there is something else here," he added, voice roughening. "Something I don't see."

Her lips pressed together.

"You're not holding out on me, are you, Chloe? Cedric asked how much danger you're in, but you didn't answer him." His hand lifted and curled against her cheek. "Baby, I am here. I am not scared of anything out there."

He'd come so far. She thought of how he'd been when they first met. He'd pulled away from everyone and everything near him. The hand that touched her so tenderly had once been used to save lives. But he didn't do that any longer.

Because he'd killed. Because he'd changed.

Just like Lucia had changed? "There will be more," she told him. He needed this warning. "I think someone out there isn't going to wait any longer."

"Wait for what?"

Wait for you. But she didn't say that. She couldn't. Because *she* was afraid—of losing Joel.

CHAPTER SIX

The line of richly dressed men and women wrapped around the Serpent. Joel and Chloe had headed to the club shortly after they'd left the police station. Reese was still in custody, but his lawyer had assured them he would be released that night. Chloe had called Marie Kim, her friend/driver/who-the-hell-knew-what-else,   to take Reese home from the station.

While Marie was taking care of Reese, Joel knew that Chloe wanted to hunt.

So the hell did he.

"Your ex isn't still in town, is he?" Joel asked as he surveyed the line. He and Chloe weren't exactly dressed for the Serpent. Not like all of those other people, but who the hell cared? He knew they'd get inside, one way or the other.

As they'd driven back to the club, he hadn't been able to stop thinking about possibilities. Suspects. Who hated them enough to pull this kind of shit?

Chloe's psycho ex jumped to the top of his list. *Morgan Fletcher.* He'd met the bastard after becoming involved with Chloe. Could the guy be capable of murder? Oh, hell, yes, Joel certainly thought so. But...

"As far as I know, he's not in town. But Marie is working to track him down." She tucked a lock of hair behind her ear. "He's good at staying off the radar."

Wonderful. "So he could be here now..." He motioned toward the crowd. "Watching us?"

She tilted her head and swept her gaze over the crowd. "We need to get inside. I don't think our killer likes loose ends."

"Most killers don't. I'm just going out on a limb to say that." He threaded his fingers with hers and marched to the front of the line. When he saw the bouncer, his shoulders stiffened at the familiar figure. Not one of the jerks who'd been with Kingston that morning, but a guy he *had* encountered before. Exactly in that same spot. "Wedge." The man was on door-bouncer duty again. *Wedge.* What the hell kind of name was that?

Wedge's eyes immediately narrowed on him. But then he saw Chloe, and the man's granite-like face softened. "Saw your brother last night," he told Chloe. "Friendly guy. Not like some people I could mention." A telling glare was directed at Joel.

"I am not in the mood for your crap," Joel snapped at him.

"Oh, yeah?" Wedge surged toward him. "I am not in the mood for—"

"Wedge, I get that you enjoy antagonizing Joel. But this isn't the time." Chloe touched Wedge's chest. "Did you see anyone with my brother?"

After shooting one more glare at Joel, Wedge focused back on her. "Nah. Came in alone. I let him skip the line because he told me you were his sister."

"How did you know he was even telling the truth?" Joel wanted to know.

"Because I'd seen him once or twice before, back when Chloe used to be so tight with King." He smirked at Joel. "Or do you not know about those days?"

"Wedge..." A warning note entered Chloe's voice.

He shrugged. "Sorry, Chloe. He just pisses me off."

"The feeling is mutual," Joel assured him.

Wedge flipped him off.

"What about when Reese left?" Chloe tapped her chin. "Did you see him then?"

Wedge scratched his rather broad chin. "Don't think I saw him. My shift ended at midnight, so he must have left after that."

Or he just hadn't come out the front door.

"Do me a favor, Wedge?" Chloe asked.

"Anything."

Well, that response had certainly been fast.

"Pass the word. I want to know if anyone saw my brother talking to...friends."

"Friends?" Wedge's face scrunched. "Something wrong here, Chloe?"

"Yeah, something is very wrong," Joel answered. "Some prick roofied her brother while he was here."

Alarm flashed on Wedge's face. "Lower your voice!" He cast an anxious glance toward the line, then added, "King will lose his mind over this. You know he runs this place with a tight fist."

"Not tight enough," Joel murmured. Obviously. Or people wouldn't be getting roofied in his club.

"He's not here tonight," Wedge added quickly. "Haven't seen him all day."

Oh, sure. That wasn't suspicious. At all.

Wedge waved them inside. Probably because he didn't want Joel talking about roofies while other people were close enough to overhear.

After they were in the club, Chloe peered up at Joel. "Why don't you like him?"

Let me count the reasons. He'd just start with reason number one. "Because the last time we were here, he tried to attack me?"

"No, I think you attacked him."

Fine. Semantics. Whatever. "He was coming at you—"

"I told you before that Wedge would never hurt a woman. He has a rule about that."

"Forgive me if I don't buy that the guy is a major rule follower." They were inside. And he could smell money. He didn't need to see the diamonds winking at the ears of the women or the pearls adorning their throats to know that big money was at play. He could feel it.

"Why do you do that?" Chloe was staring at him, not the crowd. "You were a successful surgeon, and I know you have a very large amount of money in the bank. It's just sitting there, collecting dust and interest. You have money to burn, yet you tense when you see people like these individuals."

Yes, he had been a surgeon. And before that, he'd been a poor kid with no family. "I just feel like it's all for show. No one is real in here."

"Maybe people put on shows because they're afraid. Not arrogant or cocky. Maybe they're afraid if they show who they really are, no one will like them."

He didn't get a big fear vibe in that place. Champagne was spilling out of glasses and laughter rang in the air. The laughter mixed with the soft classical music that filled the club. The music came from the black-dressed symphony performers on the stage.

"There should be security footage," Chloe decided. "King is a control freak. You might not see the cameras, but they are here." She pointed upstairs. "And I know where the security room is hidden."

Of course, she knew.

"Follow me," Chloe said.

Sure. Why the hell not? They cut a path through the crowd and headed toward the stairs. The VIP area was upstairs, and two bouncers were waiting at the bottom to stop people from heading up. One of those jerks was the guard Joel had punched earlier that day. He sported a dark bruise along his jaw. When he saw Joel and Chloe, he immediately tensed.

"Oh, hell, no—" he began.

But he didn't get to say more because an explosion rocked the Serpent. The boom was deafening. The whole building seemed to shake, and even as Joel was trying to make sense of what in the hell was happening, the windows on the second level—the windows that let the VIPs spy down on the people dancing—were shattering outward. A burst of fire rolled through the broken windows even as alarms began blaring.

Screams. Shouts. Thundering feet.

Chaos.

The guard who'd been blocking their path hurtled to the floor when a second explosion blasted through the club.

Chloe staggered, but Joel caught her in a fierce grip. Smoke was quickly thickening the air around them, and the crackle of flames could be heard even over the screams. "Baby? You okay?" Frantic, his hands raced over her body.

She coughed and glanced up at him. She looked dazed. Uncertain. So not his usual Chloe.

People were stampeding down from the top floor and mixing with the folks who'd been on the lower level. They were running for the exit, and he saw people falling down. Getting trampled. Screaming.

He scooped Chloe into his arms. "I'm getting you out of here."

The guards hadn't waited to help anyone. They'd picked themselves up and hauled ass out of there.

"Help!" A terrified shout from the second floor.

More screams. Pleas.

The glass had cut people. He could see the blood pouring down arms and necks and staining the expensive clothes that the club goers had worn. And the fire—it was spreading. The sprinklers hadn't kicked on. They should have been spraying down on them, but nothing was happening.

"Let me go, Joel." Chloe struggled against him.

He tightened his hold on her. "The hell I will." He ducked and weaved through the crowd. Saw more blood. A woman with a broken arm.

"We have to help them!" Chloe cried. "You know we do!"

He knew that Chloe had to get to safety. He almost had her at the door. He almost—

Wedge. That big, hulking sonofabitch had burst into the club. "Get out this way!" Wedge bellowed. It looked as if he'd ripped the doors straight from the frames to keep them open.

Then Wedge ran forward and picked up a sobbing woman from the floor. He carried her out—

"You're going outside," Joel snarled to Chloe as he followed Wedge. "You're staying out there. I'll go back in."

She shook her head. "Once it gets too hot, it's too dangerous to go back in. If the air temperature increases too much, you can take one breath and die and—*Joel, let me go!*" She shoved her elbow into his ribs—hard—but he just tightened his grip and rushed for the door. There was no way he was letting her go. He knew Chloe—she'd run up *toward* the bombs. And it had to be bombs. No mistaking those impact blasts. There could be another set to blow at any time. Chunks of the second floor and ceiling were raining down. The whole building was unstable.

Getting Chloe out was priority one. He had to know she was safe, then Joel would go back.

"Take her!" Joel yelled just as Wedge rushed back in again. Blood trickled down the side of Wedge's face, but the other man's eyes were sharp and focused. "Do *not* let her back in!" Joel shoved Chloe into Wedge's arms. Then didn't hesitate as he turned around and headed back toward the chaos.

Chloe screamed his name, but Joel didn't stop. People were hurt. He headed for the stairs and the desperate pleas that he could hear filling the air. Glass crunched beneath his feet.

***

"Stay out here, Chloe," Wedge told her as he put her gently down on her feet. "I need to help—women are crying in there. I have to go back inside."

She nodded and watched him rush away. She counted down in her head as more people stumbled out.

Three. Two. One.

Wedge had disappeared inside. She hadn't wanted to fight him, though she was fairly certain she could have taken him out if needed. No, Wedge was intent on helping others, and hurting him—the giant man with his equally giant heart—had never been something she wanted.

So she just waited for him to get inside. Then she rushed forward.

Joel didn't know her at all if he thought she was just going to stand safely outside while other people were dying. She didn't watch while other people suffered.

That was her mother's style.

Not hers.

***

Joel tightened his hold on the woman he'd found sprawled near the top of the stairs on the second floor. A giant gash ran the length of her thigh, at least eight inches long. He'd wrapped it with a torn piece of his shirt and tried to keep her as still as possible in his arms. She was out cold—from shock or from pain. He watched his step and dodged the chunks of wood and broken furniture that seemed to be everywhere.

A moan slipped from her lips when he was about ten feet from the door.

He hadn't seen any EMTs yet. No cops. No firefighters. They had to get there soon.

There hadn't been another explosion. Not yet.

"Anyone else upstairs?" It was Wedge. He had a man in a bloody suit thrown over one wide shoulder.

Joel nodded grimly. One of the people he'd seen up there had been far past the point of saving. But he'd heard moans from others. He needed to get this woman to safety and get back to—

From the corner of his eye, Joel thought he saw movement. A quick flash that raced by even as he was lunging for the open doorway.

Chloe?

No. His stomach knotted. Chloe was outside. She wasn't rushing back into the Serpent. She wouldn't do that.

He hurried outside. Heard the wail of sirens. A crowd had gathered. Wounded were scattered around. Most people were staring at the building with wide, shell-shocked eyes. "Somebody help me!" he thundered.

His roar shoved people into motion. Two men—young, college-age-type kids—hurried forward.

"Keep her stable. Get her into an ambulance as soon as—"

Another wail. The ambulance was coming into view.

"I'm pre-med," one of the guys said. "I got her."

Joel spun back for the building. He took about four running steps forward.

"Stay back, buddy!" A firefighter slammed his hand onto Joel's chest. "We got this. No one else needs to go back in that place."

"People are trapped inside," Joel quickly told him. "I heard voices on the second floor. Think bombs went off. At least two, but there could be more set to explode up there."

The man's eyes widened right before he grabbed his radio and barked out commands. Joel spared a glance for the crowd. "Chloe?" He didn't see her.

Because she went back inside.

Wedge was trying to get back inside, but two cops were pulling him back. The cavalry had finally arrived and they were intent on keeping civilians out. "Wedge!" Joel shouted. "Where is Chloe?"

"Out here," Wedge fired back. He glared at the closest cop. "I saw a woman in there, behind the bar. You *will* get the fuck out of my way so I can help her."

Frantic, Joel glanced around once more. He still didn't see Chloe and every instinct he possessed screamed...

Inside.

Screw it. He shoved past a firefighter and ran back inside. Wedge was right behind him. Joel didn't know if the cops had gotten the fuck out of Wedge's way or not. He just knew Wedge was going back inside, and so was he.

The smoke wasn't that thick, thank Christ. That meant he could keep breathing. There were faint flames overhead, and the place looked wrecked to hell and back. Tables overturned. Smashed. Glass everywhere.

He coughed as he rushed up the stairs. The smoke *was* thicker up there. He turned to the left, then the right, looking for Chloe, but he didn't see her. Fear twisted in him, and he hurried for the VIP rooms. The door to the one on the left hung open, smashed from the inside out by the force of the blast. That room—he'd been in it long ago. He'd played poker in that room while Chloe had sat, blindfolded, but still able to perfectly read all of the players in the room.

A man was on the floor. Sprawled. Or, what was left of the poor bastard was spread on the floor. There was nothing that Joel could do for him, so he followed the faint moans that he heard.

Moans that came from a hallway that snaked to the right. Another broken door. More glass. More chunks of debris and—

Chloe.

On her knees as she struggled to lift a giant cabinet off a softly crying woman. Joel didn't waste time. He went straight to Chloe's side and heaved that cabinet off the vic. As soon as it cleared her legs, Chloe pulled the other woman out of the way. One of the woman's fancy high heels rolled across the floor.

He let the cabinet fall. Fire crackled in the corner. The bombs hadn't set off any kind of chain reaction there. Just explosive force. They were still able to breathe and function normally—for the damn moment.

He assessed the woman. Stark white face. Dilated pupils. Trembling lips. One look at her legs, and he knew that she had multiple breaks. There was a vicious open fracture on her left leg, about two inches below her kneecap. The bone shoved through the edge of her skin.

An ominous creak sounded from above.

"Structural integrity is gone," Chloe said as she looked up. "Collapse is imminent."

Fuck. He could see that. He shot a glare at Chloe. "Get the hell out—and this time, don't come back!"

As Chloe jumped to her feet, he scooped up the woman and ran. He was only vaguely aware of the broken monitors and computers around him. The creak turned into a deep groan just as heavy chunks—wood, plaster, dark parts of the roof—

began to fall down on them. Joel dodged as best he could and he tried to keep the victim steady.

A board slammed into his back, and Joel stumbled, but he didn't go down. He ran forward and hit the stairs. Firefighters were there. They grabbed him. The victim. Chloe.

And the second floor completely caved in.

***

Joel leaned toward a man who sat on a curb. Blood trickled down the guy's face. Joel was talking softly to him. Shining a light in his eyes. Chloe wasn't sure where Joel had even gotten that light.

The area looked like a war zone. So many shell-shocked faces. Not enough first responders. More were coming, Chloe knew it. But the authorities hadn't been expecting a double bombing in their town. They were scrambling to cope.

Joel left that victim. Immediately ran to help an older man who'd just grabbed his chest. Chloe tensed. *Heart attack?* An EMT joined Joel. They got the man into the back of an ambulance that had recently arrived.

"Didn't know he was a doctor," Wedge said as he ambled closer to Chloe.

She glanced at him. "You're bleeding." She lifted her hand to wave for one of the EMTs.

"Nah. I don't need them." Wedge caught her fingers. "Been hurt much worse than this. Those people—they need your doctor and the others more than I do."

She surveyed him. Normal speech. No weaving. The blood was heaviest on his hands. "You had to dig some people out, didn't you?"

A shrug. "It's a good thing I'm so big."

"It is a good thing," she replied softly.

"I don't know how to patch people up. I-I can't help do that." He let her hand go.

She grabbed him right back. "You helped *plenty* tonight, Wedge."

He gave her a small smile.

"You need to let the EMTs patch up your hands," she insisted. The skin was torn and ripped open in spots.

But Wedge just shook his head. "Like I said, I've been hurt worse." He slipped away.

She looked back at the crowd. Not everyone had made it out. She'd seen the dead upstairs. Dead that would now need to be recovered from the wreckage. It would take time. Some of the dead—one man had been in pieces.

Her hands trembled. She clenched them into fists.

"Chloe..." Cedric's voice.

She'd texted him as soon as she'd gotten out of the building. Well, the second time she'd gotten out.

His gaze raked her. "Are you hurt?"

She probably looked like hell. She was pretty sure some of her hair had been scorched. "None of the blood is mine."

Cedric swallowed. "Knew you'd come here. As soon as your brother said this was the last place he'd been...I knew."

The cops were keeping the crowd back.

"I didn't expect this," Cedric continued gruffly. "What the fuck happened?"

"Two detonations. Both upstairs. I believe one was triggered in the main VIP room, while the second was in the security room."

She saw his features harden. "The security room?"

Chloe nodded. "I suspect the intent was to destroy any footage that may have been recorded the night my brother was here."

Cedric swore. "I really hope there is some backup in the cloud or—"

"We'll have to ask Kingston."

His attention immediately shifted to the crowd. "And where is he right now?"

"I don't know." Even as she made the confession, Chloe knew this was going to be bad. "He wasn't here tonight."

Cedric's gaze jumped back to her. "That's real lucky for him, isn't it?"

Lucky? No, she knew that wasn't what he actually meant. What Cedric was really saying was...

That is suspicious as all hell.

He wasn't wrong.

***

"You look like shit."

Reese glanced up at the smooth, female voice. He'd just shuffled out of the police station. His lawyer—who both impressed him and still scared him—was at his side. But the woman who'd done the talking? The one who'd just given the lovely assessment of his shit-looking-self?

She waited near the limo. Her arms were crossed over her chest, and her slender hips pressed back against the side of the vehicle. Her midnight-black hair, dead straight, slid over her cheek as she studied him.

"Thanks," he told her gruffly. "You always know just what to say."

Marie Kim's lips twitched, but the smile didn't reach her dark eyes. Instead, he could have sworn that she was staring at him with worry in her gaze. Crazy, of course, because Marie had made it clear—on numerous occasions—that she didn't give two flying fucks about him.

"Looks like I'm your ride." She opened the back door to the limo. "He *is* free to go, isn't he?" she asked the lawyer.

"The cops will have more questions." EG sent him a pointed look. "You will *not* answer those questions without me present."

His head pounded constantly, and nausea rolled in his gut. "I will not," he assured her. His British accent thickened the words.

She nodded, apparently pleased. "Then, yes, he is free to go tonight." Her eyes darted to Marie. "I trust you will ensure that he is watched?"

Watched?

"Absolutely." Marie didn't miss a beat. "I've got my orders from Chloe. I'll be his shadow, don't you worry."

His shadow? What was that about?

But his lawyer was ditching him, and he didn't feel like just standing around in front of the police station all night, especially when there was a limo in front of him. He walked toward Marie. "Could you have used anything less...billboard flashy?"

"I could have," she readily agreed. "But I thought you were the one who enjoyed flash. Figured a ride home in a limo might cheer you up." She motioned toward the open door.

He looked at the cavernous interior and just shook his head. Reese headed up to the front of the limo and made himself comfortable in the passenger seat. He closed his eyes and sagged against the leather.

He heard her shut the back door. Then her soft steps padded toward the front of the vehicle. Marie opened her door and slid inside.

"Are you okay?" Not flippant or mocking. How very unlike her.

"I'll live."

She shut the door. Started the car. They drove in silence. That was the thing about Marie, she was always good with silence. She didn't make small, idle talk. Didn't ramble. She loved the quiet. Peace.

When he was near her, he always felt a sense of peace.

So he didn't talk. She didn't ask him questions. They drove in silence and the pounding in his head eased. When he could think clearly again, he did manage to ask, "Why are you my shadow?"

"Because Chloe said you needed protection."

Given the recent events, yes, Chloe was probably right. And he knew enough about Marie to understand she was absolutely a force to be reckoned with in this world. If she was going to be pulling bodyguard duty, no way would he argue with her. "You want to keep my body safe, hmm?"

"Oh, feeling good enough to flirt, are you?"

Not really. But it was her. Even half dead, he wouldn't be able to pass up a chance to flirt with Marie.

"It's cute," she told him. "But know what's even cuter? You lost your accent."

Fuck.

"Not when the lawyer was present. Just with me." More silence. Then, softer, "But we both know why you did that, don't we?"

Because he was tired as shit and it was hard to think clearly?

"You trust me," Marie said.

Yes, he did.

"You know I wouldn't hurt you."

His eyes opened. He turned his head to look at her profile. "No, it's not that."

"You *do* think I'd hurt you?" The faintest hint of...uncertainty. Pain.

That was wrong, too. "It's not about you hurting me." She should already know this. If she didn't, then she was just blind. "It's because I'm in love with you."

Marie sucked in a sharp breath.

She didn't speak again.

And Reese just enjoyed the peace that he felt when he was near her.

CHAPTER SEVEN

By the time she got home, Chloe wanted to crash. Her body was torn between exhaustion and the mad surge of adrenaline that had been created back at the Serpent. She went home alone because Joel had ridden in the ambulance with one of the patients. They'd been on the way to Memorial Grove hospital. Joel was known there. He'd even been offered a position by the people in charge, but he'd turned it down in order to keep working with her.

After seeing him in action that night, she wondered if he thought the decision had been a mistake.

Maybe working with her *was* a mistake.

Maybe he was ready to go back to his old life, and if he was, she couldn't stop him.

Chloe shut the door behind her. Put her back against it. Her hair slid forward over her face.

"My, my..." Marie said as she strolled down the stairs. "And here I thought your brother looked like shit."

Her head lifted. "He's back here?"

"Yes. Currently snoring loudly enough to shake the house. Surprised you didn't hear him."

Marie reached the landing and stared at Chloe across the expanse of the foyer. "Rough night?"

"The Serpent is gone. Two explosions. One was in the security room, so the footage of Reese's night will be long gone."

"That would explain the singed hair on your left side. You'll want to trim that up later." Marie's shoulders tensed, belying her almost mocking words, then she pushed, "*You* weren't hurt in the explosions?"

"I'm fine." Chloe made a mental note to trim that hair.

"Where's the stray who usually trails you?"

Chloe swallowed. Her body ached, and she wanted to get into a shower and just wash the night away. "At the hospital. He's okay. Just—"

"Falling back into old habits. Got it."

She didn't think being a doctor was a habit. He'd studied for years to be a surgeon. He'd wanted that life. Until a monster had tried to take it away from him. "He may not stay," Chloe heard herself admit.

Marie took a step toward her. "Stay at the hospital...or with you?"

This wasn't the time. If she hadn't been so tired, Chloe would never have made that slip. "I can count on you to watch out for Reese, can't I? I will pay whatever you need for bodyguard services with him and—"

"I'll watch Reese, and you won't pay me anything else."

One problem solved. Reese would be safe. "Thank you."

Marie nodded.

Chloe headed for the stairs. As she passed Marie, her friend reached out a hand to touch her side.

Chloe stilled. "There's something else?"

"There are a few somethings."

The night was never going to end.

"Morgan Fletcher." Marie dropped the name and stared into Chloe's eyes.

She fought the urge to tense at the mention of her ex-fiancé's name. "I asked you to check up on him. Judging by your expression, I take it that you've already found something interesting."

"Oh, it wasn't hard to find info. If you hadn't been out battling explosions, you probably would have heard the news, too. Not every day that a man comes back from the dead."

Morgan hadn't been dead. He'd *faked* his death some time ago and created a whole new identity for himself. Mostly because Chloe had led him to believe she had proof of crimes he'd committed. Crimes like...murder.

"Your ex is making headlines in Boston right now," Marie revealed in a carefully neutral tone. "Seems that when his yacht went down, he made it onto a life raft. He was lost at sea for a while. Rescued by some fishermen. He was injured, quite confused. Didn't know who he was. His memory has only recently returned."

The entire story was bullshit. Morgan hadn't been lost. In fact, he'd recently been in New Orleans. Watching her. Then he'd fallen off the radar again...

Only to now show back up in Boston? "This is really not something I need right now."

"Then you should have let me kill him when I had the chance."

Yes, true. Marie wasn't wrong. The man needed killing. *Because he isn't going to stop.*

"He thinks he's in love with you," Marie added.

"I'm just his latest obsession. I fit his pattern." She looked just like the first woman her ex had killed. Chloe tried to push back the tension in her body. She hated thinking about Morgan. He reminded her of what a huge mistake she'd made.

Once upon a time, she'd thought that she had a real connection with him.

Then, of course, she'd realized the truth. Morgan Fletcher—handsome criminal defense attorney, charmer—was evil.

"It's not your fault."

At Marie's low words, Chloe realized that she'd been staring at the floor. Her gaze jerked up. "It is. I made a mistake with him. I let him get close to us all. I should have realized the truth sooner."

"The man is a world-class liar. You should see the media coverage he's getting right now."

Unfortunately, she would have to see it. Later.

"It's like a conquering hero has come home. He's feeding his tale of woe to reporters who are greedily swallowing it whole."

"He always did have a knack for being able to capture his audience." That was why he'd been such an effective defense attorney. He could make any jury believe his words. Could get them eating out of his hand.

He even fooled me.

"I'll deal with him." Chloe squared her shoulders. "At least we know where he is. If he's in Boston, holding court with reporters, that gives me time to handle what's happening here." One nightmare at a time. She put her foot on the bottom step.

"What's his plan?"

Chloe glanced back. "Mutual destruction."

Marie's eyebrows dipped low. "What?"

"He disappeared before because he thought I had intel I could use against him." Because Chloe had figured out who—what—he really was. "I think he now has information that he believes he can use against me."

"What kind of information?"

Information about her family. "I'll deal with him," Chloe said again.

"Oh, great. Wonderful. Don't share. That's the way to play it."

"It's...been a very trying day. As you pointed out before, my hair even caught on fire. I need to go upstairs." Before she collapsed. "Thank you for the information on Morgan—and for watching after Reese."

Marie pressed her lips together and looked away.

There was something else? Dread settled around her shoulders. "What is it?"

"Reese...he must still be out of his head."

Alarm flared. *Reese.* He was what mattered, not Morgan. She knew that Reese had been examined by several doctors while in police custody and they'd given him the all-clear. Yes, he'd have dizziness and headaches, but he should have been *fine*. "What happened?" Reese could not be—

"He said he loved me."

"Oh." Chloe exhaled. Relief filled her. "Is that all?"

"Is that all?" Marie stared at Chloe as if she'd just sprouted a second head. "You knew this?"

"Well, of course. Didn't you?" Why was Marie wasting time asking what had been apparent?

"No, no, I did not know. I am not psychic. I can't read the man's mind!"

She didn't have to read his mind. Chloe thought his intentions had been obvious. "He asked you out dozens of times."

Marie retreated a few feet. "Asking someone out is not love. It's lust. Vague interest. And I've been dating other men. He knows that."

"Yes. I think it was hard for him to watch you go out with the others. But he wanted you happy. When you love someone, you want them happy above all else." Didn't she want Joel to be happy? Even if it meant he would leave her? "When you love, you will lie, steal, or kill to protect the person who owns your heart. You think you won't stoop so low." She wet her lower lip. "But you do." She studied her friend. "Why do you look afraid?" Marie wasn't the fearful sort.

"Reese can't love me."

That made no sense. "He does, so...he can."

"He's a liar and a thief."

Chloe didn't deny the charges. They were true.

"A liar and a thief, in love with a killer." A bitter laugh escaped Marie. "That's hardly the way the fairy tales go."

"Yes, but we've both always found those stories to be annoyingly predictable, haven't we? And the villains from those stories could have done so much more if they were allowed more page time."

Marie took another step back. "I will protect him. You find out who did this stuff to him—find out who drugged him and put him in that house—and we'll eliminate the threat."

Working on that. One problem at a time. Sadly, her problems were piling up at a chillingly fast rate.

"I'll protect him," Marie said again. "But I will not love him." With that, she spun on her heel and hurried away.

Chloe watched her friend vanish into the shadows. She thought about calling out once more, but didn't. Marie's final words had confused her.

Did Marie not realize that she already loved Reese?

Shaking her head, Chloe climbed up the stairs.

***

He shouldn't go to her. Joel knew he needed to stay away from Chloe. He was angry. No, *furious*. His blood seemed to burn with fire. Adrenaline churned inside of him, making his emotions even more dangerous.

No, he should not go to Chloe. Not now. He should go to his place. He should crash into the bed. Wait until the morning to confront her when he could be semi-calm and logical.

But he didn't go to his home. Instead, he went straight for the main house. He had a key. Chloe had given him a key to everything. All of the cars. The houses.

Her fucking heart?

He didn't slam the door behind him. There were others in the house, and he didn't want to wake them. He just wanted Chloe.

Joel bounded for the stairs.

"You're wearing scrubs. You must have showered and changed at the hospital."

Her voice—her very awake and aware voice—came from the right. His head whipped to the side, and he saw Chloe standing in the open doorway of the study. She'd been waiting for him? "You knew I'd come to find you."

"I knew you were mad." She wore white silk pajamas. No bra. He could see the tight points of her nipples poking through the fabric of her shirt. "Did you come to voice your upset?"

Voice his upset? His hands clenched and released. He even tried Cedric's tactic of counting to ten. Cedric had assured him the counting helped when dealing with Chloe.

It didn't help Joel.

Counting to twenty didn't help.

By thirty, he was storming toward her.

She didn't move. Just waited. He was right in front of her when—

"Perhaps I should start by voicing my upset," Chole told him. Her chin notched up and her brilliant gaze hardened. "Don't ever push me outside again and then run back into danger. If you do that, our partnership is over."

Every muscle in his body locked down. "Excuse me?"

"I think you heard what I said. It's very quiet in this house right now. But if I need to repeat—"

"You are the most fucking important thing in my world," he growled. "No, you *are* my world. Nothing else—no one else—matters. You do. If a building is exploding around us, then getting you to safety is my number one priority because *you* are my priority."

She stared at him. Blinked as she processed his words.

He didn't touch her, not yet, because when he touched her, his control would be gone. There was more to say. More for her to understand. "I would do it again." Not be partners any longer? What the hell was that about?

"And I would run back inside again," Chloe returned.

His hands flew up and his palms slammed down against the wall on either side of her head. "Why the hell would you do that?"

"Because *you* ran back inside."

"I ran back inside because I'm a fucking doctor! My job is to save lives! I couldn't leave those people in there when I—" He stopped. Something had changed. He'd seen the flicker of her lashes. A very small change, but he'd noticed it because he tried to be hyperaware when it came to Chloe. When someone was your whole fucking world—and she was—you noticed shit. "What?"

"My job is to stop killers, but I don't like to leave the living hurt. I could help them. I could get them out. Watching from the sidelines while people were screaming for help *and* you were risking your life—that isn't who I am. That is not who I will ever be."

She was holding back. He could feel it. But his control was so shot to hell that he couldn't backtrack to figure out what had happened. "If you die...what happens to me?" He leaned toward her. His forehead pressed to hers.

Her hand rose and slid against his stubble-covered cheek. A careful, soft caress. "You keep living. I'm not your whole world, Joel. I'm just a small part of it."

Screw that. She was—

"You keep living. You be happy. You save lives and you do the things that bring you joy."

He damn well felt like he was hearing some break-up speech. It scared him and pissed him off even more. "Our partnership isn't over."

"No?"

"*No.*" He kissed her. He was just done. At the end of his rope and his control and his mouth crashed down on hers. He'd thought Chloe was safe, but when he'd turned around and she hadn't been on that street outside of the Serpent...

She might think she was a small part of his world. She was dead wrong. For him, Chloe was *it*. She had no idea how close to being lost he'd been before she'd come into his life.

Her mouth opened beneath his. Her tongue brushed over his, and a greedy rumble broke from him. Sometimes, he just wanted to fucking eat her alive.

She kissed him back with a hungry fury. Her teasing tongue and her lips were driving him crazy. His kiss became harder. Rougher.

Chloe pulled her mouth from his. "Marie and Reese are in the house."

And he and Chloe were making out right there where they might be discovered. Check. Got it.

He tugged Chloe inside of the study and shut the door. He flipped the lock and took her mouth again. Going upstairs to her room probably would have been the better idea, but he didn't have the control for that. He wanted her right then. His hand was snaking down her body, shoving the pajama pants—and her tiny, silken pair of panties—out of his way. He worked his hand between her thighs as she rose onto her tiptoes and held him tight.

Tight.

That was how she felt when he dipped two fingers into her. So tight that he thought he might lose his mind. Tight and hot and perfect.

Mine.

His thumb rubbed her clit, got her moaning for him. He needed her wet and hot because he had to get inside of her.

Now.

He kissed a path down her neck. Her head tipped back. He had her up against the door. His whole body was rock hard, and all he could think about was fucking her.

He pulled his hand away from her body. Shoved his scrubs out of the way. His cock sprang toward her, and he lifted Chloe up, holding her easily against the door. He sank into her, driving as deep as he could go, even as she wrapped her legs around him.

There was no holding back once he thrust inside of her. The delicate inner walls of her sex clutched him, squeezed, and he went blind to everything but need. He pounded into her. Withdrew. Thrust. Her nails raked down his arms as Chloe arched and twisted against him.

There wasn't tenderness. Gentle touches. There was only savagery. Primal need.

When she started to moan, he took her mouth again.

She was so tight and hot that he knew his sanity was gone. There was no way to stay sane when there was this much need. Hunger.

Chloe jerked against him when she came. He felt the soft contractions of her sex around him, felt the trembles in her body, and he followed her straight into oblivion.

Bam. Bam. Bam. His heart thundered. He'd squeezed his eyes shut and darkness surrounded him. No, she surrounded him. Joel could feel her soft, sensual body pressed to his. Could smell her delicious scent.

Everything else faded away until there was only Chloe. He didn't see the wreckage from the explosion. Didn't hear the cries for help.

Bam. Bam. Bam.

His head lifted. He stared into her eyes. His breath heaved in and out. "I love you," he rasped.

He thought she'd say the words back. Instead, Chloe gave him a faint, almost sad smile. "Remember that."

Remember it? He'd never forget it.

Joel kissed her once more.

***

He'd stayed in her bad last night. Unusual. Joel typically liked to go back to his place. No, he liked to take her back there, not go alone. He didn't feel confined in his place. He could look through his glass ceiling as he sprawled in bed.

But he'd stayed. Probably a testament to how exhausted he'd been. He'd slept with his arms around her, and, as far as she knew, no nightmares had plagued him.

They hadn't plagued her, either. Sometimes, her dreams became so intense that she would strike out. She hadn't done that with Joel.

Not yet.

Chloe made her way into the kitchen, but stopped when she saw Reese sitting at the counter. Even on the best of days, her brother wasn't an early riser. And this day? Right after everything that had happened to him?

He lifted a mug of coffee toward her. "Surprise, surprise."

She pulled her robe closer to her body. "You couldn't sleep."

"I slept some. But when I woke up..." He slowly put down his mug. "Want to tell me what's happening?"

"I can't tell you what I don't know."

"Chloe...it's me."

It was. Reese. The person who'd been her lifeline. Not her real brother, though very few knew that. Reese had been a con man when he first found his way into her life. Not so much a con man as...barely a con kid. But she'd needed him. He'd needed her. They'd been together ever since. "I'm so sorry you were pulled into this."

His lips dipped down. "It would help if I knew what this was."

It would help if she fully understood, too. She closed the distance between them and slid onto the barstool near him. "I think you should go away for a while," she murmured. She didn't drink coffee. Normally, she preferred a nice tea in the morning, but not today. Her hands flattened on the countertop. "You and Marie. I'll pay for everything. Go someplace nice and tropical. When you come back, everything will be fine."

His hand slid on top of hers. Squeezed. "You're trying to get rid of me."

She was, but Chloe was doing it to protect him. "I didn't see the danger coming toward you. I let down my guard. I knew the threat was still out there, but I stopped looking for him." Because she'd been so caught up in the life she'd been given. Joel. The way he made her feel.

She should have known better.

"Him?"

"Glenn Towers, the man who was killed, had one hundred and four knife wounds on his body."

Reese whistled. "Damn. Someone wanted to make sure he was good and dead."

"No." That hadn't been the intent. "Someone wanted to send me a message. Or…send Joel a message."

She saw the understanding in the widening of Reese's eyes. "How many wounds did your boyfriend get when he was attacked?"

"He had the same number of knife wounds. And Lucia's body was found in a building that connects to Joel."

"Fuck me."

"Exactly." Forget tea. She could do with something stronger. "I knew it would be a matter of time. I just…I didn't expect this development." Being caught off guard was new for her. Unsettling.

Frightening.

"You should leave today," Chloe advised him. "I know you can pack fast, and Marie always has a bag at the ready."

His head cocked. "Why does Marie—"

"I won't be able to hunt him if I think you are in danger." She stared into his eyes. "You are the only family I have."

The faint lines near his eyes tightened. "I don't want to leave you."

"And I don't want to find you covered in your own blood with your body sliced open in a dozen different ways."

"*Jesus.*"

"I'm being honest. I don't want that, Reese." Finding her parents covered in blood had been more than enough for her. She didn't want to discover him that way. "You are the only family I have left."

"Not real family," he whispered.

Real to her.

"They…they took my fingerprints, Chloe." His confession came in a rush. "What if—what if there is a way for them to—" He broke off when she shook her head. "What?"

"Any fingerprints that they took will match with those that were on file for Charleston Reese Hastings. Be assured of that." She'd taken care of that issue long ago.

His shoulder sagged. "Sometimes, you're scary, you know that?"

Not scary enough. If she was, then no one would be threatening her family. "I need you to leave because I don't know what he will do." *He.* The killer who was in New Orleans. The killer sending her messages. Screwing with her life. *Her brother's life.*

"You used to have theories. All of these ideas." His hold tightened on her. "We both know it."

The house seemed so quiet and still. It wasn't even six a.m. yet. She'd had to leave the bed because her mind wouldn't stop spinning. "I think he wants to make monsters."

"So he's your freaking opposite."

She blinked. "What?"

"You think I don't get what you do? Why you do it?" He let her hand go and touched his chest. "I'm the cheap imitation. The real deal was someone you couldn't help. You saw him going off the rails but you couldn't stop it. Just like you couldn't stop your mom. Now, what you do—you can tell the cops it's about stopping killers, but I know it's not. I know you. You've figured out how they think. You did that because you want to figure out how to stop them. How to change them before they cross the line. The bastard you're after—you say he wants to make monsters. Fine. Whatever. That's his sick deal. But for you? I think *you* want to take monsters and turn them back into men."

At first, Chloe didn't know what to say. She absorbed his words and turned them over in her mind. He...wasn't wrong. Only she hadn't been quite aware that her motivations had been so obvious. But... "Item one, there is nothing cheap about you."

His lips parted.

"You have the most expensive tastes of anyone I've ever met."

"Uh, I wasn't talking about—"

She'd been trying to make a joke. She did it so rarely that no one—save Joel—understood her attempts. "You are not an imitation. You are the good that he never was."

"I'm a liar, Chloe. A man you met when I tried to scam away your family's money by pretending to be some long-lost brother—"

"You are the man who protected me when I needed it the most. You came into my life when I wasn't sure what my next move would be." She'd been a teenager. Powerless. "You were my angel."

"That's...that's like poetic and shit."

Not quite. She let her gaze sweep over his features. "You are not a weak imitation," she said again. "You are the brother I have always needed."

His shoulders straightened.

"But you are still getting the hell out of town. And you're taking Marie with you."

"Chloe…"

"If he wants to make monsters, he could try with her." Marie had been so close to taking that step years ago. But Chloe was careful with her words now, because she knew from his expression that Reese was not going to leave to protect himself.

But you'll leave to protect her.

"I would hate for Marie to fall prey to someone who wants to use her," Chloe added deliberately.

His jaw hardened. "No one is going to use Marie."

"If you tell her that it's your idea, if you tell her that you will feel better getting out of town, she'll go with you."

His eyes narrowed. "And the cops are going to be fine with me just vanishing? I'm pretty sure my lawyer agreed that I wouldn't leave town."

"I'll handle the cops. And your lawyer." His safety came first. "You handle Marie. She told me about your confession, by the way."

"My confession?" His brows shot up.

"Don't you remember?" She'd feared he might not. It wasn't like him to admit his feelings so plainly. "You told her that you loved her."

"I did not!" An immediate denial.

"You did."

"Christ." Reese squeezed his eyes shut. "I was tired as hell. I-I…screwed up."

That would remain to be seen. "Sometimes, it is best to get secrets out. Bringing them into the light can change everything."

"You're right." His eyes opened. His gaze pinned her. "You have to tell him." His shoulders were still straight, and in that moment, he seemed determined. "It can't go on this way." He gave a firm nod.

Unease trickled through her. She could have sworn that goosebumps were growing on her arms. Chloe exhaled slowly. "I have told Joel." And it had been a major step for her. "I told Joel that I think I love him." Love. A four-letter word that she didn't use often. But everything with Joel was different. Even the way she felt. She wanted to—

"No! Jeez, no, I am not talking about how you feel about the guy." A wince. "But if you really do love him, don't you think that is all the more reason to tell the man the truth?"

The truth. A weight seemed to settle in the pit of her stomach. "I want to protect him."

His hands moved to curl around her shoulders. "I get that. I do, Chloe. But this is huge. Life-altering. Joel is going to lose his shit when he finds out."

"Why do you think I haven't told him?" Because the last thing she wanted was for, um, Joel to lose his shit.

"He deserves the truth. No matter how hard it might be for him to hear." Reese gazed into her eyes. "You know it."

"It will wreck him." Everything was different now.

"Yes, well, it's kind of wrecking information, don't you think?"

"Reese…" He didn't understand.

"You have to tell him." His hold tightened on her. "You have to tell Joel that when he crawled out of that fucking hole he'd been buried in…when Joel killed the man he found waiting for him— that bastard wasn't the sick SOB who'd tortured Joel for hours on end. You have to tell Joel that he killed the wrong man. The real sadistic prick is still out there. You have to tell him—"

"*What?*" Joel's voice. Ragged. Gruff. Stunned. "What in the fuck did you just say?"

CHAPTER EIGHT

Reese's head whipped toward him. Reese's mouth dropped open, and he sputtered, "Y-you...y-you..."

Chloe's movements were slower. Her spine straightened. Her chin lifted. Then she maneuvered her whole body around to face Joel as she used her foot to swing around on the stool. "You can move so quietly." Her voice was admiring. "And you've learned the house so well. You know every board that squeaks, don't you? You can go through the entire place without making so much as a sound."

He was frozen to the spot. Reese's words were screaming through his head.

You have to tell Joel that when he crawled out of that fucking hole he'd been buried in...when Joel killed the man he found waiting for him—that bastard wasn't the sick SOB who'd tortured Joel for hours on end. You have to tell Joel that he killed the wrong man. The real sadistic prick is still out there.

That was...wrong. Reese was wrong. Or maybe Joel had heard wrong. Everything was wrong.

The real sadistic prick is still out there.

"Chloe?" Her name was more growl than anything else.

"Reese, will you give us some time alone? Perhaps you should go pack."

For a moment, it looked as if Reese would argue. But, no, he never argued with Chloe. He jumped off the stool. Winced as he stared at Joel. Pity flashed in his eyes even as he raked a hand through his tousled, blond hair.

You have to tell Joel that he killed the wrong man. Impossible. Joel had escaped. The bastard's shovel had still been at the ready. His gloves had been dirty. He'd swung the shovel at Joel—

Reese clapped a hand around Joel's shoulder. Joel flinched.

"I'm sorry," Reese told him. "But it's going to be okay."

Joel could only shake his head. This was wrong. Nothing felt okay. "Chloe?"

Reese let him go and walked away.

She pressed her lips together.

"Reese...is wrong." His words were wooden. Hollow. He felt hollow.

"I'm afraid he isn't."

He took a step and could have sworn that he almost fell. The floor seemed to tilt under him. His hands flew out to steady himself.

Chloe jumped toward him. She grabbed his right hand.

The floor stopped tilting.

He stared into Chloe's eyes. Her beautiful, unforgettable, blue eyes.

"I haven't been completely honest with you, Joel."

Chloe loved him.

"When we first met, I didn't realize how things would go with us. You've always been hard for me to predict."

He couldn't look away from her. His heartbeat was too loud. It felt as if it were shaking his chest.

"The more I got to know you...things changed. What I thought about you changed."

What she'd *thought?* What had she thought?

"And I knew what the truth would do to you."

"The truth." He barely recognized his own voice. "What is the truth?"

"The truth is...you weren't the first he played his game with, and you were not the last."

"What?" Joel shook his head.

"Did you ever..." She bit her lip. Stopped.

"Don't fucking stop now."

He saw her throat move as she swallowed. "Did you ever do any research on the man who was there with the shovel?"

"The man I killed."

She inclined her head in the faintest of nods. "Did you ever look at his life? His childhood? His education? His criminal record—"

"He was an ex-con. The cops told me he had a rap sheet dating back to when he'd been a teen." His heartbeat felt off. Fast and jerky.

"He did have a long history with the police. Started with shoplifting. Petty theft. Moved up to B&Es. Mostly all non-violent crimes."

She'd researched the bastard?

"There was nothing there that would tie him to an attack of the nature that happened to you."

"He was fucking *near my grave*. He had the shovel. He—"

"He had a reputation for hiring out his services. He'd even rolled on a body disposal case before, in order to get out of a B&E charge. Made a deal with the DA. Honestly, all of that should have come to light after your attack, but I think the authorities wanted to just make everything go away. They wanted the city to feel safe. Perhaps it was better for everyone not to dig too deeply when the bad guy was right there."

He wasn't hearing her correctly. "No."

"He buried you. I don't deny that. There *is* no denying it. But I read your statements, Joel. You never saw the face of the man who tortured you. You can't say that it was Sam Morrow. He buried you. You dug yourself out. When Sam realized you were coming for him, he grabbed the shovel. He attacked you, so you had to defend yourself." She squeezed his hand. "You understand what I'm saying? *You defended* yourself."

He could see the shovel swinging toward him. "You're wrong."

"I found video footage of Sam Morrow. Footage taken at the time you were taken. When you were being held. Cut. While that was happening, Sam was at a strip club. He was caught on the club's security camera." Her gaze held his. "I can show you the footage if you'd like."

She had proof? The man who...

"He's still out there, Joel. The man who tortured you? He's alive. And you may not believe this next part but...I don't think he ever intended to kill you."

What the fuck? Joel yanked his hand away from her and stumbled back. The numbness was fading. Anger—rage—built. "Did you miss the scars on my body? He fucking meant to kill me."

"If that had been his intent, then how did he miss every vital organ that you have? One hundred and four slices. Some deep. Some shallow. And never once—not once—did he hit anything that would have made you bleed out."

"I was *buried*."

"A shallow grave. Shallow enough for you to crawl out." Her words came fast. "That wouldn't be normal for Sam. I told you, he was a grave digger—"

Joel flinched.

"He would have known to bury you deep. I believe he was told to put you in a shallow grave. Told to wait there, probably promised payment or something, but the truth was that the man who hurt you—he wanted you to find Sam waiting with the shovel. He wanted you to think that Sam had hurt you and then he wanted..." Her words trailed away.

"Don't stop now."

"I don't want to hurt you," she whispered.

A little late. "You've been fucking me and lying to me."

Her lips parted.

"You knew this from day one and you didn't tell me. I thought you were the one person in the world I could count on." He could only shake his head. "What was I? God, I know your obsession with killers. Was I just some kind of test for you? Some experiment? Some—"

"Not to me."

Those words chilled him. "Chloe..."

"I am sorry," she said again.

Were those tears in her eyes? Chloe didn't cry.

"You were a surgeon. You saved lives." She bit her lower lip.

His chest burned as a tear slid down her cheek.

"Don't you see what he wanted you to do?" Chloe's voice was so husky and low.

Take a life.

Another tear trailed over her cheek. "He wanted to take something strong and break it apart."

Not break it apart. Slice it apart. Joel thought of all the stitches he'd gotten after the attack.

Slice me apart...and then have me stitched back together. Except, hadn't he been put back together wrong? Hadn't he felt *wrong* since the attack? Darker? Dangerous? Shit, even his shrink had warned him, that Gordo jerk had told Joel that he was unstable. That he could be a threat to those around him...

Because I was an experiment?

No. No, that wasn't—

"He didn't break you, though, Joel."

He stared at his hands. He'd pounded his fists into Sam Morrow, over and over again. Until the only sound he'd known had been the thud of flesh hitting flesh.

"He didn't win. You aren't—"

His head whipped. "I can't be near you."

She sucked in a sharp breath. "Joel, I-I know you're angry." She stepped toward him.

He immediately stepped back. "You don't know what I am."

"I do. I know you."

What she knew was killers. And he—Every part of him hurt. "Stay away from me."

"Joel—"

"I'll pack up the guest house and be gone before nightfall." The pain was growing. "Don't come near me again."

All of the color bled from her face. A tremble shook her body. "I...I love you."

He turned away from her. Stormed for the door. Didn't look back. Couldn't.

***

Her cheeks were wet. Chloe reached up her hand and swiped her fingers over her left cheek, then her right. She'd been standing in that same spot for a few minutes, just staring.

Joel had left. She'd heard his steps thundering away. The slam of the door.

The distant roar of his motorcycle.

He shouldn't be driving when he was upset. It wasn't good. Not safe. He should be careful.

Don't come near me again.

She'd been afraid to tell him the truth. Once you started a lie, it was hard to stop. Stopping meant that people got hurt.

She hadn't wanted Joel to be hurt.

"You don't screw up." Reese's voice. He'd just walked into the kitchen. He stood near the entranceway, waiting.

I do screw up. I messed up with you. You were drugged, taken, and I didn't see it coming.

"You knew Joel was in the kitchen, didn't you?" Reese asked her softly.

Her lips were trembling so hard. She clamped them together. She couldn't ever remember feeling this way. As if someone had reached into her and ripped out something vital.

Reese crossed the kitchen and stopped in front of her. His hand lifted and brushed across her cheek.

Was she still crying? She did it so rarely. It felt odd. Her head was aching, too. A dull thud behind her eyes.

"You knew he was there. You wanted the truth to come out, didn't you?"

Joel had deserved the truth, even if it hurt.

"Because you think the man who hurt Joel is here in New Orleans." Not a question this time. "He's...the one who took me?" Reese asked carefully.

"He arranged for you to be taken." She wasn't sure he'd done it himself. There were other options she had to explore. Other people she had to check out and— "Joel left."

"I know."

Her head bowed forward. "He won't be coming back."

And it hurt. She'd lost other people before. People who'd managed to slip their way close to her. Even people who'd managed to fool her into thinking they were different than what they were.

Like Morgan...

But Joel—everything had felt better with him. Or maybe she'd just hoped it would be better.

"He'll be back." Reese seemed confident.

But then, he hadn't seen Joel's face. "I hurt him."

"Chloe, you are the only one who can help him."

Her head lifted.

"You know it. I know it. No one else was even looking for the man who did that shit to Joel. Everyone else let him go. You are the one who knows he is out there. You can find him."

"I *am* going to find him." Because of what he'd done to Joel. To her brother. To Lucia. To— "I am going to stop him."

"Damn straight, you are." He brushed his fingers over her cheek once more. "Let's get focused. You're always like a torpedo when you're focused."

Nothing was focused for her. The world was spinning too fast. *He left. He won't be back.*

"Tell me step one. What is the first thing you need to do?"

She sucked in a breath. Another. Pulled it in and released slowly. "I need to find out who triggered the bombs at the Serpent."

"Seeing the footage of that wreckage when I woke up this morning freaked me the hell out. Would have been nice if you'd let me know you were trapped at a bomb scene sooner."

She stared blankly at him.

"Right. Other things are going on. Lots seem to be going on." He cleared his throat. "Back to step one. Let's go find out who triggered those bombs."

Her brows pulled low. "You're not going with me. You were packing so that you and Marie could go someplace safe." She knew he hadn't forgotten the plan. It hadn't even been that long ago since they'd discussed the whole situation.

"Oh, yeah, about that." Another careful brush of his fingertips across her cheeks. "I was lying. That's what I do. You know this. I'm a liar and a thief."

He was so much more than that. Her head shook in a negative motion. "Reese..."

"I will never leave you when you need me. You need me now."

Her hand lifted and curled around his. "It's dangerous."

"I kinda figured that when I woke up in a strange house with no memory of the previous night."

"But what if you don't wake up next time? He could have just as easily left you dead in the bed."

His eyes narrowed. "Why didn't he?"

She didn't speak.

"You have an idea. What is it?"

She let his hand go and eased back. "I would feel so much better if you and Marie would go someplace tropical." She turned away and paced back toward the counter. "What are you going to do about the confession you made to her—"

"You won't distract me."

Her shoulders stiffened.

"You think I don't know your tricks? I've been on to the way you operate for ages. You can throw out your lines and distract others, but not me." A pause. "Why am I not dead?"

Chloe exhaled slowly. "Because I believe you were a message. A threat."

"He's threatening you."

In a way but... "If you would just leave, it would be so much—"

His footsteps padded across the kitchen. His hand closed around her shoulder, and he turned her toward him. "You're in this guy's head already. You understood what message he was sending." He searched her eyes. "Tell me. I'm not letting this go."

"When did you become so determined?"

"Probably when I started spending too damn much time with you." His jaw set. "We can stand here all day, or you can tell me what I want to know and it will speed things along. You know, speed up that whole finding the bomber situation and all."

She wondered if Reese realized how very much he'd changed since they first met. "I *think*...because you were at Lucia's...the intent was not for me to suspect you were responsible for what happened to her. The cops might believe that. They may think that you're being set up by whoever drugged you, but I don't believe that's the case."

"It sure as hell seems like the case."

No. "He could have killed you just as easily as he left you alive."

"You do keep mentioning that." He swallowed. His hand was still around her shoulder.

"I know who he is—I don't mean his actual identity. If I had his name, I'd be shouting it to the cops about now. But...I know what he did. To Joel. To others. But Joel didn't know."

His lips parted. "You're not saying...wait. Was I some kind of warning?"

She believed that he was. "When I heard what happened to you...I got the message."

"And the message was...?"

"Tell Joel the truth or I take someone that you value."

"That's...that's a huge crazy jump. People don't make jumps like that."

She did. The killer did. "I took someone he valued. Joel was his experiment. I took him. Brought him here with me. But I kept the truth from Joel about what had really happened to him."

His hand slid away from her shoulder. "So you're telling me...you...you just gave up Joel to save my sorry ass? You made your big reveal to him, knowing he'd turn and walk away from you—you did that for me?"

"I don't happen to think your ass is sorry. I'm quite fond of it. And you."

"But you *love* Joel."

Yes. She also loved Reese. Though...had she ever told him those words? Sometimes, they were so hard for her to voice.

"Fuck," he whispered. "You did that for me?"

"For you and for him." Two men that she loved, in different ways. Strange. Growing up, she'd always felt so cold. Like her heart was encased in ice. Nothing could get through the ice.

Joel and Reese had. "He deserved the truth. The lie had to end. This man...he will come for Joel." *I have to be ready for him.*

"You think he's going to kill Joel? The way he killed Lucia?"

"Kill him or use him..."

"Use him for what?"

She thought of the words she'd said to Joel. *He wanted to take something strong and break it apart.* "He isn't done with Joel."

Because to be fully done with Joel, she thought the perp would want to conclude his experiment. To make a monster.

But I won't let that happen. No matter what she had to do, Chloe would not let that happen to Joel. He might hate her, he might never want to see her again, but she would not stand back and let anyone hurt him.

"Step one," Chloe said once more as her shoulders straightened. "I find out who triggered those bombs."

"How do we do that?"

She'd noticed his not-so-subtle stress on "we" in that question. "I go and talk to some bomb investigators, and I see if I can gain access to the Serpent. *You* stay here with Marie. The cops aren't going to be down with you appearing at crime scenes."

"Hey, at least they know *I* didn't set the bombs. I was in their custody while this craziness was going down. That should make me clear as a bell."

She lifted an eyebrow.

"You can't go alone," Reese insisted.

Chloe sent him a gentle smile. "Who said anything about me being alone?"

CHAPTER NINE

He didn't even know where the hell he was going. Joel drove hard and fast and tried to escape, but the truth kept pounding at him.

I murdered the wrong man. He'd used his fists. Used that damn shovel. He'd *killed* a man. And...

It wasn't him. Joel had been so fucking wrong. All along. And Chloe had known. From the very beginning. When he replayed their conversations in his head, there had so many tells there. But he hadn't seen them. First, it had taken him too long to truly understand Chloe.

With her, half of the time, what she *didn't* say was more important than what she did.

And second, he'd been so certain. So sure that he'd stopped the bastard who hurt him. But...had he been so certain because it was easier that way? Easier to think the SOB was no longer a threat?

Yet, deep down, a whisper said...*If you didn't think he was still a threat...why did you have so many locks on your apartment in New Orleans?* When Chloe had first met him, when she'd first come to his place, she'd seen the locks. She'd asked him—

He shut down the thought and braked his motorcycle. His hands clenched around the handlebars. He wanted to tilt his head back and yell. To roar his rage because the sonofabitch was still out there. He was still out there...

And I will fucking find him.

When Joel found him...

I will kill him.

Chloe was wrong. Rare, but shit happened. She thought that Joel hadn't been broken by the bastard.

If only.

He'd been broken straight to his core. *That* was why he'd left her. He'd looked at his hands and known exactly what he would do.

Hunt. Find the sadistic bastard. Kill him.

Joel was broken, through and through, and he couldn't be around Chloe. He was too dangerous. He was a monster. Chloe knew monsters. If she hadn't already done it, she'd look at him, and she'd know...

She'll see what I am.

She'd had to stop her own brother. End his life when he grew out of control. She'd killed the real Charleston Reese Hastings after her brother had brutally murdered Chloe's mother and father. Chloe's wealthy grandfather had made sure the truth of that nightmare was hidden from the rest of the world. And in time...

Chloe had found herself a new brother. A guy to take up the identity of her brother. A new Reese...one without the killing tendencies that her real brother had possessed.

Her real brother was out of control. A monster. He wanted Chloe to stop him. And she had. Even as a child, Chloe had stopped him.

Will I get out of control, too?

One man had long told Joel what he would become. One man had told Joel all of the signs were there. That Joel had to watch out for the breaks occurring in his psyche. That he had to be careful.

Joel hadn't listened to the warnings.

Now it was too late.

His breath heaved in and out. In and out. Rage built and blazed, but he tried to push past it. He tried to think...

His hand was shaking when he hauled out his phone. He hit the contact for the person he needed. Waited impatiently for the call to be answered—

When it was picked up, he didn't waste time with words. "I need an address. And I need it now."

***

"I get this puts you in a difficult spot," Chloe said as she held her phone near her ear. "But I need you to know what's happening. I need your help." She listened. "Thank you." She slid the phone back into her bag and exited the vehicle. She stared at the house before her. Sagging porch. Faded paint. Steps that had warped from time. The shotgun house sat, waiting, for a second life. The houses around it had long since been updated. They were a vast array of colorful homes. Bright. Happy.

This house wasn't happy. She didn't know if it ever had been.

Her steps were determined as she headed for the front door. But she didn't get a chance to knock. Instead, the door was jerked open before she could even raise her fist.

"How the hell did you find me?" Kingston demanded.

Her nose wrinkled as the fumes hit her. "Did you fall into a barrel of whiskey?"

"Cute." He pointed over her shoulder. "Get your ass back in the car, Chloe."

"I will." A nod. "When you come with me." Her nose twitched. "A good thing I'm here to drive. You are certainly in no condition—"

"I'm not drunk."

"Oh, you just smell like—"

"Why are you wearing sunglasses?"

The abrupt question caught her by surprise. Chloe barely hesitated. "Because it's incredibly bright outside. The UV rays will—"

"You're pale, too."

"I'm always pale." British skin.

"Take off the glasses."

"Tell me why you smell like a whiskey distillery," Chloe returned.

"Because when I found out that some piece of shit had torched my club and that people had *died,* I grabbed the whiskey intending to get my ass drunk. But I took one swallow and realized that shit wasn't going to help. I threw the whiskey against the wall. The glass shattered. When I was cleaning it all up, the stuff got on me."

"When you throw things, they shatter." Her gaze darted to his right hand. A thick, white bandage had been secured around his hand. "Is that how you got the cut?"

"Yes."

"You're lying."

"Chloe..." He grabbed her hand and hauled her inside. He slammed the door behind her. "Why are you doing this to me? I hired *you*, remember? You are supposed to be on my side. You're not supposed to grill me and—"

"I was there last night. When the bombs went off."

His lips parted. It took him a few moments to rasp, "What?"

"I was there. Joel was there."

"You...aren't hurt?"

"No. And, by the way, you owe Wedge some sort of serious promotion. The man is being utterly wasted as a bouncer. When the rest of your guards were running for the doors, *he* was running back inside."

A muscle flexed along his jaw. "I will take care of him—*and* the others."

"I thought you would. But then...you already *have* taken care of some, haven't you? That's why you smell this way. Who did you go after? The manager? The fellow in charge of the VIP rooms? What was his name—Bruce? Boyd?"

"You damn well know it was Boyd Miller."

"Right." She did know. "You had a talk with him, hmmm?"

"Why would you think that?"

"Because someone attacked your place. Because Boyd was in charge. Because Boyd ran his ass out of there and I'm betting Wedge told you this already. So you—being the kind of man who would want to know why his place was bombed—you went to Boyd. You found him drinking while your place still smoldered. You fought him." She slanted a glance down at his hand. "I'm sure that is a cut from a broken bottle, but probably one you got when he came at you, fighting, and not a cut you got from throwing a bottle against a wall and then picking up the broken pieces."

"Broken pieces. Story of my life."

"I can relate to that."

He squinted at her. "I can never read you. Are you shitting me right now? It is not the time to shit me."

"Why haven't you gone to the FBI?"

"Fuck. Not that again." He whirled away from her.

"You cut ties, didn't you? Why?"

"Look, I told you before that I'm not an active FBI agent."

"No, but you *were* an agent. In another life. And at first, that life spilled over in New Orleans. They helped to put you in power—"

He spun back toward her. "I got my own power. I don't owe it to anyone or anything."

"You...were in organized crime."

His eyes glittered at her. "Don't touch it, Chloe. You—of all people—should know that the bad guys hide everywhere."

Yes, she knew that.

"They will completely disavow me. Just as I would them. I'm on my own. And that means if I can't prove my innocence on this...my ass will be locked away."

"Well, if you're trying to look innocent, beating up the manager of your club doesn't look the best."

Kingston shrugged. "So I was pissed. I thought Boyd might need to understand my level of anger. I also wanted to see if he'd been involved."

She didn't let her expression alter. "Because you think this was an inside job?"

He gave her a slow smile. "Ah, Chloe...don't you, love? Isn't that why you're here? Didn't you come...first, to see if I was guilty? To see if I'd set my own place to blow and if I'd killed those people?"

"No."

He blinked. Seemed caught off guard as his confidence faltered. "Excuse me?"

"No, that's not why I'm here. I'm here because I promised my brother that I wouldn't investigate alone. You're my new partner for the day."

"What. The. Hell?"

"New partner," she enunciated clearly. "Did you hit your head in the fight with Boyd?"

"You already have a partner. A jealous, possessive prick who usually trails you like a looming shadow." His head cocked. "Where is the doc, by the way?" Then his eyes widened. "Was he...did something happen to him last night?"

"Joel was not seriously injured in the events that took place last night."

He closed the distance between them. His hand flew up and snagged her glasses. He whipped them off. "Weird that you kept them on *inside*, don't you think?" His gaze hardened. "Want to tell me why your eyes look that way?"

She retrieved her glasses. "I'm assuming you are referring to the redness and puffiness of my eyes? In case you forgot, I *was* in a building that contained a great deal of smoke and debris last night."

"Didn't forget. Also don't think that is the reason."

She twirled the glasses in her hand. "Joel is no longer working with me. Because of the nature of this case, I assured my brother that I would not investigate alone today. Though, obviously, I am more than capable of handling things on my own."

"Obviously."

"Since you have a vested interest in finding out who put the bombs in your club, I thought you would like to accompany me. If I am mistaken, I can just get right out of your way. I won't waste more of your time."

"We both know you're not mistaken. We also both know I'm the number one suspect for the cops."

Agreed. "And that's why you came to your mother's old house. Because you didn't think anyone knew about it and you could lay low while you figured out which one of your enemies did this."

"Apparently, it wasn't low enough."

She inclined her head at the accurate truth. "I don't think it *was* one of your enemies."

"What?" Surprise flashed on his face, only to be quickly smoothed away. "Uh, yeah, it was. Nothing says 'personal attack' like someone bombing your club. Your VIP rooms. Your security room."

"I believe it was one of my enemies." If he was going to be working with her, he should know what he was up against.

Silence.

She waited. More time passed. He still remained silent. Her left foot began to tap against the floor. "Did you hear me? Should I repeat—"

"Your enemies tend to be twisted fucks."

"Yes." A brief pause. "Will that be a problem?"

"Not for me."

She'd hoped for that response.

"Let's go," he added. "The sooner I can make the fool pay, the better—"

She put her left hand on his chest even as her right continued to twirl the glasses. "How about you shower? When we are questioning people and looking for the truth, I think it would work to our advantage if you smelled a little less like you'd been drinking for days."

"Fair. A very fair point." He backed away. "But you stay here, got it?"

"Of course. Where else would I go?"

Shaking his head, he hurried into a nearby bathroom. She stood there and stared straight ahead. One of the benefits of a shotgun house. You could stand at one end and see clearly to the other. An old saying held that you could open the door, and fire a shotgun—the blast would go straight through and out the other side.

Because she could see so clearly in the house, she'd know the instant that Kingston stepped out of the shower. She'd see him. He'd see her. With that in mind, Chloe knew that she would have to be very fast with her search of the home.

As soon as she heard the pounding spray of the shower's water, she got busy.

***

Joel shoved open the door and marched into the small office. "Session's over." He ignored the killer view of the river. It was probably supposed to be soothing or some shit. It wasn't. "I'm sure Gordo will reschedule you for—"

"What are you doing?" Dr. Gordon Jennings leapt to his feet. His little notepad was gripped in one hand and his other fist clutched a black pen. "You can't barge in here when I'm working with a client!"

"Sure, I can. I just did." He waved to the client, a twenty-something-ish guy in a blue suit with gray glasses. He had been sprawled on the couch, but now the man was up and looking decidedly uncomfortable.

"I'm sorry," the woman who'd identified herself as Wendy Hyde, Gordon's office manager, pulled on Joel's shoulder. "I tried to stop him."

"What can I say?" Joel ignored her pulling. "I'm an unstoppable machine." His eyes narrowed on Gordo. "But isn't that what you always said?

Isn't that why you are *here* now? You followed me all the way to New Orleans."

A furrow appeared between Gordo's bushy brows. He studied Joel in silence for a tense moment, then turned his attention to the uncomfortable client. "My apologies, Stephen. It would appear that an emergency situation has developed. Please go with Wendy. She will make sure that you can get in to see me tomorrow."

Stephen shuffled toward the door. Wendy backed out with him. The door closed with a soft click.

Joel didn't move.

"I didn't...*follow* you here," Gordo began carefully. He cleared his throat. "I made connections when I previously came to the city. I was offered an adjunct position at Tulane, and the FBI indicated that they would like my help in working some cases—"

"Thought they had a whole behavioral analysis unit for stuff like that. And the last time I looked, you *weren't* FBI."

"Yes, well, neither is your friend, Chloe." He paced toward his desk and put down the pad and pen. "But she seems to get along well with law enforcement."

Not all law enforcement. She and Paul Richardson—the FBI agent who'd been the lead on the last big serial murder investigation in New Orleans—pretty much hated one another. "That why the FBI guy, Richardson, wanted you around? He thought you'd help him one-up her?"

Gordo turned back toward him. "You seem stressed, Joel. Have you been having the dreams again?" He stroked the carefully cropped beard that covered his jaw.

Joel swallowed. "I've never liked you. Not from the first moment we met."

"Yes, that was rather apparent." Gordo propped one hip on the desk.

"You didn't like me either. You told me...you thought I was dangerous."

"You are dangerous. And that Chloe friend of yours? She is dangerous *to* you. She will put you in situations that force you to face the darkness inside of yourself, and that darkness will grow, it will swallow you—"

Joel took a lunging step toward him.

Gordo's eyes widened in alarm. His hand flew back on this desk as he tried to grab the phone. Probably so he could call the cops.

Or maybe his FBI BFF. *Should have started with that move, Gordo.*

"Why?" Joel gritted out. He didn't try to stop Gordo from calling the cops or the FBI. He wasn't there to stop the man. He was there for answers.

"Why...what?" Gordo croaked.

"When I came to you before, you asked all the questions. It's my turn." He studied the shrink he'd come to hate.

Because he told me the truth? "Why did you tell me I was a threat? Why did you think I was so dangerous?"

"You were suffering from severe post-traumatic stress. You were locking all of your rage and pain inside. You didn't want to get past what had happened." Slowly, he stopped reaching for the phone. His fingers were inches from it. "The only thing that made you feel better was that the man who'd hurt you was dead."

"Shouldn't that have made me feel better?" *Except...it's all wrong. Wrong man. Wrong.* His chest burned. Joel rubbed his palm against the ache.

"It was like you'd gotten a taste for something. I feared you wanted more."

More what? More death? "You don't know me."

"Then why did you start working with Chloe Hastings? What did she offer that convinced you to join with her?"

When Chloe had first come to Joel...she'd offered him payback. A chance to stop the killers who hunted in the dark. Killers...like the man who had hurt Joel.

"I still think you are a threat, Joel," Gordo told him. "You need therapy. Medication. You need—"

"What if I killed the wrong fucking man?" Why was he still talking to Gordo? He hated this bastard.

Shock ripped across Gordo's face. "Wh-what?"

"How screwed up would that make me? That I killed the wrong guy?"

Gordo's mouth opened and closed, but no words emerged.

"That's what I thought." Joel spun away. "Figured you'd just want to know," he threw over his shoulder as he headed for the door. "You were right about me all along."

"Joel! Joel, wait! Let me help you, I can—"

He shot one look back. "No one can help me. But I think we both already knew that."

***

"Are you ready, Chloe?" The bathroom door had opened. Kingston stood in the doorway, dressed in jeans, a black shirt, and black boots. He'd applied a fresh bandage to his hand.

Chloe rose slowly from the couch. "Took you long enough. It's not like we have places to go or murders to solve."

His lips thinned. "Sorry to keep you waiting."

At least he'd apologized. "I do value punctuality."

As he closed in on her, his expression turned thoughtful. "I would imagine the cops are looking for me."

She nodded. "Yes, I would certainly imagine so, too. Lots of questions. The longer you avoid them, the more suspicious it will seem."

"But instead of going to the cops, I'll be with you because...?"

"Because I'm going to help you find the real culprit." They'd been over this. Why rehash? "Then you can take that information to the cops and hopefully clear yourself."

"Won't we cross paths with some of the cops while we are doing this investigation of yours?"

She let her eyebrows rise. "That is a possibility. I am sure I can deal with it when the situation arises—" Her phone beeped. A discordant, rough note. Chole pulled her phone from her bag. "Excuse me. That's my brother texting." She read the quick text and fired off a response. When she looked up, Kingston had a pensive expression on his face.

"There a problem?" he asked her.

"At least a dozen of them, but I'm trying to work them out." She shoved the phone back into her bag. "Shall we?"

"Where is our first stop?"

"Honestly, I'd like to take a look at the Serpent again, but that's not happening."

He shook his head. "Cops have it completely blocked off."

Because the investigation there would be quite lengthy. "So how about, instead, you take me to the facility you use to house your blackmail material?"

Kingston didn't so much as blink. "I'm afraid you're mistaken."

Chloe sighed. "And I'm afraid you're wasting my time." Her gaze darted around the house. "I'd thought that perhaps the material was here, but no such luck." Her attention returned to him. "I know you video the high stakes matches in your VIP rooms. I know that you have security *on* your security. You watch everyone who enters your domain. You find secrets that are useful, and you make those secrets work for you."

"Interesting ideas you have."

"The bomber *didn't* know. If he or she had known, there would have been an attack at the secondary location. Instead, the VIP rooms were destroyed, and the security footage room was destroyed." She glanced down at her watch. *Burning daylight.* "Don't play, Kingston." Her stare returned to him. "You have security footage. I want it. After Lucia was killed, someone at the Serpent drugged my brother. They took him and they put him in her bed. When I went to retrieve information from the Serpent—when I went to see which staff member had talked to my brother or what patron had been spending time with him—bam, the place exploded."

He swallowed.

"Inside job," she told him smoothly. "You were right on that. But this inside person doesn't know you like I do. This person doesn't know that you trust *no one*. That you have security on your security and that secrets are your business. So let's cut through the lies. Take me to a place where I can see the footage. I need to know who set this in motion."

***

"I remember you from last night." The woman in the hospital bed stared straight at Joel. "You saved my life. You and your girlfriend."

Joel had slipped into the hospital room of Kelly Addams moments before. He wasn't even sure why he was there but...

I didn't hurt her. Gordo was wrong. I saved someone. And if he had saved someone, then maybe he didn't have to leave Chloe. He was trying to think past the shock and the rage and figure out what the hell to do next.

"Are you a doctor?" She tried to push up in the bed. The machines around her immediately began frantically beeping.

"Take it easy." He lifted his hands toward her in one of those automatic, soothing motions. "You don't need to do anything to stress your body." Her legs were immobile. He moved closer to the bed so he could get a look at the work that had been performed so far.

"They put screws in the left leg." She scrunched her nose. "I heard one of the nurses saying that I'd have to do physical therapy, but that I was lucky I hadn't lost the leg."

His lips thinned.

"I don't remember what happened. One minute, I was at the Serpent, and the next, that woman with the dark hair and bright eyes—your girlfriend, I guess?—was there. She was trying to get a cabinet off me."

Chloe. For a moment, he remembered how absolutely terrified he'd been when he realized Chloe had gone back into the club. "Why do you keep saying she's my girlfriend?"

"Because I...I heard the two of you." A ghost of a smile lifted her lips and briefly lit her eyes. "You argued like a couple."

He glanced away.

"Thank you," she told him quietly. Her voice had slurred a little.

His gaze slid back to her. "You're on morphine, aren't you?"

She drifted back against the pillows. "The good stuff," she murmured.

He shouldn't be there. "Rest." Joel turned for the door.

"I...would have died in there. If you hadn't gotten me out."

"I'm glad I was able to help." His words came out sounding hoarse. "Do you...did you work at the Serpent?" Asking her questions when she was drugged up was wrong. "Never mind."

"Yeah. I help with security." Even more slurred. Her lashes were sagging. An IV dripped into her arm. "Started...last..."

She didn't get to say more. She'd drifted away. Joel figured she must have recently gotten her dosage. His gaze swept over her once more. "I'm glad I was there," he said again. *Very glad.*

She'd made it. Survived. A monster wouldn't help people to survive. He was more than that. Maybe...could Chloe have been right? Could the freak out there who'd attacked Joel—had he failed in his plan?

No, he didn't fail. You fucking killed the wrong man.

Squaring his shoulders, Joel strode for the door. He wished he could look at Kelly's file, but it was at the nurse's station, and he doubted they'd just hand it over to him. Though maybe he could bullshit his way to—

"What do you know? Chloe was right."

He stilled in the corridor. Turned his head slowly. And met the watchful gaze of Detective Cedric Coleman.

"She said you'd be here. That you would probably be interviewing the witness even though no one is supposed to be talking to her." Cedric's annoyed gaze drifted down the hallway. "Where the hell is the uniform I put on her?"

"No clue. Never saw a uniform."

Cedric shook his head. "You need to get out of here. Come on." He turned, obviously expecting Joel to follow him. "Let's get outside and—"

"I killed the wrong man."

Cedric's shoulders straightened. "Not now. Not here." He kept walking.

Joel gaped after him. Had the detective not heard what he'd just said? "Cedric—"

Cedric spun to face him. "The first time you met Chloe, didn't I warn you away?"

Yes, he had.

"But you didn't listen. Like a moth to a dumbass flame." He pointed at Joel. "Not now. Not here. You got me?"

"I got you."

"Good." Cedric whirled and started double-timing it down the hallway. As he hurried past the nurse's station he paused only long enough to say, "Make an announcement to get that uniform back at his station. If he's not there in five minutes, you call me, got it?"

"Yes, Detective Coleman."

He kept hurrying. Didn't stop until they were in the elevator. When someone else tried to join them, Cedric flashed his badge. "Totally full. Try the next one." He shoved a button on the control panel. The doors started to slide closed.

Joel kept his hands loose at his sides. As soon as they doors closed fully... "I know you heard me. I killed the wrong man. I want to go to the station and make a full confession so that I—"

"So that you can what—clear your conscience? Waste my time?"

Joel blinked. "Excuse me?"

"I read the reports. I've read them a whole lot since you walked into Chloe's life. You think I didn't get that she had an angle with you? Like Marie says, that woman is always pulling in strays. Thinks she can fix the world. She can't. Some people can't be fixed."

"I'm one of those people?" The words came out as a question.

"How the fuck do I know?"

The doors opened. Cedric continued his hurried walk, but he jerked his hand to indicate that Joel needed to speed up and keep pace.

Joel followed, mostly because he was confused as all hell. He'd just confessed to a cop so...

Cedric walked outside. Moved away from the main doors. Looked around to seemingly make sure that no one was close, then he nodded, apparently satisfied before he faced off with Joel. "Did Sam Morrow come at you with a shovel?"

"Yes, but—"

"I'm not looking for exposition here. I want a yes or no. I'll ask questions. You'll answer."

The sun beat down on Joel. Even at this time of the year, the New Orleans heat had sweat slickening his palms. "You seem pissy."

"You have no idea."

"Oh, I have an idea. My morning hasn't been so great." His fingers clenched and released.

"That's why I'm here. Your friendly neighborhood cop here to save the day."

Joel frowned at him. "Are you mocking me right now?"

"Did Sam Morrow come at you with a shovel?"

"Yes," Joel fired.

"Did the two of you fight?"

"Yes, I—"

"Was there dirt all over him because he'd just buried you alive?"

Joel's heart lurched in his chest. "Yes." Softer.

"A man who'd just buried you alive swung a shovel at you. He fought you. Were you supposed to hold his hand and say please and friggin' thank you?"

Joel blinked. "I-I killed him."

"And you were cleared. Self-defense. I read the files. Over and over. I get that you've got some extreme guilt going on, but listen to me, and listen well." Intensity burned in Cedric's eyes. "I've seen a lot of bad shit in my time. Monsters come in all shapes and sizes. Was Sam Morrow the man who tortured you? I don't know."

"Chloe said—"

"Chloe doesn't have evidence. She has her hunches and her ideas. I know. I grilled her when she called me."

Chloe had called Cedric? How had she sounded? Was she—

"She wanted to make sure you didn't do something stupid," Cedric continued grimly. "Like say, run to the nearest cop and confess you were a killer. You know, some stupid shit like that."

CHAPTER TEN

Joel's brows shot up at Cedric's comments. Taken aback, he could only shake his head. "Not the response I was expecting from a cop."

"You were already cleared in Sam Morrow's murder. The DA didn't file charges back then."

"The DA didn't know—"

"Fact one. The perp buried you. Even if he didn't slice you to hell and back, he buried you."

Joel stiffened.

"You can argue—quite successfully, I'd say—that by burying you, he was trying to kill you."

Not if he didn't bury me deeply enough. That's what Chloe thinks. That I was supposed to get out—

"Fact two. He came at you with the shovel. If you hadn't defended yourself, do you believe he would have let you walk away?"

No. The answer was immediate. Joel could still see the guy's eyes. The rage. The fear. The determination that said he wouldn't stop.

So I couldn't stop.

"Self-defense isn't murder. I've been in this business a long time. No DA will try you. It would be a PR nightmare, first of all, to try a victim that way. And even if some fool did put you in court—

which would *never* happen—you'd just get off. The evidence to convict isn't there. So how about you save us some drama time, and you stop trying to get your ass arrested just because you feel guilty."

Joel swallowed. "Are you finished?"

"I don't know." Cedric cocked his head. "Are you done being a dumbass?"

Joel's eyes narrowed.

Cedric hauled a hand over his face. "I get that nightmare messed with your head, but falling on your sword? Trying to get yourself locked away, what does that do?"

"It protects the people I might hurt." A stark and true answer. *It protects Chloe.* Wasn't that what it came down to? Protecting her? Isn't that why he'd told her to stay away? Because he was afraid of what he might do...to her.

Afraid that Gordo had been right. Afraid that deep down...a monster waited.

"Who the hell are you planning to hurt?" Cedric demanded.

Joel opened his mouth. Stopped.

"If you and Chloe know who took you, then *that* is the kind of information you need to tell me. You don't get to go off all half-cocked on your own just because you want some sort of payback."

A chill skated down his spine. "What did you say?"

"It's not an eye-for-an-eye world. My mama always told me that you go that route, and we all go blind. You don't get to hunt him down. You don't get to have payback, so if that's what you're thinking...*stop.*"

Chloe had offered him payback. The very first time she'd tried to pull him onto a case. Now he wondered, had she been offering him revenge all along? "She doesn't know who it is." Was he saying that to convince himself or Cedric?

"Knowing her, she *will*." Cedric huffed out a rough breath. "Great. Now I have to watch out for that, too. Wait..." He surged closer to Joel. "Are the deaths happening now related to the man who attacked you? Is that why you're skulking around the vic's hospital room?"

"I wasn't skulking. I was checking on a patient."

"But you're not a doctor anymore, remember?" A deliberate dig. "Wouldn't think a cold-blooded killer would care how someone was faring."

Yeah. All right. He *got* what Cedric was saying. "I understand what you're doing."

"Good. Then I don't need to waste more time." He glanced around the parking lot. Pointed. "So how about you hop on your motorcycle and go find Chloe? Because I have to tell you, I honestly feel better when you *are* near her. Of the two of you, at least you're the one more likely to go to the cops...you know, case in point and all that."

He thought of the way he'd left Chloe. Of the way she'd stared at him. Of the things he'd said. Of what he still feared he might do. "Chloe...it's not good for us to be together now."

"Jesus, man. I have to ask, as a cop and a friend...are you high?"

Joel glowered at him. "Not funny."

"It wasn't meant to be a joke. It was meant to be me trying to figure out why you're suddenly insane. Let me be clear. Chloe is your best hope. You want to know who took you? Chloe can tell you. From where I stand, she's the only one who actually was looking for the killer. You want to find him? Chloe will do it."

Chloe can't be hurt. "I don't want her in the crossfire."

Cedric just laughed, as if Joel was the most hilarious person he'd ever met. "Seriously?" His lips kept twisting. "That's her favorite place to be. If you don't know that, you don't get her at all."

Joel was worried he didn't know her. If Chloe had kept this truth from him, what else had she hidden?

"I've got people waiting on me. I need to talk to witnesses and deal with an entire *bomb* scene. And, of course, King Broussard is in the wind—which doesn't look suspicious at all—so that just makes my life harder." Cedric adjusted his tie. A bright yellow one today. "This has been fun. But let's not do it again, got me?" His gaze was suddenly serious. "I know that it's a lot to handle, but you're not doing this alone. You have friends in this town. I hope you consider me one of them."

"You just spent the last five minutes basically calling me a dumbass over and over again."

"Right." Cedric winked. "Because you are. And if your friend can't call you on being a dumbass, who can?" With that, he headed back for the entrance to the hospital.

Joel stood frozen in the parking lot. A sudden weariness filled his body, as if all of the energy had been sucked out of him. Ever since he'd heard the truth from Chloe, he'd been running blind. Moving on rage and fear. His priority had been to get away from Chloe because...

I'm a threat. If Gordo is right, I'm a threat. Chloe shouldn't be around him. And...

It had fucking hurt. Knowing that she'd stared at him, that she'd fucked him, and she'd kept the truth. This wasn't some small omission. It was a BFD. He'd trusted her completely. That trust had been rocked.

Where the hell did they go from this point?

***

"Why isn't the boyfriend here?" Kingston finally asked as they braked at the edge of a tall, narrow building near the end of a dead-end street. "I thought you were inseparable."

"He found out that I'd lied to him about something big, so he told me that he never wanted to see me again." She killed the engine. "The footage is inside?"

"Yes. I personally drop off a flash drive copy each day here. Sure, most people are probably just wired to have things sent—or stored—in drifting clouds..." He made a little swish motion with his fingers. "But I've found that online security is hacked far too often. Files can vanish in a snap. It's better to have separate backups for what I need."

"People can always just steal your flash drives. It's not like it's a perfect method of protection." So if it wasn't about protection...Chloe cocked her head. "You give the flash drives out as proof, don't you? That way, you have your prey just where you want them. It's not about online security. It's about a small delivery that shows you have control."

He smiled at her. "What was the something big you lied to Joel about?" His eyes widened dramatically. "Did you cheat on him? If so, I am impressed and wounded. Impressed because I was sure you had an extremely naughty side lurking beneath your buttoned-down exterior. And wounded because you could have come to me. I would have been happy to help you on the cheating front."

She didn't look away from him. "You're one of the few people I can't get a good handle on. I know you *were* law enforcement. I know you *are* heavily involved in criminal activities, but I've always felt like you had your own code you followed. You only played with people who deserved your game."

He was the first to avert his stare.

"Are you still sticking to those rules?" she asked him.

"Yes." A grumpy hiss.

"Then why are you trying to delay instead of taking me inside to see the footage? Or are you afraid of what I'll see?"

He shoved open the door. "I'm not afraid of anything."

Those words were such a lie, but she wouldn't call him on them. Not at the moment. They marched for the door, and she took note of the various security cameras watching them. He typed in a code at the door's control panel, used a fingerprint scan for security, then they finally eased inside. He immediately went for the second level, and she followed right behind him. Their steps seemed to echo in the building.

"A man murdered his entire family here back in the 60s. Folks who lived in the place after that reported hearing children crying. Whispers. No one would stay long." At the landing, Kingston turned to the right. "So I got the place for a steal. Ghosts never bother me."

Another door waited. One with an additional security pad. Soon they were inside that room, and Chloe did a quick double take at the sight that greeted her. So many computers. So many files. So many carefully arranged monitors and stacked DVDs and flash drives. "No cloud, huh?" Bullshit. She didn't buy that he wasn't teched out to the one hundredth degree.

He slid into a desk chair. Booted up the system. His fingers flew quickly over the keyboard. "You know about my past?"

"That at sixteen, you tapped into the Pentagon? Sure, I know. One of the many fun, interesting tidbits about you that I've managed to discover."

He kept typing. Footage popped up on the screen in front of Kingston. "Can't view it from just anywhere," he explained. "I make certain it is only accessible here. Neat little program I created."

She leaned toward him. Noted the date and time of the footage before him. Her gaze sharpened when she saw the players in the VIP room. Interesting. But for now... "I want to see the footage from when my brother was at the Serpent. Start there. Play through slowly."

He did. She saw her brother head to the bar. Saw him make an order. He chatted briefly with the bartender, then Reese looked toward the VIP level. When he glanced upward, a blonde woman slid onto the stool next to him. Her face was averted, but something about her felt familiar. As Reese kept staring at the VIP level—probably trying to figure out who the other players up there would be—the blonde slid her hand over the top of his drink. It was a quick, subtle move.

"I'll be damned," Kingston whispered.

They both already knew that, so she wasn't sure why he felt that moment was the appropriate time to point it out. "Keep playing. I want to see what happens."

Reese drained his glass. It wasn't long before his body began to slump. The blonde started talking with him. She pulled him from the stool. Led him through the crowd. He stumbled behind her.

"She's taking him to the storage room," Chloe realized.

Her face stayed averted. But Chloe was noting the woman's shoes. High heels. Elegant. Expensive. Shoes she'd seen before.

"There aren't cameras back there," Kingston noted.

"But you recognize her." Chloe was still leaning forward.

"I think so." His fingers were poised over the keyboard. "I'd like to see her face to make sure."

"Then why don't you pull up the feed from the night of the bombing?" Chloe advised him helpfully. "Go to the security room. Bet she didn't realize that you had a camera in there, so she wouldn't have been trying to hide her face."

His head turned toward her. "How do you know about that camera?"

"I know you—as I said before, you don't trust anyone easily. Thus, this entire set up." She waved one hand to indicate the room. "You would have wanted to make sure no staff members tried to erase anything important or that they didn't try to break in on your blackmail scheme."

Kingston winced. "Can we not call it a scheme? And do we have to use the word 'blackmail' to describe things? You make it sound dirty."

She thought they had to use both the words 'scheme' and 'blackmail' in this instance. "If you don't want to be described in a dirty way, then don't be dirty."

Muttering, Kingston turned back to the computer. After more tapping, she soon saw the footage from the night of the bombing. The blonde hurried into the office. Chloe noted that she was still wearing the same expensive heels. She went to the monitors in the security room. Worked on the computers a few moments. "Probably trying to delete the footage of her and Reese."

Kingston didn't speak. He'd seen the woman's face. So had Chloe. It had confirmed her suspicions—suspicions that had been born as soon as she got a look at the woman's shoes. She'd seen those shoes before. She'd actually gotten an up-close view of them.

"She's setting the bomb," Kingston said. "But she's *staying* in the security room. Does she have some kind of death wish?"

They could see the first explosion. The blonde must have triggered it remotely. Her hand seemed to curl over some object. Then the woman on the footage hurried behind a heavy filing cabinet.

"Oh," Chloe said as she understood. "She thought it would protect her from the blast, but she could still play victim." The second explosion rocked the Serpent. The woman waited a moment and sprang up, completely unharmed. She started to run for the door.

Chunks of the ceiling rained down. Parts of the wall fell in. The cabinet slammed down. The blonde turned toward it—too late.

The cabinet took her down. Her legs were trapped beneath it.

"Amateur mistake," Chloe murmured.

"She...works for me." Kingston's voice was hollow. "I-I thought I was helping her. She'd had a bad break. Her father was in the military. One of those career guys. He...he got hit by a bomb on a tour. He was an explosive ordnance disposal specialist. Poor bastard got blown to hell on the mission."

Her father had been a hero. And she'd been...

The one to set the bombs.

"This explains why the sprinklers didn't work. I'm sure she deactivated them." Chloe watched as the woman kept struggling to get out from beneath the cabinet. She was screaming for help.

"Did she get out?" Kingston growled. He forwarded the footage. When he saw Chloe rush in, he stiffened.

"She got out," Chloe replied simply. "And I know where she is." With her injured legs, the woman wouldn't be going far. "Give me her name. I need to dig into her life." She also needed to get to the hospital and talk to the woman, *ASAP*.

"Kelly Addams," he bit off. "Victim." His tone mocked the word.

She knew what he really meant. Kelly Addams...killer.

And I think Joel may be with her now...Because he didn't know the truth about Kelly. Because he thought he was a monster and he'd be looking for proof that he wasn't. He'd think Kelly was that proof. Only...she was something altogether different.

"Send that footage to Cedric. *Now*. Get backup copies for us. Then we have to get to the hospital." Her words flew out even as she spun for the door. "She couldn't have moved my brother on her own. She's working with someone. We have to make her tell us who that person is."

***

"You're still here?" Cedric shook his head when he saw Joel lingering near the hospital's entrance. He'd figured Joel would have been gone. Or maybe, he'd *hoped* Joel would be. Why hadn't the guy taken his advice and gone after Chloe? "What the hell were you doing, waiting for me?"

"Is Kelly still out?"

"Dead to the world," Cedric assured him as he raised his hand to shield against the sun's rays. "Doctors said she was in a lot of pain this morning. She should be more coherent around dinner. I'll be back then so I can ask her questions. Maybe she saw someone last night who can—" He broke off when his phone gave a little peal of sound. "Excuse me." He looked down at his device. Didn't recognize the number.

The text read.

You have to watch this.

Shit. Just what he needed. This better not be porn or some shit that a joker had sent to—

Another text appeared. *Chloe wants you to see it. Coming to hospital.*

He pressed the screen to play the video.

"Uh, Cedric?" Joel's voice was halting. "Everything okay?"

As he watched, he recognized Kelly Addams. And immediately realized what she was doing. "Fucking hell, she's not the victim." His head whipped up and he gaped at Joel. "Kelly Addams set those bombs!"

He saw the same shock he felt reflected on Joel's face. They both turned at the same time and ran back for the hospital doors. Maybe it was crazy to run back in there.

Kelly had been completely out of it when he'd stood in her room moments before. Even if she'd been faking her unconscious state, it wasn't as if the woman could run from the hospital. Not with her injuries.

But he needed to see her again. He wanted to make sure that the uniform on duty got the order that she was not to be trusted. She wasn't a victim. Kelly was a dangerous perp. Three people had died in that bombing.

He and Joel rushed into the elevator together.

"How do you know?" Joel asked quietly. "How do you know the person you thought was the victim is guilty?"

"Chloe found a video. Just had it sent to me." Could the elevator be fucking slower?

Finally, *finally,* the doors opened, and he leapt out. Even as he ran down the corridor, he could see that the fresh-faced uniform wasn't at his post. No, the kid was down at the nurse's station, leaning over the counter, and flirting with the pretty staff members on duty. The sight of that unguarded door caused a premonition of dread to weigh down Cedric's shoulders.

Cedric shoved open the door to Kelly's room.

It was the silence he noticed first. No beeping machines. No rustle of bedding. No...breath? "Jesus," he whispered. She was completely still on the bed.

"We need help in here!" Joel's voice boomed as he surged for the bed. His hand flew to Kelly's neck, and he gave a grim shake of his head right before his hands went to her chest.

Nurses rushed into the room. A doctor. They swarmed the bed even as questions tumbled from them.

Cedric had plenty of his own questions as he watched Joel try to help the woman—as Joel tried to bring her back...from the fucking dead.

I was gone maybe ten minutes. Tops. He'd hit the cafeteria before going outside because he'd skipped breakfast *and* lunch that morning. Kelly had still been hooked up to the machines when he left her. She'd still been breathing.

She was gone now. It was obvious. The medical personnel were swarming, but she wasn't responding. And Cedric had seen the dead enough times to realize the truth.

But Cedric didn't get it—shouldn't the nurse's station have gotten an alarm when her machines went off-line? Hell, they should have known she was flatlining. They should have helped her. Someone had made certain no alarms were sent.

This wasn't some random-died-from-her-injuries situation. There were too many red flags flying hard and high. He whirled and saw the uniform in the doorway. The kid's eyes were huge. Cedric stormed toward him. "Where in the hell were you?"

"I-I was right here!" The young cop looked like he might piss himself. He *should* look that way.

"No, you weren't," Cedric snapped back. "I just walked right in and you weren't here."

"At the station! I was just down at the station, less than fifteen feet away—"

"With your damn back turned," he snarled from between clenched teeth. "You couldn't see this room at all, could you?" *You couldn't see what happened.*

He couldn't see...

And now...Kelly Addams was dead.

***

Even as she ran down the tiled hospital hallway, Chloe knew it was too late. She could see the cluster of people gathered around the doorway of a room up ahead. She'd gotten the room number for Kelly Addams. She knew this was the right place.

Just as she knew...

Kelly is gone.

Hospital security personnel were standing at attention. There was a miserable-looking younger cop slouched near a wall. She didn't see Cedric, but she could hear his voice booming from inside the room that had been assigned to Kelly Addams.

"What the hell happened to her?" Cedric blasted.

The security personnel noticed Chloe and Kingston. They stepped forward with their hands up, all authoritative-like. "Stop. No one is allowed to enter this area."

The security guards were in her way. "Cedric!" Chloe called out. Her voice was clear. Strong.

The guards frowned.

"She's a personal friend of the detective in there," Kingston told them conspiratorially as he leaned forward. "I would not try to block her from getting to him. You do stuff like that, and you'll wind up on the man's shit list."

Cedric appeared—Chloe figured he'd stepped from the hospital room just in time to learn that he had a shit list. Probably good information for Cedric to know.

His gaze locked on her. "Too late," he said.

Her heart sank. She'd expected that response when she saw the guards but—

Cedric's attention whipped to her right. To Kingston. "Cops have been looking for you since last night."

"Well...here I am. Look no more."

She could feel the tension between them, and she would have addressed it—if Joel hadn't walked from Kelly's hospital room at that exact moment. He stepped out and his gaze met hers.

She saw a flood of emotions fly across his face and burn in his eyes. Need. Pain. Hunger. Anger. And—

She turned away. "Call a lawyer," she informed Kingston. "We have enough evidence that should clear you, but get the lawyer ready. If you don't have one, I would recommend Ella Grace Mitchell."

"*Chloe.*"

Joel's voice sent a pang through her. A pang that she wasn't prepared to handle. For the first time in her life, Chloe walked away from what she was ninety-nine percent sure had to be a crime scene. She put one foot in front of the other and headed down that gleaming hallway.

"Chloe, wait!" Joel's voice rang out.

She felt fingers brush over her shoulder. An electric charge that came from him. He'd always done that. Touched her and caused an instant, physical response.

Her steps quickened.

"I don't think she's waiting," Kingston declared blandly. "Now if you don't mind, my *partner* and I have things to—"

Oh, no. Wrong thing to say. Chloe whirled around just in time to see Joel lunge for Kingston.

CHAPTER ELEVEN

"Stop," Chloe said and her voice was smooth and clipped and slightly more British than normal. Her accent always became a little more pronounced when she was angry.

Joel had no doubt that she was highly furious at that particular moment.

He stood less than a foot away from King, and the jerk had the nerve to smirk at him.

"Not going to let her tell you what to do, are you?" King taunted. "Go ahead, take that swing." His words were low. Barely carrying to Joel's ears. "But be aware that I swing back, hard."

Cedric pushed between them. "This is a hospital. Get your control in place." He glared at Joel. "I do not need this from you right now." Then his head turned to King. "Though I expect nothing more from you."

"Low expectations. The story of my life," King tossed back carelessly.

"*I* have higher expectations," Chloe informed him as she came back toward their group. Joel couldn't help it. He drank her in even though her focus seemed entirely on King. "So how about you play nicely and cooperate with the cops?" Chloe asked/advised him. "Go down to the station like we talked about on the ride here. Get clear. Give them your alibi. Though I am sure the mayor will have plenty to say about it."

Wait...what? The mayor?

"I wasn't involved in the bombing. I was...involved with someone else at the time," he said smoothly.

"The mayor's wife? Are you trying to hint you were involved with Jolene?" Cedric squeezed his eyes shut. "Does everything have to be a clusterfuck with you?"

"Kingston is the one who found us evidence tying Kelly Addams to the crime," Chloe informed them crisply. "Kelly Addams—"

"Is dead," Joel finished. He wanted Chloe to look at him. Why wouldn't she look at him? "I strongly suspect that when an autopsy is performed, we'll find out that she was suffocated. So Cedric, make sure your team is bagging and tagging all the pillows and sheets in that room."

Cedric swore.

"You'll want to make sure Ruben takes a look at her eyes." That was what had tipped him off when he'd been with her. He'd taken a moment to lift up one eyelid to see the tell-tale red and purplish splotches that had already appeared on her eye. "It would have been easy enough for someone in scrubs and a face mask to just waltz right into her room and get the job done." The words felt so cold. "She was on morphine so she was probably knocked out the whole time. Wouldn't have put up any fight."

Cedric was already shouting orders to his men.

Chloe just nodded briskly and turned away.

She was leaving. Again.

King was back to smirking, even though Cedric was now telling the guy he would be getting his ass hauled down to the station. Joel moved to the right so he could see Chloe and—

"Hi, there." King blocked his path. "Just so you know, I don't like you any longer."

"Totally wrecks my heart," Joel growled back. "How will I sleep at night?"

"Stop staring after her like a lost puppy. You're done. She's marked you off her list and moved the hell on. That's Chloe for you. When she's done, she's done."

He didn't have time for King's crap. "You don't know anything about us."

King laughed. "No? Because Chloe shares quite a bit with me. Like the fact that you're the one who ended things. You burned that bridge. Chloe isn't the type to sit around and cry you a river. She's already moved on, or can't you tell?"

Chloe had told King about their fight? "You misunderstand." Joel's voice was curt.

"Then enlighten me, doc. Because from where I stand, the story was pretty simple. Chloe lied. You got pissed. Now it's done." His smirk was back. "Always thought you were playing out of your league, anyway. Why don't you run along back to Texas and leave Chloe to me?"

"That's enough." Cedric locked a hand around King's shoulder. "King, you're coming to the station. Better get that lawyer Chloe mentioned. And stop trying to push Joel into swinging at you. I am not in the mood to arrest you both."

Joel glanced over King's shoulder.

Chloe was gone.

***

She was sure they'd locked down the hospital. She'd noticed the extra cops when she first went inside. Now she got what their presence meant. Chloe would bet they were checking each person's ID at all the exits.

Cedric would want a record of every person at that hospital.

The killer would know that. So he wouldn't just waltz out one of the main entrances. No, he'd try to slip by the cops.

She suspected Joel had been right in his assessment of the killer. The perp probably had been wearing scrubs. A surgical mask over his face. Gloves. Booties to cover his shoes. A cap over his hair. The perfect disguise that also allowed the killer not to leave a single shred of evidence behind.

Annoying and vaguely impressive. She knew this hospital, though. She'd made a point of knowing because just a short time back, Joel had been in danger there. Someone she'd trusted had hunted him.

She'd gone through the corridors of that hospital. The forgotten nooks. She and Cedric had searched until they found Joel. Just as she was now going to search and see if the killer was still waiting.

Kelly's death had been recent. Nurses had still been rushing in the room.

How would he get out?

She was sure Cedric had sent his men to search the basement. That was an obvious hiding spot. And he had guards at the main doors.

To her mind, that left option number three.

There used to be a chapel on the first level. The hospital had closed it down when they'd opened a big church right outside. But the chapel had its own entrance/exit. A place that should have been boarded up.

It was easy to remove boards.

And there were no security cameras at the old chapel because the space wasn't in use any longer.

Chloe headed for that chapel. She took the twists and turns on the first level with no hesitation, but her gaze did dip toward the men and women in scrubs as she headed for her destination. She made a mental note of faces.

Everyone seemed focused on other tasks. They barely paid her a glance.

At the entrance to the chapel, she stilled. The old cross was still above the door. For a moment, she looked up at it.

Her father had insisted that she and her brother go to church every Sunday with their mother. Her mother had sat in the first row, a small smile on her face. She'd nodded at all the right times. Said the right words.

Scolded Chloe when she got fidgety.

Donned the perfect mother role.

Chloe's hand pushed against the door. If no one had been inside lately, it would have been locked.

It wasn't locked. The wood slid inward and the hinges groaned. The interior of the chapel waited, big and cavernous. A dozen, red-cushioned pews gleamed beneath the faint light that spilled from a stained-glass window over the old altar. She took one step inside and felt chill bumps rise onto her arms. The air smelled stale, as if it had been closed up for a while. On the other side of the chapel, she could see the old, red EXIT sign. The letters still glowed.

She was willing to bet the door beneath that sign would swing open easily.

No one else was in the chapel. Had the perp already left?

She took another step forward.

"You're not supposed to be in here," a man's voice said from behind her. "This chapel is closed."

Her breath eased out slowly. She hadn't heard him approach, and she had very good hearing. She was typically hyperaware of her surroundings. She'd been trained to be aware. The very fact that she had not heard the man approach told her something important.

He'd silenced his approach. Deliberately used careful steps to sneak up on her. And he was probably wearing booties on his feet to muffle the sound of his movement even more.

His voice had been a little raspy, as if he'd distorted it. There was only one reason to do that. Her hand slid into her bag. "Sorry," she said brightly as her fingers curled around the mace she kept hidden in there. "I needed to say a little prayer."

"God can't help you," he whispered.

Don't be so sure.

She brought up the mace, but before she could swing around and aim it at him, something hard hit her in the upper shoulder and back of the head. The blow knocked her off balance and sent her crashing into a pew. She sprawled and twisted, but didn't let go of her mace. The chapel darkened as pain surged through the base of her skull, but she could see his form lunging toward her.

"Didn't Lucia look just like her?" His whisper teased her ears. "You were warned not to dance with mother..."

She sprayed her mace. It erupted in a stream, and he yelled as he shot back.

He immediately ran for the old EXIT sign and Chloe shoved to her feet. But the chapel swung sickeningly around her, and she had to grab the back of a wooden pew for support. When she looked down, she saw the blurry image of broken wood. Probably the wood that had been over that back door to stop people from getting inside. He'd slammed the heavy chunk of wood into her head and shoulder.

She took another halting step forward as nausea rolled through her stomach. He was getting away. She was *letting* him get away. A guttural groan tore from Chloe as she forced her way to the exit door, one pew at a time. The back of her head pounded in a relentless agony, and if that bastard had fractured her skull, she would make him pay.

The exit door hung open a few inches. Bright light trickled inside. Chloe kept her grip on the mace and shoved the door open. Sunlight immediately had her head screaming as the agony intensified.

Wonderful. Just *wonderful*. The exit had led to a busy parking lot. Cars were zipping by, people milling about, and...

She tripped on something.

Chloe looked down to see what had tangled around her foot.

Looked like...scrubs. The pants that a doctor would wear.

He'd ditched his disguise. Blended with everyone else. She looked up again, squinting against the light. Where had he gone?

Her bag was still locked around her body, crosswise. Her fingers fumbled inside it until they found her phone. Good thing Cedric was one of her contacts. She brought the phone to her ear and tried to ignore the rising nausea in her throat.

"Not a good time," Cedric growled by way of answering. "I'm taking care of King and—"

"North lot," she told him. At least, she was about sixty percent certain it was the north lot. "Perp...just fled via the old—old chapel exit."

"What?"

Her left hand touched the back of her head. She felt the warm, wet stickiness of her blood. "And I think I need a d-doctor."

***

"What?"

Joel turned at the sharp note of alarm in Cedric's voice. And his first thought was—*has there been another attack?*

"Hurt? How? Chloe, dammit, talk to me!"

Chloe? Joel's blood iced even as he lunged for the detective.

"Your words are slurring," Cedric fired out. Joel could hear the alarm in the detective's voice. See it on his face. "Are you at the hospital's old chapel? Is that what you said?"

Joel couldn't hear her response, but he saw Cedric give a jerky nod. That was good enough for him. Joel immediately ran down the hallway.

"We'll get security there," Cedric's voice followed him. "And I'll tell my team about the perp being in the north parking lot. Don't you—"

Joel didn't hear more. He was too far away. He shoved open the door for the stairway and ran down those stairs. He wasn't waiting for an elevator. He was getting to Chloe. She was hurt. She'd been attacked—attacked by the same bastard who'd killed Kelly?

Attacked by the same bastard...who tortured me?

He couldn't let that sonofabitch get Chloe. Couldn't let him hurt her. He wouldn't torture her. He wouldn't take Chloe.

No one could take Chloe.

Joel erupted from the stairwell and ran down the hallway. His shoulder slammed into some guy who stumbled into his path. Joel kept going. His heart was about to burst straight from his chest. *Chloe. Chloe. Chloe.* Her name was a constant refrain in his mind.

Up ahead, he saw two security guards running down the hallway, coming in his direction. The chapel was about ten feet away, so he knew they were heading there, too. Must have been contacted by Cedric. He didn't stop when he saw them. Joel barreled right inside that chapel. "*Chloe!*" Joel roared her name.

He stumbled past some broken boards as his gaze frantically swept the scene for—

"Here." Her voice was weak. Low. Not like Chloe at all. He saw a shadowy figure slumped against the far wall, not too far from the altar. He rushed toward her even as the guards spilled into the chapel behind him.

As he leapt for her, he saw Chloe start to lift her right hand. She was holding mace.

"Baby?"

Her head tilted. "I see...two of you. Both h-handsome. B-but angry."

What?

"Make sure I don't...don't have a skull fracture, will you?"

What. The. Fucking. Hell?

"Thanks so much," she told him and her body began to fall.

He caught her before she could slide to the floor. *"Chloe."*

CHAPTER TWELVE

"This is completely unnecessary." Chloe glared from her position in the hospital bed. "A brief exam is certainly fine and understandable given the circumstances, but once we ascertained that there was no skull fracture, I should be free to—"

"You have a concussion, Chloe," Joel snapped as he crossed his arms and glowered from the foot of the bed. Every muscle in his body had locked down. Adrenaline, fear, and rage beat inside of him, growing into an inferno.

"I'm aware of that." She kept glaring at the doctor who'd been assigned to her, and she didn't look at Joel. She *hadn't* looked at him, not since she'd woken up.

She'd passed out in his arms. Given that some asshole had slammed a board into the back of her head, she'd been lucky to stay conscious as long as she had.

Lucky.

She'd only had her mace as a weapon. She'd been on her own, hunting a killer.

Not supposed to happen. They were partners. Or they had been, until he'd been a dick and left her. But she hadn't given up. He knew she'd gone after the guy because of who the SOB was to Joel.

You did it for me, didn't you?

And she could have died. What the fuck did she think her death would do?

"You're not immortal," he informed her. In case she'd missed that important detail about herself.

"Never thought I was." Her voice wasn't slurred the way it had been when he found her in the chapel. Her skin also was no longer bleached of color. "But I do think I am capable of recovering from a bump on the head."

Dr. Theodore Allan peered down at his notes. The light glinted off his glasses. "While there was no fracture or swelling of the brain detected—"

"Which is excellent," Chloe cut in. "Because I would hate for my brain to swell."

Joel's eyes narrowed.

"You do have a concussion as well as some pretty severe bruising on your left shoulder. I recommend that you stay overnight at the hospital," he looked up with a nod, "so that we can monitor you in order to make sure your condition doesn't worsen."

She'd been dressed in a green hospital gown. Her fingers pressed to the front of the gown.

Joel wanted her to look his way. "Worsen," he repeated. "As in...you have a freaking traumatic brain injury. That concussion will impact how your brain works for a while." She could have periods of confusion or fogginess—something he was sure Chloe was not used to experiencing.

"You'll possibly have headaches, your alertness level will vary, and you could even pass out again."

"Your vision has returned to normal." The doctor moved toward her and waved his light before her eyes. "But Dr. Landry said you reported seeing two of him when he first found you."

"Joel," he corrected. "Just...Joel."

Dr. Allan lowered his light and peered at Chloe. He lifted his right hand. "How many fingers?"

"Are we doing this again?" She sighed. "I grow weary of the finger game."

"Chloe." Joel's voice was curt and held a warning edge. "Just answer him."

"Three. It was two before. Then five. Then one. I remember all the fingers. Now can I go home?"

The doctor's lips thinned. "You could have seizures. Dizziness. I want to stress that you need monitoring and staying at this facility is the best course of—"

"No offense," Chloe said as she shook her head, "but someone was recently murdered in your facility. I don't think staying here is the safest idea for me. Actually, the facility now has a track record with incidents like this one. I previously worked a case where—"

"*Chloe.*" Joel broke through her words. Now wasn't the time to point out all of the security flaws at the place. Now was just the time for her to heal.

The doctor backed away from her. "Murdered?"

She swung her legs to the side of the bed. Because Joel was watching her so closely, he saw the flicker of her lashes and the way she sucked in a deep breath.

Still dizzy. He wondered just how many symptoms she was hiding from the doctor and why. When she pushed away from the bed and rose, Joel closed in. His hands reached out to steady her.

"I don't need you," Chloe informed him. Her words froze him as her gaze finally met his.

A chill swept over him because there was no emotion in her eyes. No anger. No fear. No love. Nothing.

"I am perfectly capable of taking care of myself," she continued. Her gaze slid away. Focused on the other doctor. "But I will certainly take your medical recommendations under advisement."

Before Joel could speak, the exam room curtain was hauled aside.

"Chloe!" Cedric shoved the curtain out of his way. "You could have been killed!" He hauled her into his arms and squeezed her in a tight hug.

Joel had wanted to hug her that way. He'd wanted to grab tight and never let go. But...a wall was between them. One he'd put there.

Chloe winced, and he knew that Cedric's hug had made her head ache again. Or, hell, her head probably was just constantly aching. She was covering up her condition, and that act was not going to fly.

"She's got a concussion," he groused. "Easy on the hugs. Her head probably feels like it got hit by a sledgehammer. Because it pretty much did."

"A board is not a sledgehammer," Chloe noted in that dead-pan way of hers. "Completely different. If I'd been hit with a sledgehammer, I would most likely be dead. I would *definitely* have attained multiple skull fractures."

"*You're not dying!*" Joel snarled.

Carefully, Cedric eased away from her. "Yes, let's make sure you stay in the land of the living. I like it when you're here." His jaw hardened. "Who was it, Chloe?"

"I didn't see his face. He attacked me from behind."

With the wounds she'd received, that story matched up with—

"At first..." Chloe added. Her brow crinkled. "When the board hit me, I stumbled forward." Her hand dropped to her hip. "Hit the edge of a pew."

He wanted to look at her hip. Everyone had been so focused on her head and shoulder that—

"Then he lunged down to me. I just lifted up my mace and fired. I only had the mace, you see. I can't bring any other weapon into a hospital."

"Uh, actually," Dr. Allan cleared his throat. "You can't have—"

"What happened after you fired the mace?" Cedric asked her. His gaze was sharp and intense.

"He ran for the old exit. By the time I could reach the door, he was gone. I saw the scrubs he'd ditched. Without the scrubs and mask, he would have blended with everyone else."

"There weren't any cameras over there. Not inside or outside." The frustration was clear in Cedric's voice. "Sure he knew that, though."

"Yes," Chloe agreed. "I'm sure he did."

Cedric was silent a moment, then he squared his shoulders. "All right. Hit me with everything you learned from him in those few moments. You might not have seen his face, but I know you—you took in plenty of details and I want to hear them."

Chloe's body swayed.

Joel's hand flew out and curved around her shoulder. "You need to get back on the exam bed."

Her head turned slightly toward him. Again, no emotion showed in her eyes. "I need to get home. I am not staying here."

"Staying here?" Cedric's voice rose. "Her injuries are so bad that Chloe needs to stay?"

Before Dr. Allan could respond, Joel replied, "She saw two of me when I found her in the chapel. Her voice was slurred. She passed out in my arms. Yes, her injuries are bad. She needs monitoring, and there is no way I am just going to stand back and let her waltz out of here."

"I wasn't going to waltz anywhere," Chloe murmured. "I was going to sit in a wheelchair and let some kind orderly push me outside where I would have a ride waiting."

"Do not push *me* right now," Joel warned her.

"Why not? You are physically pushing me. Your grip on my shoulder is getting tighter and you are trying to make me get back in bed. I don't like it. Stop."

He'd been trying to *help* her. "You're weaving on your feet." He eased his grip. He'd been careful not to apply too much pressure, but he also hadn't wanted her falling. "I want to help you."

Her lashes swept down to conceal her gaze. "Is that what you want?"

"Chloe—"

"He was tall. I-I saw the back of his head as he left the chapel. Based on the height of that door, I'd say he was over six feet. Maybe six-foot-one or two. Appeared to be in good shape. Broad shoulders." Her nostrils flared. "He certainly had a good swing but..." Her words trailed away. "I think it could have been better."

"Oh, so now you're critiquing the guy's hit?" Cedric's eyes were still intense and watchful, but a lighter note had entered his voice. "Does that mean you are feeling better?"

"No. My head hurts so badly I want to vomit."

"Chloe!" Joel was going to *put* her back into the—

"Why do you care?" Her head tilted. She winced.

She had not seriously just asked him that question. "Because it's *you*."

She blinked. Processed. Blinked. Slanted a glance at Cedric. "I'm critiquing his hit because I think if he'd wanted, he could have bashed my brains in right then and there."

Joel's heart seemed to stop.

"I didn't hear him approach. His feet were covered with the booties that the doctors wear and that I use at crime scenes. He was good at staying silent. Before he hit...he let me know he was there."

"How?" Cedric's voice was now ice cold.

"He talked to me. Something vague about how I shouldn't be there. He just said it to let me know *he* was there. His voice was muffled. Raspy." Her focus seemed to turn inward. "I knew he would attack after that, so I was able to lunge forward a bit. If he'd put more power in that blow, he could have completely incapacitated me."

Joel's teeth ground together. For a moment, he was sure the entire room went dark. He could hear the thud of his heartbeat. The slow, hard drumbeat.

"Are you all right?" Chloe's hand slid against his cheek.

His head turned. His mouth pressed to her palm. "Not even fucking close."

She held his stare. He saw the faintest crack in her no-emotion shield. Saw the flash of worry. Of longing. Then...

Her hand fell away.

"Did he say anything else that was important?" Cedric grilled her. "Do anything else? What did he—"

Her lashes swept over her eyes. "Memory loss is common after a concussion."

That wasn't exactly an answer to Cedric's question. And so far, her recall had seemed plenty sharp to Joel.

"Perhaps I will be able to tell you more after I've rested," Chloe added as her gaze seemed to find the floor utterly fascinating. "I've been warned that my mind may not work as quickly due to the injury. I could have some temporary impairments. Fogginess after a blow to the head is to be expected."

Cedric turned on Dr. Allan. "I don't want her foggy. I happen to love her brain so get her up to—"

Dr. Allan's body stiffened. "She needs rest. Not poking and prodding by a cop. I have *told* her that. She's the one who is insisting on standing even when her body is weaving. There is no sign of permanent damage, luckily. But she must allow for twenty-four hours of observation to make certain that nothing else develops—"

"I am not staying here." Chloe was definite. "I want my clothes, and I will arrange for a ride home."

Cedric stepped back so he could gesture toward Joel. "He's a doctor. He can observe her just fine at her home. Problem solved."

Chloe started to shake her head.

"Problem solved," Joel repeated, voice hard. He'd already planned to stay with her.

But, as if she'd argue, Chloe's plump lips parted.

So he took that opportunity to lean in close and whisper in her ear, "I know you don't want me near you."

She wanted to get away. After the scene at her house, he got it. He'd fucked up. Reacted and raged and he never should have walked out.

"But I am not going anywhere," he vowed.

"That's not what you said," she whispered back.

He had to make amends. He would. But he wouldn't start now. Now, he was going to have to play dirty because her safety was on the line. "If you don't agree," again, his voice was a whisper, "I'll have to tell Cedric that you just lied to him."

Her body stiffened.

"You know more," he breathed. His mouth brushed against her ear. Her sweet scent wrapped around him, and he pulled it in like a greedy addict.

Then he forced himself to step back. He gazed down at Chloe. Waited.

Her delicate jaw was tight, but she said, "Problem solved."

CHAPTER THIRTEEN

"How the hell did you let this happen?"

Joel had known that the interrogation would come. But he had to give Marie credit, she'd at least waited until Chloe was settled in her bedroom. He'd stopped by the kitchen just for a moment. He fully intended to remain upstairs with Chloe for the rest of the night. He'd be waking her up every few hours, asking her simple questions like what was her name and—

"Hey, asshole! I'm talking to you."

Slowly, he turned to face her. Marie's small body seemed to vibrate with tension. Her arms were crossed over her chest, and her dark gaze burned with anger. Joel figured he was very lucky she didn't have a knife at the ready. When Marie had a knife in her hand, the situation would be *deadly*.

"You had one job. Just one." She marched forward. Her hands fell to her sides. "Keep her safe. That's it. Simple. Straightforward. But you couldn't manage that, could you?"

"It's on me. I get it."

"Good. You should get it. I heard what she told Reese when he was freaking out and doing his mother hen impression around her." She sucked in a quick breath. "That freak attacked her when she was alone. He slammed a two-by-four into her head. He could have busted her brain wide open."

A visual Joel did not want. "It's not happening again."

"It better not. Because if it does, she'll probably be dead." Her index finger rose and jabbed him in the chest. "You said you cared."

Fuck. "I do care."

"Then why did you run as soon as things got tough? What did you think, it would be a non-stop party? That she would just suddenly learn *not* to keep secrets? This is Chloe we are talking about!"

He felt his own eyes widen. "You knew."

Her hand fell away. "I figured there was a reason she was suddenly so curious about you. There are always deeper reasons with her, so don't act all shocked." She snorted. An inelegant sound that completely mocked him. "Come on, deep down, didn't you wonder if there was more? Think about things she said. Go back through your head. Hell, are you so sure she didn't even mention it to you before?"

She'd—

"Then you fell for her, and things got complicated. Shit happens. We deal with it." Marie shook her head, and her black hair slid around her face. "Seriously, you are so lucky I don't have a knife with me." Her gaze darted to the left. To the counter. To the knife block. "Wait. Hold the thought."

He caught her wrist before she could decide to do serious damage. "I made a mistake."

"Don't I know it." She stared at him in disgust. "Pretty sure I warned you what would happen if you hurt her. And at the first opportunity, what did you do? So typical. So—"

"It's the man who tortured me. He's the one who came after her."

Her lashes fluttered. "What are we going to do about him?"

"Kill him."

"Good. If you'd said anything else, I would have wrecked that pretty face of yours." She yanked her hand free. "You going to stay with her until we get him? Or will you run again when you get scared of the secrets she carries?"

"That's not why I left. I wasn't scared of her secrets."

"No?"

"No, I left because—" *I'm scared of what I carry.* "Doesn't matter. What matters is that I am here. I will *be* here. She won't be hurt by him again."

"Not hurt by him...but what about by *you*?"

He studied her. This woman with a past that was twisted and dangerous. "Do you ever think that we might not be good for Chloe? That we're a threat to her?"

Wrong thing to say. Marie moved—lightning fast—and her hands fisted in his shirtfront as she glared up at him. "I would never hurt her."

"You were once trained to kill," he reminded Marie.

As if she needed the reminder. Her father had been an assassin, and he'd planned for Marie to follow in his footsteps.

Marie had planned for the same thing. Then Chloe had entered the picture.

"Chloe is my friend. I don't have a lot of those, so I know how valuable she is. I'd walk through fire for her any day of the week, just as I know she would for me." Her lips twisted. "And if you don't know that about her—if you don't know she'd go balls to the wall for those that matter to her, then you don't deserve her." With that, she spun and stormed away.

He didn't move. *Maybe that's the problem, Marie. I know I don't deserve her.*

But he wasn't sure he could let her go.

"Oh, one more thing…"

He'd been staring down at his fisted hands. But at her words, his head snapped up.

"Remember Morgan Fletcher?"

"What the fuck?" Of course, he remembered. Not like he could forget the guy. Chloe's psycho ex. The jerk had faked his own death, then came down to New Orleans to find Joel—

"He's back in the land of the living. Found that out earlier but then, you know, you cut out so we didn't get to bring you up to speed." She'd turned her head back to see his reaction. "The media is buying his story about him being lost at sea, then rescued, and other fun bullshit."

"Where is he?"

"Boston. For now. But we all know it will only be a matter of time until he comes after her."

Their gazes locked.

"Still planning to be *here*?" Marie inquired silkily. "Or maybe you think things are too intense? If you're cutting and running, do it now."

"I'm not going any fucking place."

"I'll believe it when I see it. Told Chloe it was a mistake to bring in strays. She should have listened to me."

***

"I need to sleep on my side," Chloe said as she settled into her bed. The pillow felt soft and heavenly as it brushed against her temple and face. "Doctor's orders."

"Which doctor?" Reese perched on the edge of the bed. "Would it be the doctor who is now back downstairs and looking more than a little unhinged? And here I thought he'd stormed off in a huff. Someone sure came crawling home quickly." He brushed back a lock of her hair.

"He's not crawling. I needed to be monitored for twenty-four hours. He's doing that job."

"Hmmm. Do we trust him to do that job? He certainly did a piss-poor performance with his other duty. You know, the part where he was hired to protect you."

"It's...complicated."

"Why not see if I can follow along?"

She closed her eyes.

"I already know about Kelly Addams. My lawyer called me before you came back here. Connected lots of dots—dots I'm sure you created for everyone." He carefully stroked her hair. "Kelly drugged me, huh? And you found proof?"

"Yes."

"I knew you would."

"I think Kingston might be in jail." She wasn't exactly clear on what had happened to him after her run-in at the chapel. "But he'll be out soon. I don't believe he was involved in what happened to you."

"Good to know."

Chloe inhaled and exhaled slowly. She felt comforted there with him. Safe.

"There's something you're holding back," Reese noted quietly.

Yes. "He...knew me. The man who attacked. He knew me."

"A lot of killers know you. Unfortunately. You do have a bit of a reputation. If you wanted to stay anonymous, I think there were other ways to—"

"No, I mean, he *knew* me. My past. I thought that might be the case when I was at Lucia's crime scene, but I hoped I was wrong." Being right—that led to more problems.

Hinges squeaked. The bedroom door had just been opened.

"She needs her rest." Joel's voice. Quiet but unyielding. "You can talk in the morning."

Her lashes lifted. She stared straight at the wall.

"I can sleep in the chair," Reese offered quickly. "In case she needs something during the night, I will be—"

"I *will* be here," Joel said. "I'll take care of anything she needs."

"Is that what you want, Chloe?" Reese asked. His tone said that if Joel was a problem, he'd handle the other man.

Except...Reese couldn't handle Joel. Reese was a great actor, a true con man, and deep down, he had a heart of gold...but in a physical match, he would also come out the loser when he tangled with Joel. After his attack, Joel had made it his mission to never be a victim. He was a fighter, through and through.

"I won't need anything," Chloe assured Reese. "Go on to bed."

He pressed a quick kiss to her temple. "I get that you were trying to help me," his words were low, meant only for her to hear, "but how about you don't put yourself in danger for me again?"

She didn't answer, and he crept away. Once again, she heard the hinges on her door squeak.

"I guess you don't oil them because you like knowing when someone is coming in and out of your room."

Yes, that was the reason she didn't oil them.

She heard the wooden floor creak beneath his feet. She expected him to take the chair near the bed. Instead, the mattress dipped a little as he climbed *into* the bed with her.

Her shoulders tensed.

"This will seem ridiculous," he said. She heard him kick his shoes off. "But knowing he's not your real brother...sometimes, I get jealous. You two are very close. Anyone can see that."

"He's very real." Reese was hardly imaginary.

"Not blood-related, Chloe. Your real brother is dead. You told me that."

"I told you...that I put a knife in his heart." Because he'd wanted her to do it. Because he'd killed her parents. Tried to kill himself. But he hadn't been strong enough. He'd wanted her to shove that knife into his chest.

And, at thirteen years of age, she had. "I pushed the knife in him."

"Because he was a killer. Because he wanted to be stopped."

She blinked away the little fog that filled her eyes. The concussion must be making her weepy. Not a side effect she'd anticipated. "He wanted *me* to stop him."

"And you did." A pause. "If something happened to me...if I went over the line the way your brother did, would you stop me?"

Her heart rate seemed to double. "You want to find the man who tortured you. Hunting a monster isn't going over the line."

"That's not an answer to my question."

Once more, she closed her eyes. "What do you want me to say, Joel? That I'll take a knife and drive it into your chest? That I will sit there and watch as you bleed out?" Just like she'd done with her brother? "Is that what you want me to promise you?"

"Chloe..." Her name was a ragged growl.

"Because I won't give you that promise. Because I won't go down that road again. I will not kill someone I love, and whether you believe me or not, I do love you."

"Baby—"

"I'm very tired. A crazed perp tried to knock my head in today, and I also had to deal with Kingston for quite a bit so that was...a lot." She swallowed. Licked her lips. Was glad he could not see her face. "You don't need to sleep in the bed with me."

"I want to be close in case you need me."

She wasn't up to dealing with him right then. She couldn't play clever games when she felt so empty and hollow and...afraid.

"I...can't handle it when you're hurt." His voice had become even rougher.

"It's not my favorite thing in the world, either."

"Can I...can I put my arm around you?"

Her lower lip wanted to tremble. She bit it. Managed a nod. She knew he'd be watching her, so he'd see the movement.

Carefully, he slid closer to her. His arm curled around her stomach as she faced away from him.

"You know why I left today," Joel rasped.

She did.

"It wasn't because you lied."

Chloe knew this.

"It...aren't you worried?"

"No."

"Chloe, how can you be so sure? I'm not fucking sure. I'm terrified that I will do something to—"

"I'm not even a little worried that you will turn into some uncontrolled killer." Just so they were clear. "I have not worried about that issue since five minutes after meeting you. Whatever he wanted to happen to you, it didn't. He failed."

Silence. The only sound was his deep breathing. "You know there's something dangerous inside me."

"You're not dangerous to me." Weariness pulled at her. Her body began to relax against his. As she drifted to sleep, Chloe thought...

Didn't he get it? She could sleep in his arms because he was safe for her. The safest place in the world.

***

"Chloe, baby, wake up." Joel softly stroked her cheek. Three hours had passed since Chloe had fallen asleep in his arms.

Her eyes fluttered open. The room was dark, with the only light spilling though her window.

"Tell me your name."

"Constance Catherine Chloe Hastings," she whispered. "But my friends call me Chloe."

He smiled. "Go back to sleep."

"I am asleep," she murmured back as her eyes drifted closed. "And I'm dreaming about you."

***

"Chloe, wake up." His fingers slid against her throat. Her pulse was steady. Strong.

She murmured his name, but didn't open her eyes.

A fission of alarm snaked through him. "I need you to open your eyes and talk to me."

Her lashes fluttered. He'd moved so that he was crouched on her side of the bed, and Joel peered at her. "Do you know where you are?"

"I was sleeping," she retorted, voice both grumpy and husky from sleep. "But then you had to wake me up."

"I'm checking on you. I have to make sure you're still making sense, sweetheart."

"I always make sense." Her eyes sagged closed. She shoved a fist under her pillow.

***

"Chloe..."

"G'away."

"I want you to open your eyes. Last time, okay? When you wake up again, it can be on your own."

Her face scrunched—pretty freaking adorably—but her eyes didn't open.

"I need to make sure you're not slurring your words and that you're not having any mental confusion." Her "G'away" had seemed slurred, so he wanted to hear more.

One eye cracked open.

"Who is your brother?" Joel asked her.

The other eye opened. "I never found his body," she whispered. "I searched and searched, but couldn't find him."

"I know. I know, and I'm sorry that you—"

"If you don't have the body, how do you know for sure someone is dead?"

Her stare was very, very alert. Her words hadn't slurred at all. Once more, he was crouched on her side of the bed, the better to see her face and check her responses. But, at her words, his shoulders straightened.

"Sunlight is coming in the window," she noted. "Day is here again."

"You don't need to get up yet. Go back to sleep."

"But if I do that, I'll just see the knife. I'm plunging it in over and over—"

"Chloe?" Did she realize exactly what she was saying?

Her lashes swept down. "I'm plunging it into you."

CHAPTER FOURTEEN

Chloe's eyes opened. The room was bathed in bright sunlight. A dull ache throbbed at the base of her skull, reminding her of the time she and Marie had pulled an all-nighter on Bourbon Street. Marie had been sure that she could drink Chloe under the table at the first stop of the night.

She'd been wrong.

Chloe sat up slowly, waiting for more pain. Her shoulder was a little stiff, and she was sure it would sport a lovely bruise, perhaps a purple or blue shade, but otherwise, she felt pretty good, all things considered.

Joel wasn't in the bed with her. Wasn't in the room at all. A long sigh slipped from her. She remembered him waking her during the night. Talking softly to her. Chloe was fairly sure she'd responded appropriately to him each time he'd questioned her, but she couldn't swear on that fact.

She pushed back the covers and prepared to face whatever madness would come that day—

The hinges squeaked.

The bedroom door opened fully, and Joel balanced a tray on one hand as he crept into the room. When he saw her sitting up, he paused. "Oh."

The tray was filled with eggs. Orange juice. Biscuits. Even beignets. No tea. Unfortunately.

"I guess I don't have to be quiet, not since you're up." He gave her a quick smile, one that flashed his dimple. The smile seemed oddly nervous.

Chloe realized that she felt nervous around him, too. "Why are you bringing me breakfast?"

"Thought it would be better if you got some sustenance in you before you went heading down the stairs." He brought the tray forward. Settled it over her. It was one of those trays made for beds—the legs slid over her body so that the top was leveled for eating. "I also just wanted to take care of you so...yeah. The beignets are probably shit. Marie watched me make them and just made fun of me the whole time. By the way, your kitchen is now covered in powdered sugar. You're welcome for that."

Chloe tried to figure out a way to tell him that she didn't have much of an appetite.

"You haven't eaten since the attack," he pointed out as he sat in the nearby chair. Her reading chair. She'd snuggle into that chair when she needed to escape the cases that haunted her. Plush, soft, it was heaven. "I need to make sure you can keep food down." Joel pointed at the tray. "So humor me and try to eat a little, would you?"

She picked up a beignet. Powdered sugar covered her fingers. "I didn't expect you to have such a...caring bedside manner."

"I'm only a jerk on certain days." His stare never left her. "Days when I think I might turn into a freak killer and hurt the only person in the world who matters to me."

"Oh." She took a bite out of the beignet. Hurriedly put it back down and reached for the orange juice. After four swallows, she was able to say, "I get that."

"Is the beignet really shitty or can you not keep down solid food?"

She tried the eggs. Much better. "I'm afraid the beignet was just really shitty."

A laugh sputtered from him. Her chest seemed to warm, right over the place where her cold, cold heart used to be. She stared at him and felt a faint smile curve her lips.

"You had a bad dream last night," he said as his eyes darkened even more. "Do you remember it?"

She often had bad dreams. And, yes, she remembered everything. Even her concussion hadn't stopped that trait. "Yes." Chloe ate slowly. She finished off the eggs. Half the biscuit. All of the orange juice. "Am I clear now? Do I get a good doctor's report?"

"Who was the man who attacked you?"

"Sneaky." She had to give him credit. "You lulled me into a false sense of security. Didn't ask me last night."

"You were weak last night. You needed rest."

"Am I not weak now?" She still felt less than top notch. Not the best situation given the items on her to-do list for the day.

"You kept down the food. If I give you much more time, you'll probably figure out a way to *try* and ditch me as you go after the perp on your own."

She mulled over his words. "You're not wrong."

"I know."

Time for her to ask more questions. "How did your meeting go with that terrible shrink yesterday?"

His head jerked. "How'd you know about that?"

She simply stared back at him.

"Or did you *not* know, until I just confirmed it for you?" Suspicion swept over his face.

She had known, and *how* she had known—that hardly required any brilliant deductive strength. "You called Reese to get the address. Did you think he wouldn't tell me?" Before Joel could reply, she hurried to say, "In the interest of being fully honest..." She *was* trying. Did he see that? "I anticipated that you would go to the shrink. You'd just found out what your attacker intended to do to you. Dr. Gordon Jennings *warned* you that it was possible you'd become a threat to those around you."

"Oh, he didn't think it was just possible. Back in Dallas, he pretty much figured it was a done deal."

"Because he's a prat."

"What?"

The British version fit him better but... "He's a fool. You can't go by what he says. I wouldn't trust his psychiatric input for even a moment."

Joel scraped his hand over the edge of his jaw. The stubble had thickened on him. Normally, Joel shaved promptly each morning. But...she rather liked the stubble on him. It gave him a rough, sexy look.

Though she honestly always found him to be sexy.

"I don't want him to be right," Joel muttered.

"Then don't let him be." Simple enough. She pushed against the tray. "I need to shower. I have to go and talk to Ruben and figure out—"

"No."

"I'm sorry." Her head cocked and her hair slid over her shoulder. "It sounded as if you told me no."

"I did."

"I don't do so well with being told what to do." He should have realized that about her by this point in their partnership. "I tend to prefer doing whatever I want, when I want it."

"Before we go anywhere, I'd like to know more about what happened in the chapel, Chloe." He rose. Moved the tray. Then sat down on the bed and put his hands on either side of her body, caging her. "I know that you held back with Cedric. I want to know *what* you held back."

"Are we to have no secrets between us? Is that what you want?" She needed to understand what the rules were going to be for them. How could she follow the rules if she didn't know them?

"Uh, yeah, no secrets. *None.* That's what I've been after the whole time."

She wanted to touch him. Instead, her hands fisted. "I thought about telling you the truth so many times. But I didn't want to hurt you." Then he had learned the truth, and the pain had been just as strong as she anticipated. "And you walked away."

"Chloe…"

"When we first became personally involved, do you remember our deal?"

His gaze held hers. "Yes."

She waited for him to say more.

Joel growled, "The sex didn't touch the partnership."

She nodded. Felt the dull throbbing at the base of her skull kick up a little. But Chloe kept her expression smooth. If Joel thought she was in pain, he would be even more difficult when it came to instituting the plans she had for the day. "Working as my partner was supposed to be completely unrelated to anything physical that happened between us."

"That was the rule. You do like rules." He leaned a little closer. "But, sweetheart, that rule was put out *before* I fell in love with you."

"Feelings can change. Perhaps…" Chloe wet her lips. "Perhaps it would be wise to re-evaluate our relationship. Take a pause. Go back to just being partners—"

His gaze *burned*.

A light knock rapped against the bedroom door. "Wake up, sleepyhead!" Reese announced cheerfully. The door swung open. The hinges creaked once more. He beamed at her. "You're awake! How's the head? Still as—"

"Not now, Reese," Joel barked.

Alarm flared on Reese's face. "Why? Is something wrong?" Instead of leaving, Reese bounded forward. "Chloe, are you okay?" He slid onto the bed, too. "Do I need to rush you to a hospital? Are you about to pass out? Do you need—"

"I have a fucking MD," Joel reminded him. "I can take care of her." His jaw hardened. "I *am* taking care of her."

"He cooked," Chloe explained. She motioned to the tray. Reese was always extra hungry in the morning, and, fearing that he might go after her leftovers, she warned, "Stay away from the beignets. They do not taste the way one would hope."

"That would explain the burning smell that filled the kitchen." Reese remained focused on her. "What can I do for you?"

"Pack your bags," she reminded him. How many times would she need to say it? "You and Marie should be gone by noon."

"That's not happening."

He was being stubborn. Chloe didn't want him to—

"Reese, get your ass off the bed!" Joel demanded, sounding seriously *done*. "Get out of the bedroom. Shut the damn door behind you."

Reese's nose wrinkled. "Someone woke up pissy."

In that, Chloe was in agreement. Joel seemed extra upset.

"Your sister is trying to break up with me," Joel fired back. "So, yes, that shit makes me pissy." His eyes were still on Chloe. And burning ever hotter with dark flames.

"Oh." Reese whistled. "Oh," he said again. He rose and stood rather awkwardly near the side of the bed. Then he patted Joel on the shoulder. "You'll...find someone else. Buck up. Other fish in the sea and all of that."

Chloe's lips pressed together.

Joel's head turned slowly toward Reese. "Get the fuck out."

Reese winced. "Some people don't take break ups well. You seem to be one of those people."

"We aren't breaking up." Each word fell with the impact of a hammer. "Chloe is trying to put up a wall. It's not happening. Now for about the tenth time, get the hell out so I can talk *privately* with Chloe."

But Reese lingered. "She has a concussion. I don't think you should be stressing her out when she's not feeling well. How about *you* get the hell out? Especially if she wants to break up with—"

Joel lunged off the bed. Stood toe-to-toe with Reese. "I've put up with your shit."

"I don't think I ever really liked you," Reese returned as he squared his shoulders. "But I put on a polite veneer, for Chloe's sake."

"You're a con man," Joel snapped at him.

"Oh, is that supposed to hurt my feelings?" He dropped his British accent. "Takes a whole lot more to do that." Suddenly, Reese didn't look so harmless and awkward. His hands had fisted at his sides. "You *hurt* her. You made Chloe cry, and no one does that, you hear me? As far as I am concerned, you had your chance, and you threw it away because you're an idiot. If she's giving you walking papers, then I will personally make sure that your ass heads out the front door—"

They were about to fight. How unnecessary. "My head is aching," Chloe announced.

Joel's attention immediately swung to her.

"Your little spat is making it worse." She motioned between them. "Could we save it for later?"

Reese glared at Joel. Joel's focus remained on her.

"It's all right, Reese," she added. "I can handle Joel."

"Fine." He sounded anything but fine. "But I'll be downstairs. You need me, I can zip up here in a flash."

"I'd rather you zipped up your luggage and left but..."

"Not happening."

"Then I'll settle for you being downstairs." She needed to finish her talk with Joel. "Thank you."

Reese grunted and stomped his way to the door.

"Don't slam it—" Joel snapped right before Reese went out.

Reese quietly shut the door.

Joel kept his hard stare on her. "That was fun."

"It didn't seem particularly fun to me." She swung her legs to the side of the bed. She waited just a moment, got her bearings, let the throbbing in the base of her skull ease, then she stood.

Oh, good. No weaving.

Before she could step forward, Joel was in front of her. "You are the queen of distraction."

"I think my grandfather was a duke, but that hardly makes me a queen."

His eyes closed. "Chloe..."

"I need to shower. You're in my path."

His eyes opened. "The attacker, sweetheart. I want to know everything. I don't want you to distract me with some bullshit about us being only partners and not sexually involved."

"It wasn't bullshit." Her shoulders straightened. She felt a faint twinge from her left shoulder at the movement. "You were very angry. Very hurt. After what you discovered, I didn't think that you would want to jump right back into a physical relationship with me—"

His hands curled around her upper arms. His touch was careful even as his eyes blazed. "I want to jump. Let me be very clear. I want to jump you all the time. I see you, and I want you. I smell you, and I want you. I hear your voice, and I want you."

She released a quick breath. "That's...a lot."

"*All the time.* So no, I'm not in the mood to back the hell away from what we have." A pause. "Are you? Do you want us to be done because I was a fucking asshole who—"

"I understood why you left. You were angry—"

"*I was afraid that I would do something to hurt you!* You must have the same fear, Chloe. Deep inside. That's why you had the dream last night."

She held herself very still. "Dream?"

"You told me...you dreamed that you were stabbing me, baby. You must be afraid that I'll cross the line. That I will be a monster, and that I'll have to be put down."

Put down. No. Chloe shook her head. Her hand rose and her fingertips trailed lightly over his cheek. "Oh, Joel, that's not what the dream was about."

His brow furrowed.

"I don't worry about you becoming a monster." She trusted him completely. "I worry that I will become one."

"Chloe...?"

"My mother was a monster. She killed and got away with her crimes. One after the other. My brother turned into a killer, too. He stabbed her and my father so many times..." She swallowed. Her voice was low and thready as she asked, "What will I become, Joel? Sometimes, I do worry that it's only a matter of time."

"It's *not*." Adamant. Absolute.

If only she could have his certainty. "How do you know?"

"Because I know *you*." His forehead leaned forward and rested against hers. "I trust you completely, and you are not like that, baby. I know you. I know—"

"And that's it," she whispered back to him. "That's how I know you aren't a monster, either, Joel. Because I trust *you* completely. I know you. So don't let anyone else in your head, okay? Don't let anyone shake your faith. You don't need to be afraid of the dark."

"Neither do you," he rasped back.

Of course, I don't. I am the dark.

CHAPTER FIFTEEN

"You're not leaving my sight." Joel fully got that he was stalking Chloe. Guilty as charged. He'd stayed outside of her bathroom while she showered. He'd shadowed her down the stairs in case she stumbled. And now he was dodging her steps as she strode through the house.

"I was rather thinking you'd come with me on this trip, so I will certainly be within sight."

She was back to being all cool. Composed. She wore black pants, a loose, red top, and black flats on her feet. Her hair swung over her shoulders, and she'd applied a small amount of makeup to her face. Makeup to hide the fact that she was still too pale, and faint shadows *had* slid under her eyes. The shadows were cleverly disguised, she looked absolutely beautiful, but he could feel her delicacy, and it was making him extra protective.

Hell, who was he kidding? When it came to Chloe, he was always protective.

Marie and Reese sidled out of the study. Their gazes instantly settled on Chloe. "Going hunting, are we?" Marie asked.

Chloe shrugged. "Going to see Ruben about a dead body."

"With a concussion." Marie nodded. "Because, sure, why not?" Her eyes drifted to Joel. "And you're down with this?"

"I'll have a doctor monitoring my every step. How much safer can a woman get?" Chloe returned before Joel could answer.

A whole lot safer. She could stay *in* the house and not go out searching for a killer but...that wouldn't be Chloe.

Chloe headed for the front door.

Marie and Reese moved into her path.

Joel closed in behind her.

Chloe's shoulders stiffened. "What is this?" Her right hand waved vaguely in the air. "You are all surrounding me."

"Good eye to detail," Marie returned. She smiled. It wasn't a particularly warm smile. "We're done, Chloe."

"Excuse me?"

"We're done waiting. You're not leaving this house without answering our questions."

"But—"

"While you were showering, Joel texted us. We all want to know what happened with that bastard last night."

Chloe glanced over at her shoulder to assess Joel. "A group attack? Truly?"

He shrugged. Was he supposed to feel guilty? He didn't.

"Fine." An exhale. Then she moved a bit to the right—the better to allow her to see them all at the same time. "I went to the chapel. He announced his presence. He swung a board at my head. I mentioned *all* of this to Cedric, by the way. He is fully informed—"

"Tell us what you *didn't* tell Cedric," Joel ordered. He knew she was holding out on them. "Because we're going to make sure you don't leave until we all know everything."

"I think this is a mutiny," Chloe decided. "I don't like it."

Marie didn't appear concerned.

Reese had guilt written all over his face. Of the three of them, Reese was the one most likely to break and slip to Chloe's side. Joel glared at him and mouthed, *Keep your shit together, man!*

If anything, Reese looked even more miserable. Wonderful.

"Just get on with it," Joel urged Chloe. Reese could be miserable, but Joel didn't feel bad at all. He'd called in the troops, hell, yes, because he wanted everyone on guard. He didn't like where this case was headed. Liked even fucking less the idea of that SOB out there *ever* getting his hands on Chloe again.

"He knows me," Chloe said.

"Well, sure…" Marie squinted at her. "If he's read the papers or watched any news show, the bad guy *will* know who you—"

"No. He knows me…as in…he knows things about me that he shouldn't." Her hands pressed to the top of her thighs. "My mother was a dancer. Did I ever mention that?"

She hadn't. At least not to Joel. Reese didn't look particularly surprised. Marie had a *so-what* expression on her face.

"A ballet dancer, back in her youth. From all accounts, she was quite amazing. I remember once, I found her in our ballroom. She was spinning round and round. And...there was blood on her dress."

First, the woman had had a friggin' ballroom in her house?

And, second, jeez, Joel knew this story was going to have a messed-up ending. Chloe did not have any warm and fuzzy family memories.

"She was asking me to dance with her. She reached out her hand, but my brother..." Chloe's gaze flickered to a watchful Reese. "He stopped me. He got really angry. Told me to never dance with her."

"Oh, shit." From Marie. She rocked back onto the balls of her feet. "Guessing he wasn't really talking about dancing, was he?"

"I was worried that she'd hurt herself." Chloe's gaze fell to the floor. "But he told me the blood wasn't hers."

Marie took a step toward Chloe.

Joel beat her. He was already *at* Chloe's side. His hand curled around her arm. "Baby..."

Her eyes lifted. "Years later, I learned that one of her friends had been stabbed that weekend. An intruder came into the house. Stabbed her five times and stole her diamond necklace. The intruder was never caught." A pause. "After my mother died, I found a beautiful diamond necklace hidden in one of her drawers."

Her voice was so calm. He knew she was blocking all emotion from her tone. Knew, too, the price it had to cost her.

"When we went to Lucia's crime scene, I remembered my mother. I thought it was all just in my head...but when I looked at the mirror and I saw the blood trailing down...it was like I had blood on my hands."

"You *don't*," Reese denied at once. "You don't, Chloe."

"He knew," she admitted.

Joel didn't let her go.

"When we were in the chapel, right before I sprayed my mace at him, he asked me...said, 'Didn't Lucia look just like her?'"

"Oh, damn." Reese blanched. "*Damn.*"

Chloe nodded, as if she felt the same way. "Then he told me, 'You were warned not to dance with mother...'" Her head turned so that she was looking at Joel. "I didn't tell anyone about that. But he *knew*. He knows my darkest secrets. He knows things I have kept from the world. That makes him very, very dangerous."

How the hell had that sonofabitch learned about those details?

"I don't think you are his only experiment, Joel. I-I think I am one, too."

***

"You nailed it, Joel." Ruben inclined his head toward Joel as the two men stood on opposite sides of the body. "Kelly Addams was suffocated." His gloved hand reached for one of her eyelids, and he pulled it up. "I noticed the splotches in her eyes right away. Dead giveaway that our vic didn't just peacefully drift away. Then when I looked at her lungs, I found evidence of petechial hemorrhages that put the nail in the coffin for me."

Joel leaned closer to stare in Kelly's open eye.

Chloe watched them from a few feet away. Chill bumps had risen on her arms the moment they entered the lab. Ruben had been waiting for them, his body almost vibrating with excitement.

"I also recovered some small fibers from the vic's tongue," Ruben was saying. "I will bet a month's salary they will match up with one of the pillows that Cedric and his team collected for evidence." He let go of Kelly's eyelid and glanced over at Joel. "Suffocation with a pillow. That's something you see on TV shows like...*all the time*. But I have to confess this is my first actual incident of this type of murder."

Well, that might explain his excitement. Chloe sat on the edge of his desk and flipped through his files.

"Oh, Chloe...you probably shouldn't do that." But despite his words, Ruben didn't sound overly worried about what she was doing.

Curious, she glanced up. "Why not?"

"Because Agent Richardson already called this morning. He told me, quite specifically, that I was to not let you get your hands on my files." He straightened. "Your hands appear to be on them."

"Richardson." A curl of disgust lifted Joel's mouth. "Is he being pulled in on this case?"

"Unfortunately." Ruben turned away from the vic and pulled off his gloves. "Let me tell you, Cedric will *less* than thrilled." He sniffed as he threw the gloves into a nearby garbage can. "He doesn't need that jackass heading in on *his* turf. You would have thought Richardson would have learned his lesson last time."

"He doesn't learn lessons easily," Chloe pointed out as she put the open file onto Ruben's desk. "That's part of his problem."

"Uh, Chloe, you're still looking—"

"My hands are not on your files. I'm not touching them at all. My eyes are just scanning through your notes." And what she saw interested her. "You noted some old fractures that Kelly Addams had on her body. On her hands." She glanced over at Ruben. "They occurred about ten years ago?" Kelly would have been a teenager. Ten years ago...that would have also been right around the time that her father had died.

Chloe had started digging into Kelly's past on the drive over. Joel had been her driver, so she had made use of her time in the vehicle.

"They were old, my estimate was ten years, but that could be off some. They hadn't set properly, so I don't think she ever saw a doctor about them." His expression tightened. "I *have* seen those types of injuries before. Typically, they appear in child abuse victims. The kind of breaks and fractures you get when someone slams your hand in a door."

Chloe absorbed that information. "Thank you."

Both Kelly and Lucia had pasts that seemed to have been filled with abuse. And the two women had become killers.

Victims into killers...

Her gaze darted to Joel. She found him already watching her.

"Are you concerned that our least favorite FBI agent is going to be dodging our steps?" he asked her.

"Potentially." But she had bigger concerns at the moment. One in particular was nagging at her mind. "He's lower on the list." Chloe jumped away from the desk. Her nose twitched at the antiseptic smell in the lab.

"Why is he being brought in?" Joel asked as he pulled off his gloves and tossed them into the trash.

That answer was easy. "Because his boss thinks we have a serial on our hands."

A pause from Joel. "His boss got that impression because you told him?"

"No, I believe Cedric did." She slanted a glance at Ruben. "Am I right?"

"How would I know?" His voice rose.

How indeed. "I'll have to call Richardson's boss later," Chloe murmured. "Make sure he understands that his agent is already not playing nicely." Wanting her to keep her hands off Ruben's files. What utter nonsense.

"Are you going to tattle on the man?" Ruben wanted to know.

"Of course." But she had other goals at the moment. "Thank you for the assistance, Ruben. And are we still on for our hurricane date this weekend?"

"Uh, Chloe..." He crept closer to her. "Cedric told me what happened to you. And though I do certainly think you look gorgeous—as always..."

His hand rose and his index finger gently slid under her eyes. "I know how to see through makeup." His lips turned down. "How badly were you hurt? And are you still hiding that pain from everyone?"

"I got a bump on the head. A slight bruise on my shoulder. Nothing I can't handle," she assured him.

He didn't look assured. "You went off on your own."

Cedric had certainly been the over-sharer. She'd have to talk with him about that.

"If you have a partner, why were you on your own?"

"I had a new partner. Cedric was taking him into custody, so I was improvising."

Ruben's eyes widened. "A new partner?" He nearly rubbed his hands together as he came even closer. "Tell me more."

She let her gaze drift over him. "I like the new hair color. I don't typically picture you as a blond, but it really works."

His right hand flew to touch his hair. "Do you? I mean, it's not too much?"

"It's perfect. Brings out your eyes." She glanced over at Joel. "If you need to examine the body more, I can wait for you outside."

"I'm done." Clipped.

Ruben side-eyed him. "Are you mad about the new partner? You are. I can tell."

"She doesn't have a damn new partner. She has *me*."

Ruben fanned one hand. "All this tension...."

"Do *not* play with me right now, Ruben," Joel warned. "This is not the day."

"Fine. I'll leave the playing to Chloe." Now he made a shooing motion toward the door. "It would be better if the two of you are not here when the Feds arrive. Less stressful for me that way. And I am trying to cut out stress. That's why I am trying yoga. Also why I will need at least *two* hurricanes when we meet for drinks, Chloe."

She strode for the door, aware that Joel was shadowing her steps. She held the door while he turned back to Ruben—

"Thank you," Joel told him.

Ruben beamed. "Still working on those magic words, are you? Have you noticed what an incredible tool they can be?"

A growl was Joel's response.

"If you try saying 'please'," Ruben added, "maybe you can replace the new partner that Chloe has. Just a word of advice, you know. Though I do think I've advised you to use 'please' with her before. Remember that time when I told you to try saying, 'Chloe, please let me—'"

"Good-bye, Ruben." Joel marched out the door.

Chloe met Ruben's stare. "Was that fun for you?"

"The highlight of my day, thanks for asking." But his expression sobered. "You...will take precautions, won't you? I don't like hearing that my drinking and gossip buddy got her head bashed in." His nostrils flared. "That type of news quite upsets me."

"I will take precautions," she promised. "I would hate for you to be upset."

He nodded. "Good. Because the last thing I would *ever* want..." A slow exhale. "Is for you to come across my table."

There were many things that she wanted to accomplish that day but... "Believe me, that item is not on the to-do list."

***

"What's the next stop?" Joel asked as his fingers curled around the steering wheel.

"I have a suspect that I'd like to interview."

"A suspect." His head swiveled toward her. "You know who the sonofabitch is?"

If only. "There is someone who is conveniently here when I do not think he should be."

"Chloe..."

"I know you do not like the man, but I think it is necessary for us to pay a visit to your former shrink."

"What?" His jaw dropped. He quickly closed his mouth. Shook his head. Then... "You think Gordo could be guilty of—"

"He's a suspect in my mind because of his tie to you. I'd like to interview him, but I completely understand if you do not want to be present," Chloe added carefully. "The last thing I want to do is make you feel—"

"Where you go, I go." Immediate. "But...Gordo? You think it could be him?"

She noticed that Joel's knuckles had whitened around the wheel. "He relocated to New Orleans. He knows your past. He knows killers." Her voice remained steady. "We can't overlook him."

"If it's him..."

"We'll find proof," she finished. Because there would be no mistakes. They would find their prey. And then he would pay.

CHAPTER SIXTEEN

"Not again!" Dr. Gordon Jennings leapt to his feet as alarm flashed across his face. "You cannot barge into my office a second time while I am with a client—"

"Certainly, he can," Chloe replied before Joel could. "He just did it." She turned her head to the woman at her side. "I will need you to stop touching me right now. I don't like it. I don't know you, and I do not want your hands on my person."

Gordon's office manager let her go. But glared. "You should *not* be here. I will call the cops and let them know—"

"Excellent idea," Chloe praised her. "I should have thought of that myself. When you telephone them, do me the courtesy of asking for Detective Cedric Coleman, would you? I think he might be interested in our visit today. And..." she added, almost conspiratorially, "Cedric is a good friend. He'll leap into action."

The office manager didn't seem to have a ready comeback, Joel noted. It was the same woman—Wendy Hyde—who'd been there the previous day, and, as luck would have it...the client was the same, too. Same guy with the sturdy build, glasses, and tousled hair. Standing nervously and with a definite what-the-hell expression on his face.

"If you want to see me," Gordo snapped, "then make an appointment. The same way that everyone else does!"

"Oh." Chloe nodded. "Brilliant. We will." She pointed at Wendy. "We would like to schedule an appointment to ask Dr. Jennings about a series of murders. Not because we think he may have some amazing insight, but because we believe he may be directly involved—"

"No!" Gordo cried out.

The client ran for the door.

"Stephen, wait!" Gordo hurried after him. "Everything is under control. Just give me a moment to—"

Stephen was gone. Gordo grabbed the doorframe and frowned after him. Then he spun toward Chloe and Joel. "Are you trying to destroy me?" he demanded.

"Absolutely not," Chloe returned. "If I wanted to do that, I would be blackmailing you with the video I recently saw in which you were getting high and looking to buy the services of a prostitute."

His eyes bugged. "Wendy, please leave us alone. *Now.*"

The office manager—her eyes just as wide as his—hurried out. Gordo slammed the door shut behind her.

Joel cast a quick glance Chloe's way. At this point, he wasn't surprised by the information she rolled out. Well, fine, he was semi-surprised by it this time. A video?

"Stephen looked vaguely familiar to me," Chloe murmured. She turned to Joel. "Have we met him before?"

"I met him," Joel returned. "He was in for a session with Gordo when I came by yesterday." He wasn't sure when she might have encountered Stephen, but knowing Chloe, anything was possible.

"Hmmm." Chloe's head cocked.

"You do have an impressive memory, sweetheart. So if you think you know him, you do."

"*What is the meaning of this?*" Gordo demanded.

"But you did take that blow to the head," Joel reminded her. "Maybe it's slowing you down."

Her spine straightened. "I am *not* being slowed—"

"It's a tactic." Gordo strolled back to his desk. If he hadn't been breathing so heavily, Joel would have thought the man was relaxed. He wasn't. "You two are trying to throw me off. Doing this rapport thing that alienates me even as it is designed to confuse me. It won't work. I'm far too adept at these games myself." He propped a hip against his desk. Studied Joel. "You seem calmer."

Joel clenched his back teeth. He actually wasn't very calm. But Chloe was close by, and he knew she wanted answers, so he was keeping his veneer in place.

"I thought you might be on the verge of a breakthrough when you came by yesterday." His gaze seemed to weigh Joel. "If you want my help, threats are not necessary, I assure you. I have always wanted to do what is best for you."

Huh. How about that? The shrink almost sounded sincere.

Gordo's gaze slid to Chloe. His eyes narrowed on her.

She stared back at him.

A long sigh slipped from Gordo as their stare-off continued. "I was concluding Stephen's session, anyway. If you had just given me five minutes, we could have avoided any unpleasantness." He lifted one eyebrow. "Though I suspect that you quite enjoy unpleasantness, don't you, Chloe?"

"Oh, is this where you try to get into my mind?" She smiled, then hurried to take a seat on his couch. She waved one hand regally. "Please proceed. But...will you call me Constance or Ms. Hastings? Only my friends call me Chloe."

What was she doing? Joel schooled his expression so it would look as if he knew what the hell was happening but really...

Gordo turned his focus to Joel. "How did you sleep last night? Were the dreams back?" He made a tut-tut sound. "Especially with your new discovery, I feared you would regress."

"He's not regressing," Chloe informed him from her position on the couch. "So you can focus on all of the other fears that you may have."

Gordo's cheeks reddened. "I do not believe she is a good influence on you."

I believe she's one of the few things keeping me sane.

"Why not?" Chloe asked. She was still sitting—all prim and proper with her feet pressed together and her shoulders squared—on the edge of the couch. "What is so very bad about me? I hardly think I am the boogeyman."

Gordo's gaze hardened as it swept over her. "Why do you think you are drawn to killers?"

"I know why I'm drawn to them. I don't have to wonder." She tipped her head toward him. "Why do you think you were drawn to psychiatry? What was it about the field—and it's various disorders—that attracted you in the first place?"

His breath huffed out. "I got into psychiatry because I wanted to help people." His attention shifted to Joel. "I still do. Look, I get that you don't like me. And you don't trust me. Sometimes, my methods can seem unorthodox—"

"Oh, that is an intriguing word," Chloe proclaimed. "Unorthodox." She seemed to taste it.

"But I always have my patients' best interests at heart," he finished doggedly. "You think I was too harsh in our sessions. That I should have sugar coated with you. Is that truly what you would have preferred?" Gordo shook his head. "That's not how I work. I believe you could be a threat, Joel. If you are not managed appropriately, the danger you present will grow." He pointed toward Chloe. "She increases that threat potential because she deliberately puts you in life-or-death situations. She has you involved in physical altercations with others, she takes you into seedy locations..."

"We should discuss the seedy locations." A quick chime in from Chloe. "Since we seem to like the same spots. That video I referenced was taken at a club owned by a friend of mine. I'm sure you remember...the Serpent? Were you aware that you were being recorded?"

Gordo's hand fell back to his side. His chin notched up as he maintained his stare on Joel. "I think she wants you uncontrolled. You, uncontrolled—that would not be a good situation for anyone." His fingers curled under the edge of the desk. "I want to talk about why you came to see me yesterday."

Sure, that was an option. Just not one that Joel was interested in. "I'd rather talk about why I'm here to see you right now."

"You said—you indicated that you believed you had killed the wrong man when you rushed to see me yesterday."

Joel could feel Chloe's stare on them. She wasn't speaking now. No more Chloe taunts for the shrink.

"What makes you believe it was the wrong man? Or do you perhaps think..." Gordo rose and headed toward Joel. He put a hand on Joel's shoulder. Joel looked at the hand, then back at Gordo's face. "Do you think you are the man who should have died that day? Is the guilt getting to you? Joel, are you experiencing any self-destructive urges to—"

"Are you dead from the neck up?" Chloe's accent sharpened. "Because when I think you cannot be more of a tosser, you just have to prove me wrong."

Gordo swallowed, but kept his focus on Joel. "We should talk without her here. You and I need to discuss details about your case that are confidential."

"I don't have secrets from Chloe."

"But does Chloe have secrets from *you?*" Gordo threw right back.

Joel schooled his expression, but he could tell by the satisfied look in Gordo's eyes that the man thought he'd scored a hit on Joel. "Move the hand."

Gordo slowly let his hand drop. But he kept looking all smug.

"Oh, for goodness' sake..." Chloe rose. "Have you ever treated Lucia Rossi?"

Gordo squinted as he angled his head back toward her. "Are you asking me about my patients? My interaction with any patient would be strictly confidential."

"Truly? You wish to play the doctor-patient confidentiality card *now?*" She didn't sound impressed. Didn't look it, either. "What about Kelly Addams? Did you treat her, as well?"

"First, I never said that I treated Lucia. I said that my interaction with any patient would be confidential—"

"Why did they come to you?" Chloe asked. "And when? You haven't been in town that long."

"I never said that I had treated—"

"After Joel came to see you yesterday, what did you do?" Chloe's questions fired one right after the other.

Gordo exhaled. "Are you interrogating me?"

"She is," Joel told him. "Glad you noticed." It had sure taken the guy long enough.

Gordo stepped toward Joel. "I tried to catch you when you stormed out yesterday. I was concerned about you—about what you might do. To yourself or to others. But you didn't wait, and I had other patients that I had to treat." His gaze was steady. "I was at my office until almost five p.m. If you suspect me of something, if you are looking for an alibi, then I can assure you, I have one. My office manager Wendy can vouch for me, and so can my patients, though, of course, you understand that I do not want them pulled into any kind of circus."

"It's not a circus." Is that what Gordo thought? Joel should clarify for him. "It's a murder investigation."

Now Gordo retreated. "Wh-what?"

"Murder investigation," Joel repeated.

Alarm flared on Gordo's face. "I have certainly not been involved in any murder! Now, if that's all you both wanted, then I shall kindly ask that you *leave*."

Gordo seemed to have an alibi, so it didn't appear likely that he'd headed to the hospital and shoved a pillow over Kelly Addams's face.

"I have one more question." Chloe had come to Joel's side. "If you answer it for me—honestly—I will answer any question about myself that you would like to know."

Gordo raked her with a hard glare. "What makes you think I want to know anything at all about you?"

"Call it a guess," Chloe returned.

But she never guesses. She'd told Joel that on more than one occasion.

Gordo inclined his head. "Fine. One question each, then you leave."

"Would you like to go first?" Chloe waved one hand casually toward him. "That way, you can see that I will be completely honest. In return, I'll expect complete honesty from you."

Joel didn't like the way Gordo was suddenly studying Chloe. Not with a physical attraction. But with an avid stare that made alarm bells ring in his head.

"What is the greatest regret that you have, Ms. Hastings?"

"Not saving my brother." An immediate response.

"Your brother?" Gordo frowned. "But what does he need saving from—"

"We all need saving from something. By the way, you asked two questions, not one, so it's now my turn to ask a question."

He jerked his head in agreement.

"Nature or nurture?"

"Excuse me?"

"Come now. You know what I mean. You're a psychiatrist, after all. When it comes down to the behavior that people exhibit, do you believe that behavior is due more to nature or nurture?"

"It's a mix, of course. We are who we are born to be...and also who the world molds us into *being*."

"Um." She looked at Joel. "I'm ready whenever you are."

He reached for her hand. Threaded his fingers with hers and stalked for the door with her.

"But what about you, Ms. Hastings?" Gordo's voice drifted after them. "Nature or nurture?"

"That's three questions," Chloe responded without looking back. "Sorry, but you've passed your allotment for the day." With her free hand, Chloe reached for the door.

"*Joel!*" Alarm flared in Gordo's voice.

Real alarm. That was new. Joel glanced back at him.

"I would like to talk with you, privately, for five minutes."

Not gonna happen. "Whatever you have to say to me, you can say to—"

"Just you, Joel. We need this talk. After yesterday, we need it more than ever."

Chloe rose onto her toes and brushed her lips across Joel's cheek. "Do it," she urged. "It will give me a chance to question the touchy office manager while he isn't watching." Her words whispered into Joel's ear.

His hold on her hand tightened. He didn't want her out of his sight.

"I'll just be beyond the door," she said, as if reading his thoughts. "Five minutes?"

No, he wasn't down for this plan. Not one damn bit.

"He'll reveal more to you without me here." Another low whisper. Her breath teased him, and she slid another quick kiss against his cheek.

Then she let him go. "I'll be right outside," Chloe said loudly.

The door shut.

For a moment, Joel stood, unmoving. Then he squared his shoulders and faced the man who'd told Joel that he *would* become a monster.

***

The office manager wasn't at her desk. Chloe tip-toed around the outer office and small lobby. She didn't see any other patients. When she peeked through the blinds on the window, she was given a great view of the street below. *Ah. There.* The redhead who'd tried to bar the door was down there, taking a smoking break.

Chloe glanced at the computer. Yes, what she wanted to do wasn't legal but...

She sat in front of the computer. Her fingers flew over the screen. Legality had never stopped her before.

Password required.

Now, that was going to be the tricky part. She fumbled around the desk, looking for something that would help her. She didn't know a whole lot about Wendy Hyde. There was a framed picture of a cat on the woman's desk. A hidden stash of chocolate bars.

Chloe helped herself to a chocolate bar.

Then she kept searching.

And just as she opened the bottom desk drawer, she remembered why Gordo's client had seemed familiar to her.

Chloe sucked in a breath and jumped to her feet. She flew toward the blinds to look out on the street below.

Oh, no.

***

"You want my help." Gordo had taken a seat behind his desk.

Joel remained standing, and he laughed. "No."

"You came to me yesterday because—deep down—you know that I am one of the few people in this world that you can count on. You might not like me, but you know I have always been straight with you."

Was the guy serious? "You called me a monster."

"I said...that if you didn't keep your control, you could become a danger to those around you. That a monster lurked within." Gordo flattened his hands on the desk. "That is true for us all. But for you especially. You lived through a nightmare situation. That attack left physical scars on you, but emotional wounds *within* you. You haven't faced those wounds. You haven't healed them."

"I'm doing just fine."

"Why do you think you killed the wrong man? If you're so fine, why did you believe that?"

This was pointless. Gordo wasn't revealing anything new to Joel. The shrink just wanted to pick him apart.

Joel turned and marched for the door.

"She failed her psychological evaluation."

His hand was poised over the doorknob.

"Your precious Chloe. Did you know that? Did you wonder why she didn't work *for* the FBI but was only a freelance operator?"

He looked over his shoulder. "Chloe has no interest in working for them."

"Because she couldn't pass their evaluation. Agent Richardson knows. He's seen the results of the evaluation."

"Agent Richardson hates Chloe because she has a tendency to make him look like an asshat." Joel considered the situation. "No, he makes himself look like an asshat."

"You need to find out what was in her report."

"Seems like you already think you know *exactly* what was in that report."

"And you aren't curious?"

"No."

"But you—"

The door flew open, narrowly missing a collision with Joel's shoulder. "I need you." Chloe's breath heaved out. "We have a problem."

His gaze raked her, searching for an injury, a threat, a—

"Call the cops," Chloe ordered Gordo as she grabbed Joel's arm. "I think he took your office manager."

"What?" Gordo's voice rose. "Who? What on earth are you going on about?"

But Chloe and Joel were already running away. "He was familiar," she said as they raced through the building. "He was the right height, the right build, and he fled so fast when he saw me because I think he was worried I'd figure it out. And I was suspicious. He kept nagging at me. I looked out the blinds again, and I saw her being hauled into the van—"

They were outside. Their SUV waited a few feet away. Joel looked to the left. To the right. But he didn't see any sign of the office manager.

"The van went to the left." Chloe pointed. "Let's go that way and find them before—"

She didn't finish. Just jumped into the passenger side while he hopped in the driver's seat. Joel knew exactly what she meant, though.

Find them before she dies.

He started the SUV. And shoved the gas pedal down to the floor as they surged away.

***

Dr. Gordon Jennings raced outside of his office building and gaped after the speeding SUV. He had his phone to his ear as he watched Joel rush away.

"Sir, sir, I am going to need you to slow down and tell me the nature of your emergency," the nine-one-one operator spoke crisply.

"I...I'm not sure." Everything had been so confusing. "I think...someone may have taken my office manager?" The words sounded like a question because they were. Chloe had spit out her orders and dragged Joel away, and now Gordon didn't know what he was supposed to do.

"Sir, what do you mean?"

"I..." There had been no sign of Wendy when he searched the office. "I need police officers here." He rattled off the address.

"Is this a joke?" The woman's voice had taken on a distinct edge.

A joke? Gordon couldn't see the SUV any longer. Chloe Hastings didn't strike him as the type of woman who joked about things. "I think you need to contact Detective Cedric Coleman." Gordon had observed how close the two of them were when he'd worked a case with the local authorities and the FBI. "He can vouch for what's happening. Tell him Chloe thinks someone has been taken. And get a team to this address."

"But—"

"A woman has been taken!" Gordon was no longer using *may* because that wasn't getting an appropriate response. He needed help. His tone hardened as he ordered, "Get the police!"

CHAPTER SEVENTEEN

"Brake! Brake!" Chloe yelled.

Joel slammed on the brakes. He'd almost missed the van. It was crammed inside a narrow alley, and the back door hung drunkenly open.

Before he'd turned off the vehicle, Chloe was already jumping out. "Chloe!" He rushed after her. Caught her before she could get too close to the van.

The vehicle looked abandoned. He didn't see any sign of—

A low moan reached his ears. Weak. Pain-filled. He leapt into motion and surged toward that sound even as Joel made damn sure to keep Chloe behind him. He wrenched the back door of the van open even more and found Wendy Hyde.

She was sprawled in the back of the vehicle. Another moan came from her as Wendy's body trembled.

He jumped into the van and maneuvered toward her—*Jesus*. Joel's breath hissed from between his teeth. Blood soaked her shirt. Gray duct tape covered her mouth and bound her wrists and ankles. The moans were coming from behind the duct tape as tears trailed down her cheeks.

He grabbed the bottom of her shirt. Yanked it up. The slice was about two inches long. He tried to examine how deep it was—

Sirens shrieked in the distance.

"Joel. We need to get her out of here. *Now*." Chloe's voice.

"She's losing a lot of blood, but I don't think anything—"

"I've seen that device before. We have to get her out. Now."

Device? Joel's gaze lifted...and he realized that something was positioned in the back of the van with Wendy. A black box, with wires sliding out of the side and—was that an old phone attached to the front?

"It can be triggered at any time. She was the bait to pull us into the trap. The cheese for the mouse. *We are the mouse*."

Okay, yes, he was getting that.

"That bomb is just like the one I saw in the video footage at the Serpent." Chloe's words came out quickly, the only sign that she was shaken. But for Chloe, that *was* a big sign. "We have to get her out of here. Now," she said again.

Joel glanced down at Wendy's face. Her eyes were open and filled with terror. The duct tape was still on her mouth. He should take the duct tape off.

After they got the hell out of there.

"Go," he snarled at Chloe as he hauled Wendy into his arms.

Wendy was moaning again. Thrashing in his hold. Chloe jumped from the van and turned back toward him. Her eyes were huge, the fear in them was new, and he wanted to tell her that everything was going to be fine. He leapt from the van. "Chloe—"

The little black box exploded.

***

Joel was on the ground. Chloe couldn't hear anything. Not even the sound of her own breathing. The explosive force of the blast had propelled Joel forward. She'd watched him fly toward her. Seen the woman's arms float into the air helplessly as they were thrown. But Joel had maintained his grip on Wendy the entire time.

Chloe had been tossed back, too. She'd hit the ground hard, but other than some scratches, she thought she was fine.

She just couldn't hear. Everything was muted. She stumbled toward Joel because she needed to help him. He was breathing. She could see his body moving. His chest was rising and falling. Wendy Hyde slumped beside him.

Joel. Chloe reached out her hand toward him.

And felt a sharp prick in her neck. Like the quick sting of a bee. Her hand flew up—but she didn't touch a bee. She pulled hard and tugged a syringe toward her.

Dazed, she stared at the syringe.

Then a flurry of sounds hit her ears as they popped and seemed to throw out the muted world around her.

Sirens...shrieking. Wendy...moaning.

And a man next to her whispering, "I've got you."

Chloe slumped back against him even as the syringe dropped from her fingers.

***

Fucking hell.

Joel's eyes flew open, and he surged up. His breath heaved in and out even as his hands automatically slapped against his body as he looked for injuries—

A moan.

His head turned. Wendy Hyde's eyes were on him. Her face twisted as she fought the tape on her mouth. A ringing filled his ears. Blood dripped from a cut near his right eye. He heaved over and yanked the tape off her.

"Help me!" she screamed. Her words reached him over the ringing. A ringing and a rush—like waves. *Help me!*

He'd been trying to do just that—and then they'd both got blown the hell away from the van. His gaze jumped back around the area. Where was Chloe? "Chloe!" Her name choked out of him as a growl. "Chloe!" Louder.

"Help me!" Wendy's scream.

He couldn't see Chloe. "I am going to help you," he promised. The ringing had dimmed.

"Th-there is a second bomb in the van. I saw him put it there!" Her head shook frantically. "Get us away from here. We have to run!"

A second bomb? Fuck. Just like at the Serpent. He grabbed Wendy. Hauled her into his arms and spun to look for Chloe.

Where was she?

She'd gotten out of the van first. He'd made sure of it. The blast would have sent her stumbling at the impact, too. Where—

"R-run!" Wendy's cry. "H-hurry!"

He looked up to see people running toward him. Hell, no, those good Samaritans couldn't come close. If there was another explosion, they could get hurt. "Back!" Joel yelled as he surged forward with Wendy against him. "Get back—" He stepped on something.

Joel glanced down. Saw the broken syringe.

His head whipped up. People were ignoring his warning. They were coming in close but Chloe—Chloe wasn't there. "Bomb!" Joel shouted. "Get the fuck back! Everyone—back!"

There were screams. The group of would-be rescuers scuttled back. The group was blocking his view and he couldn't see—

A man at the back of the crowd had a woman in his arms. A woman with dark hair who was far too still.

Chloe?

"Stop!" Joel yelled.

A patrol car was racing to the scene.

"Let her go!" He tried to run to Chloe.

The man had stopped. Looked back. He—

The second bomb exploded.

***

Joel's eyes opened, and he immediately surged upward.

"Easy." Cedric locked a hand around Joel's shoulder and shoved him back against the—wait, what the hell was he on? A stretcher? Yeah, it was a stretcher. And Joel was inside a damn ambulance.

"You need to get checked out. It's been a fucking bad day for you, and I need you to just stay still." Cedric's voice was grim. "You're bleeding from a gash near your eye that is going to need stitches, and I—"

"Chloe." It was all he could say. All that mattered.

Cedric swallowed. "I was hoping she hadn't been with you."

"Where. Is. Chloe?"

For the first time since Joel had met Cedric, fear filled the detective's eyes. "I don't know."

***

She opened her eyes, but it didn't make any difference. Pitch darkness surrounded her. Chloe's fingers lifted and stretched in front of her. She tried to keep track of the distance. One inch. Two. Three. Four. Five and—

Stone. She was touching cold stone. Six inches above her.

She could feel the same cold stone beneath her.

Her breath hitched, for just a moment.

Then she reached to the right. Counted again as she did it. One. Two. Three—Only three inches of space on the right side of her body before she touched stone once more.

Chloe swallowed. The sound of her breathing seemed too loud. Loud...when before there had been nothing. After the bomb had gone off, she hadn't been able to hear for a few precious moments. Those moments had allowed her attacker to get close. He'd snuck up on her.

Injected her with something.

Taken her.

She understood where she was. She understood exactly where he'd put her.

Joel had been buried alive. But he'd been put in a shallow grave. He'd gotten out. He'd crawled out of the dirt.

Chloe wasn't in a grave. She couldn't dig herself out.

New Orleans was filled with old cemeteries. The dead were put inside tombs and vaults. Above the ground, not below. The tombs were better than being put in the earth because when the floods came—and they always seemed to come—the tombs stopped the dead from being washed away.

The cemeteries were filled with maze-like streets of tombs and monuments. So many...

She'd studied the tombs. Been intrigued by their stories.

She'd never thought to be in one.

Joel's fear is being confined. Not mine, you bastard. This would not break her. She didn't fear being trapped in the dark.

Take stock, Chloe. Find your resources. She'd measured above her. To the right. Now she counted to the left as she tried to figure out a plan.

One, two, three, four, five, and—

She touched something. Something that felt soft, like fabric.

Once more, her breath hitched even as her hand stretched to examine the *thing* next to her.

Her fingers closed around—an arm? Yes, it felt like an arm. *He'd sealed her in with someone.* So someone else had been occupying the tomb before he dumped her inside. Probably some person who had been embalmed and put to rest long ago.

Chloe had often thought that if she was going to get rid of a body, her plan would be to put the body in someone else's grave.

My attacker must've had the same idea.

Perhaps the poor soul sharing the tomb with her would have something on him—or her—that could help. The dead were often buried with sentimental items. Steeling herself, Chloe reached out again. She touched a shirt. She touched—

The shirt was wet. Sticky. And the body wasn't quite hard. No...it still felt soft. As if...as if the person had not been dead for long.

Chloe's hand snatched back. Even though darkness surrounded her, she still squeezed her eyes shut.

The body is fresh. If she'd been able to see, Chloe knew she would have found blood on her hand.

She'd been wrong when she thought *this* was the nightmare Joel feared. It wasn't. The attacker had planned well. He'd trapped Chloe with a dead body. And now her nostrils were flaring as she pulled in the coppery scent of blood, a scent she'd missed—or ignored—before.

The blood was on her fingers. The body was so close to her. She was trapped in the dark with the dead.

And blood was on her hand...

Chloe's bloody fingers flew up and slammed into the stone slab. She had to get out. There had to be a way out. She kicked up at the stone. Twisted her body. Shoved harder.

The stone didn't move.

Her heart pounded frantically in her chest.

And the scent of the blood seemed to deepen around her. A scream wanted to rise in her throat, and she choked it back. The stone would be too thick. No one would hear her screams. She'd just waste precious oxygen. Lose valuable energy. She had to think of another way. Had to try something else...

Joel had escaped. She would, too.

She would get back to him.

***

"I'm not going to a fucking hospital! I'm finding Chloe!" Joel jerked free of the EMTs who were trying to hold him back, and he leapt from the ambulance.

Cedric frowned at him. He'd been pacing outside of the ambulance while the EMTs poked at Joel. "How many times did I tell you to calm down?"

Screw being calm. "Chloe."

"We are going to find her. Look, we aren't sure that she has been taken. I mean, this is Chloe. For all we know, she went off hunting the killer."

"She wouldn't leave me."

"No?" Cedric's brows climbed. "I'm pretty sure she left your ass at the hospital and went off on her own—"

"We have a deal. She *wouldn't*."

Cedric glanced away. "I don't like anything about this," he muttered.

Neither did Joel. He sure didn't—

A phone was buzzing. *His* phone was buzzing. He hadn't even realized the damn thing was still in his pocket. Joel fished it out. The screen was smashed to hell and back but—

Chloe?

It was Chloe's number texting him. His finger flew over that broken screen.

A video had been sent to him.

It was...

Chloe wasn't moving. Her body was still. So still. Stone surrounded her. And...stone was pushed over her. Closing her up. Sealing her inside.

"That's a fucking tomb," Cedric said as he leaned in close.

It *was* a fucking tomb. It was a video of someone sealing Chloe inside a *fucking* tomb. One of those above-ground tombs that he'd seen in plenty of cemeteries. There were hundreds of those tombs in the city.

Thousands?

He played the video again. Ignored the way his heart froze at the sight of Chloe's still body. The footage was careful. Close up on the one tomb. A white tomb. A fast shot. Then...nothing.

"Send it to me. *Now*. I'll get the techs in the department to rip it apart. If it's got metadata on there that we can use, we will find it. Locations are often embedded in photos and video files—"

Joel was already sending him the text.

Cedric turned away and went to work typing on his phone. Joel knew he was sending the text to his team.

Joel stared down at the video. The bastard who'd sent the pic had used Chloe's phone. "Trace her phone," he managed. He barely recognized the hollowness of his own voice.

"What do you think I am telling my people to do right now?" Cedric groused back. "Getting them to ping towers so we can find where the hell she is, but I also want them analyzing that video."

In case the bastard who'd sent the video still had her phone close to him, Joel fired out a text of his own.

You're dead.

He saw the little dots moving at the bottom of his phone. "The bastard is about to respond."

Cedric whirled back to face him.

Joel's phone buzzed. A text—

No, but Chloe is.

CHAPTER EIGHTEEN

She pulled the ring off his finger. A man. She'd figured that out during her search. She'd had to touch him...because she needed a tool. She needed a way out. And he was it.

The bastard who'd put her in there expected her to freak out. Bloody—bloody bodies...they'd always made her uneasy. Because of her past. Because of the night she'd found her butchered parents and been forced to kill her real brother.

A few people close to her knew how blood got to Chloe. It was one of the reasons she liked to have a doctor for a partner on her cases. An MD could handle the bloody work. Literally.

Joel knew about her issue. Reese. Marie. Ruben. Cedric.

Her ex knew. Morgan Fletcher had been particularly intrigued by her response to blood. That had been one of the first major warning signs for her. The criminal defense attorney had seemed so perfect. He'd responded so well in every situation, but then the cracks had appeared in his polished veneer.

Six people. There could be others who knew. Because, obviously, her attacker knew.

But he was a fool if he thought her weakness was going to stop her in any way. The slab above her was too heavy to lift. The longer she was trapped, the weaker she would become so the less likely she would be to maneuver the damn thing off her.

So if she couldn't move it, she had to get someone else to do the job.

Her fingers clenched around the ring she'd taken from the victim's finger. A big ring, heavy. It reminded her of the first case she'd worked with Joel. The victims in that case had all worn similar football championship rings. The rings were very sturdy, like this one. Maybe this ring would work well for what she had in mind.

What time was it? Chloe didn't know how long she'd been out. If it was nighttime—and she was where she suspected she was, in one of the infamous cemeteries in New Orleans—then it was unlikely anyone but her attacker would be around. The cemeteries were closed down at night to stop vandals from getting inside. But...

There were still ways to slip into the cities of the dead. The voodoo group she'd watched had slipped in.

So maybe...*maybe* someone would be there.

She turned to the side, *away* from the body, and her fingers lifted the ring. She began to tap the ring against the stone. The clanging contact would make a sound that she *hoped* would carry.

Especially since she was sending an SOS...

***

"We have teams separating and searching as many cemeteries as they can," Cedric said as he turned toward Joel. They'd left the bomb scene. Finally gotten Joel the hell away from the EMTs.

Joel hadn't let them stitch up the cut above his eye. He'd demanded skin glue and called the job done because he damn well wasn't going to waste more time.

I have to find Chloe.

When Cedric had left that scene, Joel had jumped into the car with the detective. He hadn't even been sure where they were headed, Joel had just known he could not be cut out of the investigation. *I'm coming, baby. I am coming.*

"We couldn't trace her phone, and so far, the techs are turning up jack with the video." There was no disguising the frustration in Cedric's voice. "Looks like our guy was smart. He stripped out the useful metadata before he sent the file to you."

"Wonderful. Glad to know he's fucking smart." Joel's voice sounded strange to his own ears. Rough. "Why are we starting at this one?" He jerked his hand toward the heavy stone walls that wrapped around the cemetery. This place had been Cedric's destination.

The sun had sunk low in the sky, and darkness stretched around them. The day had been a blur. A nightmare that he couldn't wake from.

He and Chloe had lingered at the house. He'd insisted she tell him everything that she could about her attacker. Joel didn't get how the bastard had known private details about Chloe's life. She sure wasn't the type to share that shit with anyone.

Then they'd gone to the morgue. Seen the body of Kelly Addams. Chloe had stayed back. She'd scanned the file. He'd stared at the woman he thought was a victim, but Kelly had turned out to be so much more.

Then on to Gordo. And to the abduction of Wendy. *Wendy*…She was all right. An ambulance had taken her to the hospital, and Cedric had insisted that a cop stay with her for protection.

The hours had twisted together. They'd lost the sun.

How much time does Chloe have? She hadn't moved in that video, but Joel would *not* believe that she was dead. She was still alive. But she couldn't stay that way, not unless he got her out of that tomb.

So why are we just standing here?

Cedric motioned to the uniforms who'd rushed to greet him. They'd all just arrived at the scene—the St. Louis Cemetery Number One. There were several St. Louis cemeteries in the city, but Cedric had been adamant that he and Joel needed to begin at this spot.

"This is the most secure cemetery that we have in the area," Cedric explained. "Only way folks can get inside these days is by guided tour. Got too many vandals, so the people in charge make sure it's locked down."

But if it was locked down—

"That means our perp wouldn't have to worry about being disturbed. *If* he found a way inside, this place would give him the most privacy."

Privacy...to seal Chloe in alive.

The uniforms weren't going inside. What in the hell were they waiting for? Joel surged forward. If they weren't heading in to search, then he'd do it.

But Cedric put a hand on his chest. "The guy didn't just wake up today and decide to do this. He planned it out. Like I said, I think he's smart. Smart enough to know that no one would be inside to see him here. Smart enough to get past the security that keeps others out. Smart enough...that he might have a surprise waiting for us."

"I need to find her!" They didn't have time to piss away.

"Look, I get that you want to search, I do, but I'm telling you—we have to be careful. The guy has bombs, we know that. He just used two to wreck that van. We can't overlook the possibility that maybe he's got others in there waiting for us."

"I don't care, I—"

"I care." Flat. "It's my job to care." Cedric didn't drop his hand. "You're a civilian. I can't risk you. You *will* stay out here."

More men and women arrived, only they were wearing tactical gear. What the hell? Bomb squad? Yes, that's what they were. His stomach twisted. "Cedric..."

"You stay out here. Let us do our jobs. If we find her, I will bring her straight to you."

He was supposed to stand there and wait? With his thumb up his ass? "Cedric, *no*."

"I don't want to have to cuff you and shove you in a patrol car, but I will, if necessary."

Cedric's stare was unflinching. "You go in there and you trigger a bomb, then what happens?"

"I don't think *we're* triggering the damn bombs. Chloe said she'd seen the device in the van before, that it was just like the one Kelly had used at the Serpent, and Kelly triggered that herself and—*shit, I am going in there—*"

Once more, Cedric signaled to the uniforms. Two hurried forward and grabbed Joel's arms.

"Oh, the fuck, no—" Joel snarled.

"The fuck, yes," Cedric fired right back. The bomb squad rushed into the cemetery. "Maybe the perp is watching. Maybe Chloe *is* the trap. You get close to her, and he triggers the bomb. Isn't that what you think happened with Wendy Hyde? He used her as bait, got you in close, then triggered the bomb?"

Yes, that was what Joel thought. "Get your hands off me," he snapped to the cops.

They didn't let him go.

"I'll find Chloe. She's my friend. I won't leave her trapped." Cedric pointed at Joel. "Keep your ass out here because if you get blown to hell, how am I going to explain that to her?" He turned away. Squared his shoulders.

No, *no.* "Cedric!"

"Put him in the patrol car." Cedric didn't look back. "Do not let him in this cemetery. That's an order."

No, fucking—

Cedric disappeared into the entrance of the cemetery.

***

"I want to see Reese." Chloe stood in front of her parents. They were in the garden. The sun beat down on them. Warm. The flowers smelled sweet.

Too sweet.

Her mother laughed. "Darling, we would all love that." She trailed her fingers over her husband's arm. "But he's missing. You know that. He disappeared—"

A lie. She'd known the truth for quite some time. "I think I can make him better."

Her father stiffened at Chloe's words.

Her mother just laughed once more. "Are you confused, Chloe? Child, run along and play with—"

"I'm not a child." She didn't feel like she ever had been. "I'm thirteen."

Now her mother's laughter faded. Her blue eyes seemed to ice. "And you think that means you know everything now?"

"I know Reese isn't missing. I know where you sent him."

Her father rose from his seat on the bench. Concern flashed across his handsome features. "Chloe…"

She didn't want him to lie to her. He lied too often, in order to protect her mother.

Her beautiful mother, who watched with such a careful gaze and a now expressionless face.

"He was never missing." Chloe's hands were tight at her sides. "That was just a story you told."

"How long have you known this?" her father asked. No denial. No lie. He crept closer to her.

"After the fire, there wasn't a choice." That was what they must have believed. "Mother was in the barn when the fire was set. She could have died. You wanted to protect her, so you gave in and you sent him away."

"Chloe, your brother is dangerous."

Is, not was. "I think I can help him."

Again, her mother laughed. Only this time, the laughter held a...sad edge. Strange, her mother was many things. Sad was not one of them. Even Chloe's father glanced back in confusion.

"There is no helping," her mother said. Lower, "I wish there was."

Chloe would not believe that. "I can help him."

Her mother rose. The sunlight glinted in her hair. Her blue eyes sparkled. Chloe had her eyes, but she had her father's dark hair. Reese was the blond, just like their mother.

"Let me talk to her for a moment," Chloe's mother urged her father. "I can make her understand."

Her father's hand reached out and curled around Chloe's shoulder. "I'll take care of Chloe."

Her mother shook her head. "It will only be for a moment. Just a mother-daughter talk. She will understand."

His hold tightened. "I don't want her to understand you."

Chloe glanced at him. Realized that he knew the secrets, too.

His stare was on Chloe. "I don't want you to understand." Now those words were for Chloe. Only for her.

Her mother's soft laughter filled the air. As warm as the sun. As sickeningly sweet as the flowers.

Chloe had the urge to grab her father. To hold him tight. But her mother was there. Smiling her innocent smile. Pressing a soft kiss to his cheek. He always did anything for her mother. Love. That was what he called it.

Chloe didn't believe it. She thought it was something else. Something darker. More consuming. An obsession.

He slipped away a few moments later, but he didn't go far. Never, too far. Chloe saw him watching as he stood near the red rose bushes.

"You are still such a child." Her mother touched her cheek. Even though her hands were warm, the touch sent a chill through Chloe.

"I'm not..." she denied.

"Only a child would think you could change what was meant to be."

"Reese doesn't have to be locked away. I can help—"

Her mother bent her head. Stared straight into Chloe's eyes. "Darling, I worry that you won't even be able to help yourself when the time comes."

Chloe wanted to back away. She couldn't move.

"Don't you feel it, too? I was only a little older than you when it called to me the first time."

When Chloe saw the memories, she didn't see the darkness of her tomb.

She tapped with her ring. Three short taps. Three long. Three short.

***

"Get your hands off me!" Joel snarled. "You're not putting me in the fucking—"

"Let him go."

Joel whirled at the nasally voice. A voice that he hadn't particularly wanted to hear again—because it belonged to a jerk he normally disliked but...

"You heard me." FBI Agent Paul Richardson lifted his ID and flashed it at the two cops who'd been working to shove Joel into the back of a patrol car. "FBI Agent Richardson. I'm in charge of this scene now, and I'm telling you, take your hands off him."

They slowly let him go.

Joel immediately ran for the cemetery's entrance.

Richardson grabbed him, and Joel turned ready to swing—

"Hey, how about try *thank you* instead of a fist to the face," Paul huffed as he lurched back to avoid the blow. "Look, I'm on *your* side. So calm your ass down!"

"*Chloe.*"

"I know. I've been briefed. And the FBI is in charge because this case is a clusterfuck." He jerked his thumb toward the entrance of the cemetery. "You want in there? I'll get you in. But you stay at my side the whole time. I heard what Cedric said. He isn't wrong. The place could be rigged to explode."

"Then why are you letting me in?"

"Because I don't really give a shit if you explode." A shrug. "I'm not attached to you the way Cedric is."

Fine. Fair enough.

"And I also think this killer *wants* you in there. That means he's got some kind of message in that place for you. You see it, and maybe we can figure out who the hell he is and why there is a line of bodies in this town."

Joel didn't need to hear more reasons. He just wanted *in*.

Once more, he took off for the entrance. This time, Paul was at his side.

***

"I-I...I didn't...want this..."

Her brother was bleeding. Chloe stared down at him. A tear had leaked from the corner of his eye and slid into his hair line. The scent of blood was so strong.

And it was everywhere.

Her nightgown was soaked with blood. A white gown, stained red.

Her mother had once danced in a white gown that had been stained with—

"Push it in deeper, Chloe. I need you to take the knife and push it in deeper."

She shook her head. She didn't want to do that. "I don't want to hurt you."

"And I don't want to hurt you."

Her lips wouldn't stop trembling. There was no way for her not to know. She'd found the bodies. Her father. Her mother...

"If you don't stop me..." His hand closed around hers. His fingers were covered in warm blood. "I'm scared I will hurt you."

"Reese..." Her whole body was shaking apart.

"I love you." He squeezed her hand. Yanked down.

The knife sank deep. "I-I love you," she whispered back. And then she couldn't stop crying.

Chloe kept tapping with the ring. Three short taps, three long taps, three short. A pause. Three short taps, three long, three short. A pause.

I love you.

After her brother's death, she'd never said those three words to anyone again...until Joel.

Three short taps, three long, three short.

Pause.

Three short taps, three long, three short.

***

"What the actual hell?" Cedric clawed at his tie and glared at Joel and Paul. "What part of the civilian stays outside did you not get?" He had a flashlight in his left hand that he shone at them.

"I'm afraid it is not your call any longer, Detective Coleman," Paul replied as his hands went to his hips. "I've been placed in charge. Dr.

Landry knows the risks, and he's accepted them. If he gets blown to hell, that's his prerogative."

Cedric shook his head. "Because you don't give a fuck about him, right, Agent Richardson?" He stomped toward them. "I do. Chloe is my friend and so is Joel, and I am not going to watch while—"

"I think we may have something!" A young cop rushed forward, with his light bobbing. Excitement had his voice cracking. "I heard something about twenty yards away!"

"Heard something?" Cedric's light immediately swung toward him. "What?"

"It was...a tap?"

"A tap? Show me."

They flew after the young cop. Joel was aware that the bomb squad members were still there, and he was also aware of the fact that he wasn't slowing down. He was running hell fast, and the place was like a maze. The cops had lights, and the lights were swirling and bobbing and bouncing off the monuments and the white vaults that rose from the ground—

The young patrolman froze. "I was right here when I heard it."

There was a murmur of excitement.

"Shut the hell up!" Cedric boomed. "Quiet, everyone. Just *listen*."

Silence.

Joel strained, his whole body vibrating with tension. *Chloe, baby, please, if you are here, then help us to find—*

Tap, tap, tap. Three fast taps. Then...Tap. Tap. Tap. Longer taps. They were—

"SOS," Cedric breathed the words. "That's SOS!"

That was Chloe. And the taps were close. Joel spun to the right. Saw the vaults that spread as far as he could see. Chloe was there. Chloe was in one of those vaults. She was tapping SOS. If she was tapping, she was alive.

"I want the bomb squad team checking this area! Make it clear—then let's *go!*" Cedric was still giving orders. Paul Richardson was watching in silence.

And Joel was fighting to cage the monster inside.

Chloe.

His phone rang. Shit. He ignored the ring because Chloe was close. Chloe mattered. Chloe was—

Understanding broke through the madness in his mind. "That's her ring tone," he said. He yanked the phone to his ear. "Chloe—"

"I'm watching," a man's raspy whisper told him. *"I'm right outside the cemetery."*

The call disconnected.

Silence.

Tap, tap, tap. Three short. *Tap. Tap. Tap.* Three long—

Joel shoved the phone at Paul. "The fucker is outside. Just called from Chloe's phone." He didn't race toward the cemetery's exit. He rushed toward those taps.

He joined in with the search. He put his hands on top of one thick, heavy, white slab and then crouched beside it as he felt for—

Tap, tap, tap. He could feel the vibrations. "Chloe!" Joel shot up and heaved against the heavy lid.

"It could be wired!" Cedric's frantic voice. "It could be—"

"Then get the hell back!" Joel yelled. "Clear the scene because I am not leaving her!"

***

"You know, don't you?" The man with the carefully styled blond hair and ever-so-correct British accent shifted his body to the right as they sat in her grandfather's drawing room.

Chloe swung one sneaker-covered foot as she sat on the couch and watched him. "You aren't my brother."

He swallowed and glanced toward the door. "I-I—"

"It would save us both time if you didn't invent a lie." She kept swinging her left foot. Impatience slid through her.

"I've been missing for a long time. I get that you, uh, you—"

"It was better when you led with the whole 'you know, don't you' part. Don't backtrack now." She studied him with a sharp eye. "The appearance is very close. Same jaw. Same nose. Same eye color. And I like your accent. Your 'a' sounds tend to dip every now and then, so you should watch that. Otherwise, you are quite good."

He gulped. "You're going to tell them I'm not him, aren't you?"

"*Why do you want to be him?*" The question probably didn't need to be asked. The estate they were in was huge. The furniture ridiculously expensive. The Hastings fortune was enough to tempt anyone.

"It's...better than being who I was."

Now she rose. Headed straight toward him so she could take his measure. "Don't be too sure of that."

His laughter was rough. But not cold. Not fake warm. "You have no idea, kid."

"You might be surprised. And I'm not a kid."

"You look like a kid."

She stared at him. "And you look like my brother, but you're not him."

"Uh, are you going to call the chief inspector? Tell him—"

"The chief inspector is a tosser. I will tell him nothing." Her head cocked. "Have you ever killed anyone before?"

"God, no! Why would you even ask that?" He gaped at her. "Look, look, I'm sorry, spooky kid— and you are a kid, hate to break it to you. I just saw an opportunity. I-I didn't mean any harm."

"Pretending to be someone else isn't harmful?"

He yanked his hand over his face. "I'm going to jail. I am going to jail. They will lock me up and throw away the key." His hand fell. "I just...I didn't think it would hurt. I mean, your real brother isn't here. I'm sorry to say it, but I figure he must be dead."

"That's an accurate statement."

"Okay...spooky. You're not supposed to be so cool about this." He shook his head. "Listen, just—give me a minute to explain, would you?"

"That's exactly what I was doing. Please continue."

"I've never had anything. I grew up dirt poor, and when I say that, I mean it. When I was your age, my clothes were always torn and dirty, second hand that I'd taken from a thrift shop. I had to steal everything I ever had. It's second nature to me, and I just—"

"Thought you would steal someone else's life, too?" Chloe studied him.

His gaze fell. "I wanted to see what it would be like if I could be him."

"You don't want to be him."

"Huh?" His head jerked up.

The door opened. The chief inspector—the man who was slated to be her guardian—came inside with his arrogant swagger. The scent of cigars followed him. He met her gaze, then looked over at her "brother" with a hooded stare. "Did you enjoy the little talk?" His hands settled on her shoulders. Too heavily.

She didn't like his touch.

Didn't like him.

Mostly because...the chief inspector had been the one to hide her brother's body. Her brother, killing her parents...no, no, a scandal of that nature couldn't be tolerated. Not by her powerful and connected grandfather. It was a good thing her grandfather had so many good friends who wanted to help him out.

Friends like the chief inspector.

And now that her grandfather was dead, the chief inspector thought he'd get his hands on all of her family's money. She was alone. He would be her guardian. Unless...

She looked at the stranger who'd come into her home. The man with her brother's hair and jaw. The man who now had slumped shoulders and was already sending out an air of fear. When she'd asked him if he'd ever killed...his response had been so fast...

"Chloe?" The chief inspector still had his hands on her shoulders. He shouldn't do that. He knew she didn't enjoy being touched. "How was the talk?"

She knew what he wanted. He wanted her to give a reason why this man couldn't be her brother.

The chief inspector had hidden her real brother's body. Not like he could go dig it up to prove that Charleston Reese Hastings was dead.

And since he couldn't prove that he was dead...

Chloe smiled at the stranger in her house.

He nervously licked his lips. Even looked over his shoulder as if he thought she might be smiling at someone else. She wasn't. She was smiling at him. Her unlikely savior.

She shrugged off the chief inspector's fat fingers and hurried across the room. She threw her arms around the blond. "Oh, I've missed you so, Reese!" Her voice rang out with joy. "My brother, finally home!"

"Chloe..." the chief inspector began.

The door opened again. More people trickled inside. The solicitor. The butler. One of the bodyguards who often dodged her steps...Ah, yes, a nice crowd.

"My brother is back!" she told them all. "This is Reese! We finally have him back!" Then she gave her savior another tight hug.

"Do you know what you're doing?" he whispered in her ear.

She had a pretty good idea.

Tap, tap, tap—fast. Then...Tap. Tap. Tap. Slower. Three more fast—

Chloe stilled. Had she just heard something else? Like...stone scraping? "Is someone out there?" Screaming would waste precious air. It wasn't logical to scream when the tapping should help the sound to travel but...

Suddenly, she didn't feel so logical. A tear slid from her eye. Fell into her hairline. *Just like Reese.*

"Help me!" Chloe screamed. "Please, help me!"

***

FBI Agent Paul Richardson raced to the front of the cemetery. Two uniformed cops—the same cops who'd fought with Joel—were waiting there. "Search the area, now!" he ordered them. "Dr. Landry just received a call from Chloe's phone, and the perp said he was here, now, watching!"

The men leapt into action. Richardson swept his gaze over the street.

Joel had gone to help Chloe. This was Paul's opportunity to prove to his boss that he did have what it took to work violent crimes. He wouldn't be showed up again.

This case was his chance for exoneration.

He walked into the middle of the street. His eyes were on a parked car that waited about half a block away. He strained to see in the dark and...

The car's headlights flashed on, temporarily blinding him with their intensity.

Then the car's engine growled, and it shot right for him.

Fucking sonofabitch. Paul yanked out his gun and aimed it at the vehicle. He was conscious of the cops running toward him. "FBI!" Paul yelled. "Stop! Stop right—"

The fucker wasn't stopping.

Paul jumped out of the way right before the bastard would have plowed into him. He rolled across the pavement and felt it rip into his skin.

"Agent Richardson!" One of the cops was trying to help him.

Paul threw his left hand up and motioned after the car. "Get him! Get all units on him, *now!*"

CHAPTER NINETEEN

"Get it the fuck off her!" Joel shoved with Cedric as they used all of their strength to push that freaking slab. Even as he pushed it, he realized just how heavy it was. So heavy that it was taking both of them to move it—

Two people must have been needed to seal her inside. Had to be two perps. What the—

Three slender fingers—red with blood—poked out of the little space he'd just created. "*Chloe!*" He shoved with all his strength, and he knew Cedric did the same. Adrenaline burst through Joel, and they sent that slab slamming to the ground where a heavy chunk shattered.

A uniformed officer shone his light into the vault. Chloe was lying on her back. Her right hand was clenched around something and just to her left—

Oh, fuck me.

Joel grabbed Chloe and hauled her out. Her body was so tense and chilled. He was shaking. Holding her too tightly. He didn't care. He locked his arms around her and got her the hell away from the vault.

"Chloe!" Cedric tried to take her, but Joel just held her tighter. "Dammit, man, I have to make sure she's okay!"

Okay. Make sure Chloe is okay. Joel lifted his head. She was curled against him. Barely moving. "Baby?"

"I'm okay." Her voice was soft.

"What the hell happened to him?" The question came from one of the cops. Joel knew the woman was talking about the dead man who'd been in the vault with Chloe.

"I have his blood on me," Chloe said, her voice expressionless. "I checked to see if he had a pulse—he didn't. And I-I had to take his ring." Her head tilted so she was looking up at Joel. "Did you hear me scream?"

His heart broke. "No, baby."

"I didn't think you could." She wet her lips. "But you heard the taps?"

Yes, he'd heard the damn taps.

She looked down at her palm. "This is his ring. Cedric? Cedric, it might help you ID him." She lifted her hand—and Joel saw the ring she held. Her fingers were trembling.

He realized Chloe hadn't looked at the man's face. If she had...

"Evidence bag!" Cedric called. Someone shoved a plastic bag toward him, and he let Chloe drop the ring into the bag. His gaze held hers. "Are you all right?" Tender. Careful.

"He...drugged me. I don't know with what. I woke up in there." She bit her lower lip. "How long has it been?"

"Too fucking long," Joel answered.

Her head pressed back down against his chest. "I'd like to leave now."

So the hell would he.

"Could...could someone please get the blood off me?" Her voice was even lower. Almost weak. *"Please?"*

***

"In-ground burial isn't possible," Chloe said as she sat on the stretcher inside of the ambulance and let the EMTs poke and prod at her. "The high water table down here makes that an impossibility. The bodies would float to the surface." A light was shined in her eyes. An annoyance. She could see fine. "The St. Louis Number One cemetery is the oldest one in the city." She winced when antiseptic was applied to some of the scratches on her hand. "It was built in 1789."

"Chloe, just rest." Joel's voice. Worried. Ragged. He stood a little beyond the open ambulance doors. His gaze hadn't left her. She knew he hadn't wanted to stop touching her. It had taken him a few moments to actually let her go after he'd tucked her into the back of the ambulance. That ambulance had come screaming up just as he carried her out of the cemetery.

"Did you see the oven vaults near the entrance?" Chloe asked, and the question was vague—not specifically to Joel or the EMT. "Those were the ones on top of each other. You can have several family members all in one of those vaults." She should probably stop, but it seemed oddly important to explain all of this. "You put the body in and leave it undisturbed for a year and a day, then you can push those remains back to the rear of the vault. Make space, you understand? That way, another body can be placed inside."

The EMT was staring at her.

"You live in this town," she chided him. "Don't you know about the cemeteries?"

He shook his head.

"*Chloe.*"

She looked toward Joel.

"They're going to take you to the hospital. Blood work needs to be run in order to find out what he used to drug you."

She didn't like that plan. Squaring her shoulders, Chloe released a long, slow breath. "I would rather go back and look at the vault." It had to be done.

Joel's jaw locked.

"I'm sure there is a syringe in this vehicle." She motioned toward the EMT. "Can't you take a sample of my blood and let me be on my merry way?"

"No." Joel's fast denial. "You're going to the hospital." He jumped into the back of the ambulance. "We are going to get every inch of you checked out."

Unnecessary. Physically, Chloe assessed herself as being fine. "How did you find me?"

"Cedric picked the cemetery. Said it was the place least likely to have any other visitors so that would give the man who buried you—" Joel broke off. "Fucking *hell.*"

"Uh, sir," the EMT began as he eyed Joel nervously.

Joel crouched on his knees before Chloe. He caught her hands. "He buried you."

"I'm okay." He hadn't technically *buried* her. She hadn't been beneath the ground. She'd been sealed away. Though Chloe didn't think that Joel was in the mood for a clarification. "I'm okay," she told him once more.

He shook his head. "Don't." He peered up at her. "Don't reassure me. *You* are the victim, Chloe. You. God, he *took* you from me. He left you in there to—" He stopped.

She knew what he'd nearly said.

He left you in there to die.

But...was that what he'd intended? Chloe wasn't so certain. If he'd wanted her dead, there were plenty of ways to guarantee her trip to the afterlife. While she'd been unconscious, why hadn't he just slit her throat? "I'm a little unclear on the things that happened while I was...otherwise occupied."

His eyes narrowed. "You're going to the fucking hospital."

"I will but...can I see the crime scene again first? It doesn't feel right." Now that she could think past her fear and see beyond the fog of memories that had clouded her mind, Chloe was certain she was missing something. She didn't like the feeling. Then again, there was very little about the day and night that she had liked.

"Nothing feels right about this shit." He still crouched before her. "You were taken, Chloe.

Wendy was bait to get us near the van. The bombs were triggered—"

Now this part, Chloe understood. "I think they were Kelly's bombs. She must have made more before the explosions at the Serpent. Whoever she was working for—or with—he took the extras. Put them in the van." A worry nagged at her. "How is Wendy? There was quite a bit of blood on her." And Chloe didn't have any recollection of the woman after the explosion.

"She's fine. The wound in her side didn't go deep. Missed anything vital."

Just like with Joel's wounds. He'd gotten so many wounds. Wounds designed to hurt so badly, but none of them had hit anything vital. Even as Joel said those words, Chloe could see him making the connection himself.

"Fuck," he growled.

She nodded. "You'll take me back inside?"

"Cedric probably won't even let us in. The guy has bomb squad members all over the place. He tried to keep me out when he started the search, and, hell, as much as I hate to admit it, now I owe that jackass Richardson because he took over the scene and he let me—"

"Speaking of the jackass," Chloe murmured. Because she'd just seen him shove his head in the open back door of the ambulance.

"Chloe." Paul Richardson quickly assessed her with a hard stare. "I see you're still in the land of the living."

But she hadn't been. For a while, she'd been sealed up in one of the cities of the dead.

His nostrils flared. "The sonofabitch just tried to run me down. He was waiting outside of the cemetery…" He motioned to Joel. "Just like you said. And by the way, I'll be keeping that phone of yours. If he tries to reach out again, he'll be getting me."

Chloe was missing important points. She knew it. That happened when you were sealed in a vault and not participating in the investigation.

While she wanted to catch up, it was just hard to focus. The past kept clawing at her. She could smell blood. And the darkness of the night was surrounding her just like that vault had done—

"Hey, look at me." Joel's quiet voice.

Her gaze darted back to him.

He let go of her right hand. His fingers lifted and brushed over her cheek. He wiped away a tear that she hadn't even felt escaping. "You're safe," Joel assured her. "Baby, I've got you."

Once more, her breath released on a long exhale. She'd once practiced meditation and she knew the deep breaths were supposed to help calm her. So far, though, they were hardly being effective. Yet…

I feel calmer when Joel touches me.

"Hospital, then home," Joel declared. "There is a whole crime team here. Cedric is barking orders like a boss, and he isn't going to miss anything."

Yes, Cedric was thorough, but she *needed* to do this. If she ran away without a backward glance, what did that say about her? "He put me in that vault for a reason. I didn't even look when you pulled me out. I have to go back."

Joel shook his head, but she knew he was going to give in even before he said, "You know there's nothing I wouldn't do for you." His left hand still held hers. He brought it to his lips. Pressed a kiss to her knuckles. "Nothing."

Once more, tears stung her eyes.

"Uh, yeah..." The EMT had been watching the whole time. He cleared his throat. "You get that she needs to rest, don't you? She can't just rush back in there—"

"I'll carry her," Joel assured him. "I've got her."

Her gaze drifted over his face as she ignored the EMT and a lingering Paul Richardson. "What happened to your eye?" Not actually his eye, but above it, along the edge of his brow—

"Nothing a little glue couldn't fix."

He didn't even seem mildly concerned.

"Chloe," Paul said her name deliberately. "I need your help for a minute."

He needed her? And he was admitting it?

Surprised, she turned her head toward him. Chloe was vaguely concerned she might be having some sort of auditory hallucination. She had to bite back the urge to tell him...*Say it again.*

The faint lines near his mouth had tightened. "Do you happen to know anyone who drives a silver Porsche?"

She swallowed.

"I got the tag, but the number turned out to be bogus. Seems like an odd car choice for our perp. You would have thought he didn't want to stick out. The Porsche was damn flashy."

"What did I miss?" she whispered to Joel.

"After you were taken, the SOB sent a video to me. He showed you being sealed up in the tomb. It was a close-up video, though, so I didn't realize you, ah, you weren't alone in there."

Don't think about him, Chloe. Don't.

"Then when we were searching for you here," Joel added, voice hard, "he texted. Said he was right outside."

"Joel could have gone after him," Paul supplied. "Or he could have stayed in and searched for you. Obviously, we all know what choice he made."

Silver Porsche.

Sealed in with the dead man...

"Didn't Lucia look just like her?" the gruff voice whispered through her mind. Her attacker's voice. Such a deliberate word choice. Because Lucia's crime scene had been deliberately staged for Chloe.

She felt a tremble sweep her body. "I need to go back inside. Now." She surged up, but Joel caught her.

"Like I said, I've got you."

He carefully took her out of the ambulance. Held her in his arms. Strode back to the cemetery. "I can walk," Chloe informed him. "This is completely unnecessary."

"You were drugged. You have five minutes in here, then we are getting you to the hospital."

"You were nearly blown up," she reminded him as her arm looped around his neck. "You should get to the hospital, too."

His jaw hardened.

She was aware of Paul trailing behind them. He wasn't as adversarial as he usually was. He almost seemed to feel sympathy for her. How odd.

As they crept closer to the crime scene, Chloe couldn't help but tense.

"Seriously? What the hell?" Cedric demanded as he glowered at them. "You just took her *out* of here. This is an active crime scene. You can't just waltz back up with her—"

"Can you shine a light on the nearby tombs?" Chloe asked quietly. "Then we'll get out of your way."

Cedric jerked his hand. Beams of light immediately hit the nearby vaults.

Chloe read the names. Memorized them.

Julia Wellington.

Shamus Gray.

Jeremiah Landry—

"Damn," Joel breathed. "I...know that name."

So did she. Jeremiah Landry had been his grandfather.

"We can leave now," she whispered. She very much wanted to leave. Joel swung around, and they found Paul blocking their path.

"Didn't answer my question," he stated as he stood with his feet braced apart and a holster beneath his arm. "Do you happen to know anyone who drives a silver Porsche?"

She swallowed. "I do. My ex-fiancé, Morgan Fletcher, has always been partial to that vehicle. I was told that he was currently in Boston, but I suspect he has found his way down to New Orleans. He should be approached with extreme caution. I cannot stress to you enough just how very dangerous he is."

Her stare darted to the vault—the vault she'd been sealed inside. A crime scene tech was leaning over it and snapping some photos.

She'd handed Cedric the dead man's ring earlier. Been certain that it would help to identify the man who'd been in the vault with her, but there was something about the way Joel was trying to keep her away from the vault...He could be doing that because she'd just been buried in the thing but... "You know."

His gaze dipped to her face. "Excuse me?"

"You know the identity of the man who was inside the vault with me. That's why you rushed me out so quickly. That's why you didn't want me to come back inside."

"Chloe, I wanted you out because you're a *victim*—"

"I want to see him."

"Active crime scene," Joel said as his grip on her tightened. "Let's go—"

"Joel." Cedric had moved closer. "Can you ID that guy?"

Chloe saw him swallow.

Her gaze darted to the vault.

"Got a first name for him," Joel muttered. "Stephen."

Stephen. The client who'd been with Gordon Jennings. The man who'd been familiar to Chloe. The man who'd attacked her at the hospital?

"Stephen took a knife to the heart." Cedric's voice was grim. "So if you have more intel, I need to hear it."

"I don't," Joel bit off. "But I'd suggest you talk with Dr. Gordon Jennings. Gordo is the shrink who was treating your dead man. And you probably should know, the dead man is most likely the person who stabbed Wendy Hyde."

Before he'd been killed with his own knife?

A shiver slid over Chloe. "I think he was the man who attacked me at the hospital. The one who smothered Kelly Addams."

Cedric swore. Very inventively. He'd always had a phenomenal vocabulary.

Paul had been watching the byplay between them, and he'd been uncharacteristically silent. He broke his silence to ask, "And who the hell killed him?" But his eyes widened, and she knew he'd just made the same jump that she had made.

"That dangerous ex you mentioned?" Paul answered his own question. "The one who was just outside of the cemetery, trying to run me down?"

Joel's hold was so tight around her. She could feel his tension and worry. He was right to be worried. "I would say that is a very strong probability. If Morgan is here, his presence is no coincidence." She'd always known that—sooner or later—she'd have to deal with Morgan. What she hadn't anticipated? That he'd seal her in a tomb. "I'd like to go home now," she said as she put her head against Joel's chest. She needed to escape for a little while. To feel safe.

She needed to be with Joel.

He was her safe place.

***

Cedric watched the ambulance drive away. His hands were on his hips as he stared after the vehicle. He'd had to see for himself that Chloe was leaving. The woman needed care, not a crime scene.

"Are you familiar with Morgan Fletcher?"

He wasn't surprised that Agent Richardson had sidled up beside him. Slanting the man a glance, Cedric noted, "Your right arm is bleeding. You probably want to get that checked out." He swung back to the cemetery.

Surprise, surprise, Richardson had angled himself in Cedric's path. "I'm not here to take over your turf."

"No? Feels that way to me." The last thing he wanted was for the FBI to be in his way. "But then again, we saw how that worked out for your last time, didn't we?"

Paul's lips thinned. "Morgan Fletcher. Tell me what you know about him. The bastard tried to run me down tonight, and I take that shit personally."

"Oh, do you?" He moved to stand toe-to-toe with the other man. "I take lots of things personally. Like a friend being sealed in a vault and left to die. That's pretty personal to me. I also take it personally when innocent people are caught in explosions. When women are murdered. When—" Cedric broke off. He had to get his control back. This whole scene was playing with his head.

Chloe would have said that was the perp's intention. To throw him off his game. To throw them all off.

Cedric sure knew Joel had been anything but controlled when the man left the scene. Hell, Joel hadn't even been able to let Chloe go. He'd carried her. Held her tightly.

What had been the point of Chloe's abduction? If the perp had wanted her dead, he could have killed her while she was unconscious. No, Cedric didn't believe that death had been the goal.

As far as putting her in a vault close to Joel's grandfather, Cedric figured that had been a message for both Chloe and Joel...

If she stays with you, death is what she'll get. That was what Cedric thought it meant, but he couldn't be sure.

Just as he *thought* taking Chloe had been about breaking Joel.

About unsettling Cedric, himself.

About confusion.

"Morgan Fletcher," Cedric said slowly. Talk about a man he'd prefer to avoid, forever. "He's a criminal defense attorney from Boston. I'm sure you made the connection, though, seeing as how the guy has been hitting the news recently with his miraculous rise from the grave."

Paul furrowed his brow. "That's not what I meant."

"What? You're looking for a profile? Thought that was your department, not mine." He shouldered around the agent.

"We both know you understand criminals far better than most of the behavioral analysts at the Bureau. Chloe clicked with you because she likes the way you think."

"You know nothing about me and Chloe."

"I am *trying* to make a difference here. Can't you see that? I know I screwed up before. I've screwed up a lot," he admitted bluntly. "And people have died. If you don't think they haunt me, you're wrong. If you don't think I see the women who died on my watch, then you are *wrong*. They come into my nightmares, and they won't let me sleep."

Cedric glanced back at him.

"I'd like to sleep through the night again," Paul told him. "I *can* do better. I can prove myself."

Fine. Paul wanted his take? *Here you go.* "Morgan Fletcher is a smart, sadistic prick. Chloe didn't ever talk to me much about him, but I got the impression she thought he'd killed before."

"Oh, you got that impression, huh?"

Cedric counted to ten. *Don't let him piss you off.* "I hope you find him before Joel does."

"And why is that?"

Cedric marched into the cemetery. He had a crime scene to supervise. But...

I hope you find him first because if Joel gets his hands on Morgan Fletcher...if Morgan is responsible for Chloe being sealed in that vault...

Cedric had no doubt that Joel would kill Chloe's ex.

CHAPTER TWENTY

"You didn't think it was important that I know my sister had been abducted?" Reese's entire body was bow-tight with tension. "She was *buried alive* and you didn't tell me?" His voice rose to an alarming level.

Joel rolled back his shoulders. "There wasn't anything you could do."

Marie lunged for him.

Reese grabbed her and hauled her back against his side. "You can't cut him up until I'm done yelling at the bastard!"

Chloe rubbed her left temple as she sat on the couch. The night had been killer so far, and she just wanted to collapse. She also wanted her brother and Marie to not attack Joel. "He's right, Reese. There was very little you could do."

He let Marie go and hurried to her side. He glowered down at her. "You were in a vault?"

"Yes, but don't worry. I'm quite fine now. The people at the hospital said I was perfectly—"

"That's not exactly what they said, Chloe," Joel rumbled right back. "They said for you to take it easy. They said for you to avoid chasing down murderers. They said for you to stay home and let me look the fuck after you."

"Ah, Joel." She cocked her head. "You know they said none of those things."

"*This shit isn't funny!*" Reese thundered. "You can't get sealed in a tomb! You can't be kidnapped! What in the hell would I do if you died?" Stark. Ragged.

Chloe stared up at him as he loomed over her. He was so very different now from the stranger who'd come into her grandfather's drawing room. "You would be fine," she assured him.

He shook his head.

Chloe rose. Stood before him. Her hand pressed to his chest. "You would be fine," she said again. "You were always stronger than you thought."

His gaze searched hers. "Who is it? Who is coming after you?"

Silence. She looked around the room and found Joel and Marie watching her with hard stares, too. Joel knew this, but for the others, she said, "It is suspected that Morgan was at the cemetery."

"I should have killed him when I had the chance!" Marie's immediate explosion.

Chloe figured she should have done the same thing. "Before we kill him, I need to talk to Morgan."

"Talk to him?" Marie began to pace. "Why would we waste time doing that?"

"Because Morgan wasn't behind the bombs at the Serpent. Because he wasn't the one who hurt Joel." Her head throbbed but she plowed on. "He might have put me in that vault—"

"Uh, *might?*" Reese piped in.

Joel didn't speak.

"If he did, he was trying to punish me." That was what she figured. "He wanted me to face my nightmare."

"Uh, but your nightmare isn't being buried alive." Reese jerked his thumb toward Joel. "I thought that was his particular nightmare of choice?"

"There was a...fresh body sealed inside with me." She looked at the hand she still pressed to Reese's chest. All of the blood had been removed from her fingers. "It made me quite aware of my own past."

"Jesus." His arms flew around her in a bear hug. "Why can't you have a knitting hobby? Or why don't you do gardening? Why do you have to be obsessed with killers? My heart can't take this."

Over his shoulder, Chloe met Joel's unflinching stare. "In my defense," she felt duty bound to add, "sometimes, I think killers are obsessed with me."

Joel looked away.

Her breath caught. She hadn't meant— "Joel?"

"I'm taking Chloe to bed. I want to make sure every bit of security is running at this place. If that dick Morgan is running around the Big Easy, I don't want him stepping foot on this property."

"Believe me, he won't," Marie promised him as she marched for the door.

Reese slowly eased away from Chloe. "What can I do?"

She'd asked him to leave over and over. He hadn't. She knew he wouldn't. "Stay on guard."

A nod.

"This is one of those times," the words just came from her, "when his life doesn't look so good, does it?"

Reese inhaled. "A little danger wouldn't make me turn away."

It was hardly little.

"But, yes, I still think this life is good. It's the best thing that ever happened to me." His knuckles brushed under her chin. "Why?"

She knew what he meant. It was a question that had come up many times with them in the past. Usually, she just shrugged it away. Chloe had never been overly comfortable with feelings. It was easier to just block them off.

But when she'd been sealed in the dark, she hadn't exactly been able to do anything but feel.

"Because without you, I worried what I would become." He had never gotten that. He thought he was the weak one. He wasn't. He was the one who stood by her side. The one who'd sought help when he thought an addiction was taking over. The one who worked to protect her over and over again. "The idea of killing has always been abhorrent to you. Almost like something you can't comprehend."

His lips parted as if he'd speak.

Chloe plowed on. "You were good. At your core, I could see that goodness. And I thought that if I had someone like you in my life, I might become the same way."

Reese squinted at her. "Chloe, did you hit your head again? What the hell are you talking about? *You* are good."

Not exactly.

Her gaze slid to a watchful Joel. "If it's all right with you, I'd prefer to sleep at your place." She could use a glass ceiling and plenty of windows. The idea of being surrounded by thick walls didn't exactly appeal to her.

He offered his hand to her. Chloe walked toward him. Took it.

And as always when she touched him, some of her fear slid away.

***

"Why would Morgan put you in the tomb?"

She had stripped, then put on one of Joel's oversized shirts. It was soft and comfortable, and it smelled like him. "I like the way you smell." She was in his bed. With his arm wrapped around her. "Warm and outdoorsy."

"Chloe."

"Your scent is far better than the coppery scent of blood."

"Baby, I'm not going to be distracted."

She looked up at the glass ceiling. Night still reigned. She figured it was somewhere between two and three a.m. The glass was specially designed. When the sun did rise, light wouldn't flood the room. She'd still be able to sleep easily.

"Whoever put me in that vault did so because he wanted me to understand that he knew what I feared. He put me in there and sealed me up so that I had to face the fear—face my own past."

"*They* put you in there, Chloe," he corrected. "It took me and Cedric both to get that slab off you. No way one person did the job alone."

She'd figured that out, too. The adrenaline that had filled her body was gone. Chloe knew she was about to crash, and crash hard. And when she slept that deeply... "I could have nightmares."

"I'll be here."

"I might hit out at you. You haven't seen me when the nightmares take control. I can be dangerous."

He brushed a kiss against her cheek. "Sweetheart, you're dangerous even when the nightmares don't take control." He gazed tenderly down at her. "But I can handle it."

"I was so glad to see you," she confessed. "When the slab slid over a few inches, I could hear your voice, and I knew everything was going to be okay." Because Joel had been there. She'd known he would get her out.

Trust.

"I just had to hang on until you got there. I understood that."

"Chloe, I will *always* come for you. Always. There is nothing I wouldn't do for you."

She believed that. It was both humbling, and a little scary. She didn't want him to lose his soul, not for her. "You'll be here when I wake up?"

"Where else would I be?" Another tender kiss.

Sleep pulled at her, but his answer had been wrong. So carefully worded. Almost...

The way she spoke sometimes.

And even as her lashes closed, Chloe knew that Joel planned to sneak away. When she woke, he would not be there.

***

Paul Richardson still had his phone, but the guest house had a landline, and when he heard a ringing three hours later, Joel wasn't particularly surprised.

After all, he'd been waiting for the call.

He eased away from Chloe. Crept across the room. He answered the phone before it could ring again. "Hello?"

"I was protecting her."

Joel didn't need the caller to identify himself. "Morgan."

"I saw him drug Chloe. Take her from the bomb scene. You were hardly helpful, considering that you were sprawled on the ground. How is that being a good partner?"

Joel's hold tightened on the phone. "I thought you were supposed to be in Boston."

"I was. But I got word about the things going on down here. Realized Chloe needed me."

"She needed you to seal her in a Goddamn vault and let her fight for air?"

"Oh, please. Chloe had plenty of air. I don't make mistakes like that. And I sent you a video that would help you figure out her location. Is it my fault you're slow?"

The sonofabitch. "I'm going to kill you."

A laugh. "Why? I'm not your enemy. That was Stephen Wakefield. He abducted that poor office manager. He even set those bombs for you in the van. I am certain he had some very unfortunate plans in place for my Chloe, so I had to take his knife from him and stab the fellow in the heart."

Morgan had confessed to murder in the same easy tone that he'd probably use to talk about the weather. And as for the "my Chloe" bullshit… "She's not yours," Joel gritted out.

"I think she is. I think a part of Chloe—the very darkest part—will always be mine. I understand that part of her. Just as she understands that part of me."

And I understand that you are a freaking madman. "You know how she feels about blood. You have to know. That's why you left her in there with him—"

"Consider it immersion therapy. I've heard it can be quite beneficial. Want to know who told me that?"

How long had they been talking? How had—

"Your shrink told me. Gordon Jennings. Though I believe you call him Gordo? He told me lots of things. Like the fact that Lucia Rossi and Kelly Addams *were* his patients. Like the fact that he manipulated them. He used them. And he manipulated *you*."

Joel was rooted to the spot.

"You know what he did, Joel. You know exactly what he did to *you*. Even Chloe knows. I'm not sure why she hasn't told you. Maybe she's afraid that will be the final nail in the coffin of your broken psyche."

Joel glanced back toward the bed. He'd kept his voice low, and Chloe did not appear to have stirred.

"I thought about killing him myself, then realized...why not let you get that pleasure? Closure, I believe it's called."

Voice low, Joel demanded, "What the fuck have you done?"

More soft laughter. "I've taken your shrink. I've got him strapped down to a table in front of me." A pause. "Sound familiar?"

The bastard knew it was familiar. "You're not serious. You—"

A scream filled the line. Long. Desperate. Pain-filled. And the scream...was of Joel's name.

Shit. He's got Gordo.

"I have him waiting for you. But if you don't want to come and kill him, I can always do it myself."

"Morgan, *don't!*"

"Then get your ass over here."

"I don't even know where you are!"

"Sure, you do. I'm doing to your shrink exactly what he did to you." Then, rougher, angrier, "Figure it the fuck out." He hung up.

Joel's gaze was still on Chloe. They'd analyzed her blood at the hospital. Found trace elements of the drug that had knocked her out. Nothing that would cause any permanent damage, but she would be sleeping deeply as she worked through the last of the drug's effects.

It was likely that Chloe wouldn't stir for hours.

He lowered the phone back into the cradle. Only moments passed before it rang again. Joel picked it up mid-way through that first ring.

"How the hell did you know?" Cedric demanded.

While Chloe had been changing and showering earlier, Joel had taken the liberty of calling Cedric. Of asking his friend to set up a monitor on the phone at Joel's home. "He went to far too much trouble to just disappear."

"I don't have an exact address. He didn't stay on the line long enough for that, but I can narrow it down to a five-block radius—"

Not necessary. "I know where he is."

"Then share with the freaking group, would you?"

Joel exhaled as he watched Chloe sleep. "I'll do one better. We'll go after the bastard."

***

"She will hate this," Marie warned Joel as he straddled the motorcycle. "There is no way Chloe will want you going after Morgan on your own."

"I won't be on my own. I'll have Cedric and the resources of the NOPD at my back." He leveled his stare at her. "In case this is just a trick to pull me away, Cedric is also putting undercover cops around the perimeter of this place. And I need *you* to make sure Chloe stays secure."

"Secure is my middle name." Her tone was flat.

He started to wheel the bike away—

"*I* hate this." Marie's hand pressed over his. "Morgan is as deceptive as they come. I don't buy that he wouldn't have figured out that the cops were monitoring your line. He knows it's a trap."

An option Joel had already considered. "Then he must think he still has a way out."

"That's what worries me! How do you know he doesn't?"

He didn't. Joel just knew... "He has a hostage, Marie. If I don't go in there, Morgan said he'd kill Gordon Jennings."

"Why do we care about him? Isn't that the shrink asshole you hate?"

"I have to go. I'll be back, I promise. You just make sure Chloe is all right."

"Do you know how furious she will be with me?"

He had a clue. Because she would be just as furious with him. "I love her," he said simply. "If I can protect her, I have to do it. He put her in a vault, Marie. Trapped her in a nightmare. I can't let him get away with that. I won't."

Her hand fell away. "At least make him suffer, will you?"

The sun was starting to rise. Time to get this show moving. His head inclined as he steered the motorcycle away. *Make him suffer?*

She could count on it.

***

Marie slipped into the guest house—Joel's place. Her footsteps were soundless as she made her way into the den, then toward the bedroom.

She just wanted to check and make certain that Chloe was okay in there. Once she had a visual on her friend, then she would feel better about this whole mess.

She could see the huddled form on the bed. The covers were pulled up high, hiding Chloe's face. Relief swept through Marie.

Chloe appeared to be sleeping soundly. Hopefully, Joel would be back before Chloe woke. Cedric could toss Morgan in jail and throw away the key, and they could all get on with their lives.

She turned away.

Stopped.

Chloe had been sleeping very, very soundly. So soundly that...she'd barely appeared to breathe.

Marie spun on her heel. Stared at the mound. Correction, that mound was not moving at all. *Not breathing*. She lunged across the room and grabbed the covers. She ripped them back—

Pillows.

No Chloe.

Dammit! She yanked her phone out to call Joel. The line rang once, twice. He was on his motorcycle, but he could stop to answer her—

"Hello?"

The voice drew her up short. "You're not Joel."

"No, this is FBI Agent Paul Richardson."

Richardson? She knew the name.

"Who is this?" he asked.

She was the one with the questions. "Why do you have Joel's phone? Look, forget it, I need to talk to him, right away, and—"

"What's happening?"

She looked back at the bed.

"I'm an FBI agent! Joel gave me his phone because he wanted my help in stopping the man who'd taken Chloe. So I ask you again...*what is happening?*"

A faint movement by the door caught her eye. Her lips parted as Reese put his finger to his mouth.

CHAPTER TWENTY-ONE

"If we go in with guns blazing, he might kill the hostage." Cedric stood in the shelter of the alley, with his body hidden from view. "It's not just Gordon Jennings who is inside. Security footage from the business nearby showed that Wendy Hyde walked in the place an hour ago, and she hasn't come back out since. I don't know why the hell she isn't still in a hospital. But now we have *two hostages.*"

Joel had asked to meet near Gordo's office—because it was the only place that fit, given Morgan's clue. Joel had been attacked and tortured within his own hospital. It made sense that if Morgan was going by the same rules, then Gordo would be held in his own office, too.

The fact that Gordo's office fell within the five-block radius that Cedric had created after the phone call? That just made Joel all the more certain that Morgan was inside.

"He wants me," Joel returned evenly. "If he sees signs of cops, we don't know what he'll do."

"Unfortunately, we also don't know what he'll do when he sees *you.*" Cedric tapped Joel's collar. "Is this thing secure enough?"

This thing—the listening device that Cedric had brought for Joel to wear. Cedric wanted a confession. Both from Morgan…and from Gordo.

Joel had briefed Cedric on everything Morgan had said. And if Morgan was right, then Gordo was a killer, too.

If Morgan was right? Joel wasn't even sure when he'd started to half-believe the freak.

"When you want backup, use our codeword," Cedric instructed him. "We'll storm the building, and we'll get your ass out."

The codeword. Right. *Jazz.* Like he was supposed to figure some casual way to drop that word in a conversation. Then again, nothing about the conversation he intended to have with Morgan would be casual.

"I don't know how many more surprises I can take," Cedric muttered as he slipped Joel a gun. "Did you know that Kingston Broussard actually worked for the FBI? Past tense, but turns out, he's not the total nutjob I thought."

Joel tucked the gun beneath his shirt.

"He's getting out, by the way. Richardson said there was some more paperwork that he had to complete, then Kingston gets to walk." He nodded. "That means there will be a jail cell just waiting for Morgan and Gordon Jennings. So how about we lock their asses up?"

Sounded like a great plan to Joel.

"You heard the 'lock' part, didn't you, Joel?" Cedric pushed with a tight voice. "I gave you that gun to protect yourself. Not so you could go in there and shoot the bastards to hell and back. This isn't about revenge."

He smiled at Cedric. "I understand."

Cedric's eyes widened. "Wait...*do you?*"

"Thanks for the gun." He strode away, knowing Cedric couldn't leave the shelter of the alley.

"Joel...*Joel!* Wait! Freaking sonofa—"

***

The elevator doors dinged. As they swept open, Joel wasn't sure who would be there to greet him. For all he knew, Morgan could be there with a gun drawn—

Wendy Hyde jerked back when she saw him. "Y-you didn't bring any cops."

"Do you see any with me?" He was using Chloe-speak. Just easier that way. He hadn't straight lied, but...sure, the cops were definitely close.

A tear slid down her cheek. "I want—I'd like to go home."

He stepped out of the elevator. Motioned toward it. "Get on. Get the hell out of here."

"He'll kill Gordon." More tears fell. "He told me if I didn't come back, he'd kill him."

Joel bent toward her ear. "Here's a secret," he whispered. "Even if you come back, he's planning to kill Gordo."

She shuddered.

"Get on the elevator," he advised her grimly. "Get the hell away from here."

Sobbing, she jumped onto the elevator. Joel didn't wait to watch her go down. He was already striding for Gordo's office. He passed the small lobby and waiting area. Marched straight into Gordo's inner—

"Ah, right on time!" Morgan Fletcher announced. He beamed at Joel from his position in Gordo's chair. He was sporting sun-streaked, blond hair, and his dark eyes gleamed. "So glad you could come for our appointment," he said seriously.

Joel's gaze swept the room and stopped on the exam table that had been set up about five feet away. Gordo was on the table. Strapped down. A surgical tray waited by the table.

"How did I do?" Morgan wanted to know. "I get that it's not exactly a hospital, but hey, I brought in the table for you. Would you believe the movers didn't even ask me questions? For the right money, I discovered no one ever asks questions."

Joel surged toward Gordo. "I'll get you out—"

"Why?" Morgan was still lounging in the chair. His feet were on Gordo's desk. "Why would you want to do that? I had to go to all of the trouble of drugging the man—by the way, I used the same drug that Stephen asshole used on our Chloe—and now you want to just let Gordon go?" A sigh. "You just aren't getting things, are you?"

He didn't see a way to undo the straps. What the hell? Joel reached for a scalpel. "I'll cut you out. I'll—"

"Now we're getting somewhere," Morgan assured him.

Joel threw a hard stare back at Morgan. He didn't like turning his back on the guy for even a moment.

Morgan lowered his feet. Sat up straighter. "You have the means in your hand. The means to achieve your vengeance. It's just you and me in this room. You can cut him to your heart's content, and then, if you want, you can let the cops think I did it." Morgan smiled as he rose and slowly closed in on Joel. Like a snake slithering ever closer. "How is that for a deal?"

He wouldn't take any deal from that jerk. "Why in the hell would I want to cut Gordo?" Joel demanded.

Morgan blinked. He looked down at Gordo. Gordo's mouth was covered with duct tape, and his eyelids were flickering as he fought to wake up. "Well, because he cut you, of course."

Joel shook his head.

"No? You don't think so? Don't believe me? You should. I studied him. When I made my first trip down to New Orleans, he caught my attention. He's been pulling the strings, and now it's time for those strings to get cut. Luckily, you are armed with a scalpel. We call that a fortuitous event."

"You don't have any proof. Gordo didn't—"

"I had some time to read through the not-so-good doctor's case files recently. You know, while I was enacting my evil plan. He treated Lucia Rossi. She was abused by her stepfather, but I suspect you know that. Your, ah, Gordo pushed her to liberate herself. To reach her full potential." A wince. "I guess she did that, didn't she?"

Gordo groaned.

"Then there was Kelly Addams. The woman adored her father. Serious hero worship. Then he died in an explosion and she was left with a drunk for a mother—a woman who abused her. Kelly started having terrible episodes as she aged. She wanted to strike out at those who hurt her. And what better way to strike out than with the instrument that took her precious father away?" He tapped his chin. "That's going full circle, I believe. Your shrink was very into closing circles."

Joel put the scalpel down on the tray. He reached behind his back and pulled around the gun. "Step back and put your hands up."

Morgan frowned at the gun. "Why are you pointing that at me? I'm on your side. I'm *helping* you."

"Bullshit. I don't know your angle, but it's not to help me."

Morgan's gaze rose to pin him. "Gordon Jennings viewed you as a psychological experiment—that is how he viewed many of his patients. He wanted to push you until you turned from healer into killer. As I said, I read his notes. He had quite a bit to say about you and the monster he believed you have inside."

Gordo. Chloe had suspected him, too, but...

"The scalpel is right there. Just pick it up. Slice it over his skin. See what it's like when he bleeds—"

"No," Joel snarled.

Instead of backing away, Morgan stepped even closer. He shoved his chest against the muzzle of the gun. "Do you know what the plan was for Chloe? Stephen was taking her to kill her. It wasn't going to be fast. Stephen Wakefield's file showed that he had quite the sadistic tendencies.

He enjoyed inflicting pain. He would have inflicted a great deal of pain on Chloe."

Joel's jaw locked.

"Lucia, Kelly, and Stephen are all tied to the bastard on the table. The bastard who tortured *you*. I have fucking wrapped him up in a bow for you, and still, you stand here and do nothing? You are such a disappointment. I don't know why Chloe bothers with you."

"I think I hear jazz music," Joel told him in a voice thick with rage. "Coming from the street below. Guess we had all better just wait and—"

Morgan laughed. Then he reached under Joel's collar and jerked away the listening device. He balled it in his fist. "Better now?"

Joel didn't even breathe.

No, things were not better. They were one hell of a lot worse.

***

"I lost him." Cedric yanked out his earpiece. "Sonofabitch!" But, before they'd lost the connection, one thing had been very, very clear...

Jazz.

"Move!" he snapped to his men. "We are going in, now!" They swarmed forward and as they burst from the alley—

A redhead ran out of Gordon's building. Wendy Hyde. Tears streamed down her cheeks, and her body seemed to shake uncontrollably. Cedric grabbed her. "It's all right, it's all—"

"B-bomb!" she gulped. "Don't go in! He is going to make the building explode!"

Cedric's stare whipped to the building. *Fuck me.* "Everyone, get back! We need to get the hell back and set up a secure perimeter!"

***

"I'll need you to put down the gun," Morgan directed with a congenial smile. "If you don't..." He uncurled his left hand. He appeared to be holding some kind of key fob. The fob was in his left hand, and Joel's now useless listening device was in his right. Morgan lifted the fob. "If you don't get rid of the gun, I'll just have to blow us to hell."

"You're bluffing."

"I don't bluff. That is insulting. That's like saying Chloe guesses." He shrugged. "After Kelly Addams suffered that unfortunate fate at the hospital, I took the liberty of sneaking into her place before the cops could get there. I helped myself to a few of the bombs that she had ready. Now those bombs are here. So put the gun down, or we will all go...boom."

Joel laughed. And didn't put the gun down. "Bullshit."

Morgan lost a bit of his confident grin.

"You weren't in town then." He didn't think Morgan had been, anyway. "You were still giving your cover story to the media. You couldn't have gone in Kelly's place. You didn't do that—"

"You're right," Morgan allowed with a sigh.

Joel nodded. *Shit. I was guessing. It worked. It—*

"It wasn't me. It was my partner."

Now Joel did tense.

"You realized I had a partner, of course, when you found Chloe stuffed in the vault. It took two of us to seal her in. My partner got the bombs. He set them here, and then he gave me the trigger device. Happy now? You've pulled the truth from me. I think Chloe would be impressed."

Nothing about this nightmare made Joel *happy.*

Morgan waved the fob. "Give me the fucking gun, or I will blow us all to hell."

He studied Morgan. Tried to see…was this the kind of man who would kill himself? From what Joel knew, Morgan was an arrogant, manipulative, controlling SOB who liked to play with other people's lives.

"My finger is twitchy. Give me the gun, *now.*"

Joel heard the elevator ding. He'd been staring straight at Morgan, Morgan had been smirking back, and the air had been so still and silent. The ding of the elevator seemed incredibly loud.

"Who could that be?" Morgan mused. "You sent Wendy downstairs—how very chivalrous of you, by the way. So now who do we have coming to join our party? It won't be the cops. Wendy will have told them about the bombs, so they will be staying back. *Who. Could. It. Be?*"

It was obvious by his confident air that the jerk figured his partner would be coming in to help him. "You're going to kill me and Gordo," Joel said as he realized the plan. "Then trigger the bombs. You'll be long gone when you trigger them—guessing you can be a pretty good distance away from the building to get them to explode, but the cops won't realize that. To them, it will look like you're dead." Disgusted, Joel shook his head. "Another fucking fake death? Don't you get tired of repeating yourself? Someone needs to learn new tricks."

"If it ain't broke, why fix it?"

Why the hell—

"He's almost here," Morgan proclaimed. "I hear his steps. Don't you? You know, my partner could just shoot you in the back. How would that be for fun—"

"I don't think it would be fun at all," Chloe announced.

Joel's spine snapped straight. "You heard the phone ring, didn't you?" Joel asked without looking back. "Dammit, I thought your breathing seemed a little too steady."

"No." Her steps tapped across the floor. "I didn't hear the phone ring. I had a nightmare." She'd moved to his side.

Morgan's hungry gaze was on her. "Dream of being with the dead, did you, Chloe?"

"No, I dreamed that I never woke up. That I'd stayed with you all this time. The images were so terrifying that I jerked awake just as Joel was slipping away. Couldn't very well leave my partner to face all of..." She looked around and motioned vaguely with one hand. "All of *this* on his own, now could I?"

"You shouldn't be here," Morgan seethed. "You don't know what you've walked into. You don't know—"

"I know that you've been played, Morgan. Not a situation that happens often, but it did occur this time. The man you have bound on that table isn't the one who set up the murders in this town. He's not the one who hurt Joel."

Morgan's brow scrunched. "Oh, no?"

"No." A definite reply.

"Then who the hell did?"

***

"You can't go in," Wendy Hyde said tearfully as she wrapped her arms around her body and rocked back and forth. "There are bombs on the first floor. He'll trigger them as soon as you go in the front doors. If you want that man—J-Joel—to live, then you will stay out here. You'll wait—"

"She is a fantastic actress," Marie announced to Reese as they strolled up on the scene. "Look at those tears. That emotion. She should be in a movie or something. She gets to me, you know?"

Reese nodded. "Um, me, too. I want to believe her."

Cedric frowned at them. "What in the hell are you two doing here?"

"Chloe sent us. She wanted you to be distracted so she could get into that building." Reese waved his hand to said building. "But you were already distracted by this sobbing woman."

Wendy rocked back and forth, harder now.

"Chloe is *in* the building?" Cedric thundered. "With Joel? Jesus, I need to—"

"Chloe wants you to call the FBI Brass," Marie chimed in.

Cedric put his hands on his hips. "Why the hell would I do that?"

"Why, indeed…"

***

"Morgan, don't you see what happened? Your partner thought you would kill Gordon. That was his plan. He gave you enough rope so that you'd think Gordon was guilty of the crimes, and then he figured you would rush in to eliminate him…especially if you thought Gordon had been planning to kill me," Chloe added as she continued to stand at Joel's side. "Spoiler alert, he wasn't, by the way."

Behind the tape, Gordon groaned.

The muzzle of the gun still pressed to Morgan's shirtfront.

Chloe continued, "I know you like to think that you are a master manipulator, but in this case, you have been played."

"The hell I have!" Morgan threw back. "I have the power here, Chloe. Now get your boyfriend to drop the gun before I trigger the bomb—"

"Trigger it," Chloe advised him. "Go right ahead."

What? Joel's head whipped toward her. "Uh, Chloe…"

"You can squeeze the trigger and put on a lovely show for us all, but nothing will happen. Because the building isn't wired. There are no bombs stashed on the first floor. I checked before I came up to this level. Your partner lied to you. As I said, he wanted you to kill Gordon, but after you did that, then he thought that Joel would kill *you*. Everything would be tied up nicely, and he'd be free. But that's not what happened. And you don't get to—"

"He's going to pull the trigger, Chloe," Joel snarled. He could see the truth in Morgan's eyes.

Shit. He was—

Morgan squeezed the device in his hand. Joel automatically whirled and grabbed Chloe. He wrapped his arms around her and held her close as he waited for the explosion—

Nothing happened.

"Like I said," Chloe murmured, as cool as could be. "There were no bombs on the first floor. How many times must I tell you? Your partner lied to you, Morgan. He set you up—"

Joel glanced back at Morgan. Morgan threw the trigger to the floor. He grabbed the scalpel from the table and lunged for Joel.

Gordo grunted frantically.

Joel lifted the gun Cedric had given him—and he fired.

CHAPTER TWENTY-TWO

Morgan jerked when the bullet sank into his shoulder. He didn't let go of the scalpel, but he stumbled back, and his face was twisted with such rage and hate—

Joel fired a second time. Morgan staggered. Slipped. He fell onto his side even as Gordon grunted and struggled frenziedly against his straps.

Chloe's hand had reached for Joel as he fired. Her fingers hung in the air.

"FBI!" Agent Richardson burst through the open doorway. "Everyone *freeze!*"

They had frozen. Joel seemed rooted to the spot. Gordon had stopped fighting against the straps. Morgan was barely breathing. And as for Chloe...

She crept forward.

"I said *freeze!*" Richardson bellowed. "Joel, drop the gun, right the hell now!"

"He was attacking!" Joel shouted back. "Didn't you see him? I didn't have a choice! I had to shoot!"

Chloe knelt beside Morgan. There was so much blood. Her hand reached for his. Curled around his fingers.

"Get away from him!" Richardson ordered. "Back away, Chloe! Do it! Now!"

She didn't. "Joel, don't drop your gun. Do *not.*"

"What?"

Morgan's grasp was so tight. She needed him to loosen his fingers. "Don't drop your gun. If you do, Paul will shoot us both instantly." She looked up at the FBI agent. "Won't you?"

***

"You should call the FBI Brass because Chloe doesn't believe Paul Richardson was given any authority to take over your crime scene last night," Marie revealed as she stood just a few feet away from a sobbing Wendy Hyde. "Chloe suspects he lied about that. That he was at the cemetery for an entirely different reason, and when he was spotted, he just lied to cover his ass."

Cedric peered up at the two-story building. "Why else would he have been at the cemetery?" But the twist in his gut told him the reason.

Paul Richardson always hated Chloe.

"The question Chloe asked," Reese chimed in, "was this...is Richardson really such an inept FBI agent? Or perhaps were some of his mistakes deliberate? As in, he's been covering his own crimes for quite some time?"

Cedric whipped out his phone.

"And you shouldn't trust her, either," Marie warned as she pointed at Wendy. "Because everyone else in this little play is dead, but she miraculously survives with only a little flesh wound? I don't buy that."

Wendy's breath caught. Then she ran. But she didn't get far. Marie pounced on her almost instantly, and Marie brought her knife up to press against Wendy's throat. "You don't want to piss me off," Marie warned her. "I am not the enemy you want to have. Trust me, you push me, and I *will* carve you somewhere vital."

***

Joel didn't drop his gun. Paul didn't drop his.

"Chloe," Joel growled. "Come back over here." He wanted her *behind* him because he wasn't sure what in the fuck was happening.

Chloe's purse had fallen to the floor when she dove for Morgan. "In case there's a weapon in there..." Paul kicked her bag across the room.

Chloe kept pulling at Morgan's hand.

Paul shook his head. "Always have to be ahead, don't you, Chloe?"

"I feel behind, if you must know the truth," she replied. "I feel quite foolish for not having seen your true nature sooner. I just thought you were an incompetent wanker, but all along, you were a sadistic manipulator with low self-esteem who only felt powerful when he was driving others to—"

Paul put his gun to Gordo's temple. "Drop the gun, Joel, or I will kill him right now."

Desperate murmurs and groans came from Gordo as he heaved against the straps.

"You're not going anywhere," Paul assured the shrink. "If you don't take my word for it, Joel can back me up. He struggled for hours to get out when I had him on my table, but he did nothing except lose his energy and his blood."

He struggled for hours to get out, but he did nothing except...

Joel shook his head.

Then Paul...laughed.

Joel's blood iced.

It was the same laugh Joel still heard in his nightmares. The mocking laughter of the man who'd sliced into his skin, over and over again.

"Come on, Joel." Paul was taunting him. "You're the doctor. The healer. Aren't you supposed to do no harm? If you just stand there and let me blow Gordon's brains out, then doesn't that make you a killer?"

"No!" Chloe surged to her feet. She hadn't been able to get the scalpel out of Morgan's hand. Joel saw that the bastard was still clinging tightly to it. "It doesn't make Joel a killer. *You* are the killer. It's always been you. Never Joel. And if you shoot Gordon right now, that will still be on you."

Joel grabbed her arm and hauled her back behind him. He kept his gun aimed at Paul.

"Joel, the first time we met, I wondered if you would make any connection to me," Paul said. He laughed again. "Hell, I even taunted you back then with a profile about you. But you didn't put it together. You didn't see what was right in front of your face." His chin jutted up. "Neither did Chloe. Not so smug now, are you, Chloe? Here I thought you knew killers so well. But you didn't know me."

"Actually," Chloe's crisp voice rang out from behind Joel, "I knew there was a reason I didn't like you. I didn't realize initially that it was because you were a sadistic killer, but I did eventually put two and two together. Better late than never, am I correct?"

His face hardened. "You know *nothing*—"

"I know that you are the reason Gordon Jennings moved to New Orleans. I didn't get why he'd moved here originally. It seemed so suspicious to me. Then when the bodies began to mount—victims that I now know he treated—it looked ever so worse. Gordon seemed like the monster we were after."

Gordo emitted a muffled scream.

"The perfect fall guy," Joel agreed. Too perfect. He hadn't lowered his gun. He *wasn't* going to lower it. "You were setting him up every step of the way."

"I think Paul was involved with Wendy Hyde," Chloe added as her voice carried clearly. "She gave him access to Gordon's patient files, and then he moved in on his prey. He was in a position of authority—an FBI agent—so they trusted him. They let him get close. But he just manipulated them. He got them to do exactly what he wanted."

"Puppets on a string," Paul declared. "They were so damn weak. Getting them to kill was *easy*. Point and aim. Didn't even have to pull the trigger." His eyes gleamed. "Glenn Towers was a piece of work, let me tell you. I offered to look the other way for some of his activities, but the man told me to go fuck myself. Can you believe that shit? So I fucked *him* over."

"You are ever so clever," Chloe said. "I assume you were also sleeping with Lucia? That was why she trusted you and let you get so close to her in the dance studio. Did seducing Lucia give you an extra feeling of power over her? Lucia and Wendy. At this rate, I'm wondering if you were involved with Kelly, too. You seem to have serious issues with women. If I poke into your past, will I find some deep-seated mommy problems? Did you not get enough love as a child or were you just rejected so many times that you strike out now at the things you want so—"

"You're the one with the mommy issues, Chloe! I heard all about them. Like mother, like daughter, eh?" Paul taunted. "Speaking of family, I got your brother in my web, didn't I? Could have killed him if I wanted."

Joel took a step back. He wanted to maneuver toward the door and get Chloe the hell out of there. He knew Paul wanted her dead. Paul had always hated Chloe.

"You had Kelly blow up the Serpent to get rid of the security footage," Chloe announced. She didn't seem even vaguely worried that a rogue FBI agent might start shooting. Joel was stressed the hell enough for them both. "But it was more than just the footage, wasn't it?" Her voice was musing. "You were angry at Kingston. Why? Did he tell you to, ah, go fuck yourself, too?"

"Kingston should have been there that night! His ass should have been in the VIP room and he would have been gone!"

"I take that as a yes," Joel said as he angled his body to shield Chloe a bit more. "King told him to fuck himself."

"I wanted a cut of his take! That bastard was raking in the money!"

"That bastard worked for the Feds," Chloe informed him crisply. "So when you threatened him, you basically outed yourself. You realized that mistake too late, and you tried to cover your tracks with Kelly."

"This asshole is just making mistakes left and right." Joel realized that by talking to him, they were distracting Paul. If they could just distract the SOB enough that he lifted the gun from Gordo's temple, then Joel would take his shot.

"I didn't make any mistakes!" Spittle flew from Paul's mouth.

"Someone is bragging," Joel deliberately needled him. *You sonofabitch. You tortured me for hours. You thought you had the power. The control.*

"I got Stephen to shut her up for me before she could talk." Paul seemed so fucking proud of himself. "Wendy told me all about him. How he liked to hurt women but that he wanted help. Oh, I gave him help all right."

"Okay. I think that about covers it." Chloe's hand slid to the side of Joel's body, and she waved her fist toward Paul. "I believe everyone heard you. Thank you very much for speaking clearly."

"What the hell are you talking about?" Paul boomed.

But Joel knew. Hell, yes, he knew. He'd realized Chloe's game.

"I wasn't trying to get the scalpel from Morgan. Why would I bother with that when Joel has a gun? I just wanted the listening device." Her hand opened. "I turned it back on. Cedric and the others on his team just caught your full confession. I do appreciate your cooperation. Now, I'm turning it off once more."

Joel saw it happen. First in cracks—a tremble of Paul's lip. A flicker of his eyelid. A jerk along his cheek. Then the rage shattered through as he let out a guttural roar and he brought his gun up to aim it at Chloe and Joel. He was going to pull the trigger and—

Joel fired. He fired over and over again until the bullets ran out. The booms echoed around him, but he didn't stop. Paul's body jerked back like a puppet on a string.

Boom. The man in the dark stood laughing as he cut Joel.

Boom. Dirt rained down on Joel's face as he was buried.

Boom. His hands were shaking when he tried to return to his job at the hospital. Tried to work on a patient. Shaking so hard he couldn't hold a scalpel.

Boom. Chloe was lying so still. Being sealed inside a vault.

Boom. Paul was aiming his gun at Chloe. He was—

"It's okay, Joel." Chloe's soft voice. "You got him."

Joel's breath shuddered out. Paul was on the floor, and his body was twitching. Blood pooled around him. Slowly, Joel stalked forward. Paul still held the gun in his hand, and Joel kicked it away.

Paul's eyes rolled toward him. Blood spilled from his lips, but the bastard tried to smile. *Smile.* "S-see..." A hiss. "Told y-you..." His body jerked and shuddered again.

Then he went still.

Chloe's hand curled around Joel's. Her body pressed to his. "He didn't tell you anything. Like *I've* always told you, his profiles were shit."

Joel's head turned toward her.

"You saved my life. You saved Gordon. Something tells me your shrink will never call you a monster again." She stared straight at him, and Joel could *see* the love in her eyes. Chloe was unflinching. Strong. Determined. And standing by him. As she'd always done. As he knew she always would do.

"I fucking love you," he said.

"And I—"

"*Chloe...*" A ragged growl from Morgan.

Joel spun around.

Morgan had the scalpel still gripped in his hand. He was trying to crawl toward them—no, toward Chloe. As he stared at her, he lifted the scalpel.

"Morgan!" Chloe shouted. "Don't—"

With his right hand, Morgan drove the scalpel into his chest.

"No!" Chloe rushed to him. She fell to her knees beside him. Grabbed for the scalpel.

Morgan didn't let go. "H-help me..."

"No, no, you do not get to do this!" Chloe tried to pull the scalpel back.

Morgan's left hand came up and locked around hers. "I...can't...do it...my own..."

Joel flew toward them. "Let her go!"

Morgan didn't look at him. His eyes never left Chloe. "I'll...h-hurt...y-you..."

"Morgan, you sonofabitch, do you think I don't know what you did?" Her voice had gone ragged. "I figured it out. You bribed one of the staff members at my brother's treatment facility. You found out that he was admitted when he was fourteen, and you bribed them to get his case files. You learned what he was. You read his case notes. *That's* how you and Paul knew about my mother. You told Stephen to taunt me. You knew what my mother was. You knew what my brother was." Her words tumbled out as she glared at him. "And when you realized the Reese who lives with me now—when you realized he wasn't a killer—you knew that my real brother was dead."

"You killed h-him," he whispered. "My...b-beautiful Chloe...So d-dark..."

"I killed him, but I'm not killing you!"

Joel grabbed her arms and heaved her back. "You're going to jail, asshole. You're not going to force Chloe into killing you." He crouched over the bastard. Assessed the wounds. Tried to determine where he would begin—

"I'll...keep coming..." Morgan promised. "I w-won't ever stay away from her."

He'd already sealed Chloe in a damn grave.

"Stop me," Morgan wheezed. The words were almost a plea. "S-save...her..."

Joel reached for the scalpel.

"NOPD!" Cedric bellowed as he rushed into the office. He was immediately followed by about a dozen uniformed cops, men and women. They swarmed the scene.

Joel stared down at Morgan. The cops were watching. Guns were aimed. Joel swallowed. "He...needs an ambulance."

Gordo grunted.

"And Gordon probably does, too," Chloe added in her cool and collected way. "But FBI Agent Ricardson does not. He's far past the point of saving."

Cedric crouched near Paul's body. A low whistle escaped him. "How many times was he shot?"

"Were you counting?" Chloe lifted her brow as she studied Joel. "Because I couldn't be bothered."

***

The first ambulance sped away. Morgan Fletcher had been on the gurney inside, and a cop had ridden in the vehicle with him. Two other police officers had followed in patrol cars.

"Aren't you going to ask me?" Joel watched as the ambulance's lights whirled in a sickening blur.

"Ask you what?" Chloe stood next to him.

"Was I going to try and save Morgan...or drive the scalpel in deeper?"

"I don't need to ask."

He slanted a glance down at her. "No?"

"No."

Gordo was wheeled out of the building. He was on a gurney, too, only he wasn't strapped down. His hands were waving frantically and—

"Joel!" he yelled. He spied Joel and motioned desperately for him.

"Your cue," Chloe noted.

Joel ambled forward. "You need to settle your ass down," he warned Gordo.

Gordo grabbed his hand. "You saved my life."

"Saving your life also saved me and Chloe, so, yes, I guess I—"

"You're a liar," Gordo breathed. "You came here to save me. You're...you're not what I thought."

That was what he'd told the prick from the beginning.

"Uh, sir?" From one of the EMTs as he pressed his hand down on Gordo's shoulder. "We need to get you checked out."

Gordo let Joel go. The EMTs pushed the shrink toward another waiting ambulance. More lights flashed. More sirens wailed.

"Is it over?" Marie wanted to know as she strolled away from the side of a nearby building. Reese shadowed her movements. "Or will another bad guy pop out and attack us?"

"It's over." Chloe's words were confident, but when her gaze darted to Joel, he caught the uncertainty in her stare.

It's over. Those words had better be about the case, and not about them.

Chloe tucked a lock of hair behind her ear. "There'll be questions to answer. I'm sure the FBI and the NOPD will need to grill us. The FBI is certainly not going to like the fact that one of their own was a killer. Every case that Paul worked will be called into question."

"How many?" Reese asked gruffly.

"How many cases did he work?" Chloe lifted her brows. "I can't say for—"

"How many victims do you think he had?" Reese clarified.

Chloe swallowed.

Joel knew Paul's body hadn't been brought out. Not yet.

After a moment, Chloe answered her brother. "I-I fear there were a lot. He didn't just start with Joel. You don't wake up and suddenly attack someone that viciously without a build-up." Her stare fell. "You start when you're younger. You work your way up. Your confidence gets stronger. You develop a methodology. You get bolder with every success."

"Unless you're stopped," Joel pointed out.

Her gaze lifted. Met his. "Yes."

Reese slapped his hand on Joel's shoulder. "Then it's a good thing you stopped him."

Joel held Chloe's gaze. "How many times did I fire?"

"The gun jammed after the seventh bullet."

He'd known that she was counting.

He extended his hand toward her. She stared at his fingers. Then reached out to him. When his fingers twined with hers, Joel slowly exhaled.

CHAPTER TWENTY-THREE

Machines beeped all around him. A steady, monotonous beep that pulled him from sleep. Morgan opened his eyes and squinted at the brightness that filled the room. He tried to lift his hand up to shield his eyes, but something tugged on his wrist.

"That's a handcuff. Cedric cuffed you to the bed."

His head turned to the left—toward the voice with the slight British accent. Chloe.

She smiled at him. "There's an IV in your other arm. Try not to pull it out. I'm afraid you are quite in need of the drugs that are being pumped into you."

"You...care." His voice was rusty, and his throat hurt like hell.

Chloe leaned closer to him. "I care...that you stay healthy enough so that you can fully enjoy the life that waits for you."

His eyes swept over her face. "You're beautiful."

"And you're on a great batch of drugs. I do hope you'll be able to remember the words I tell you now."

"Don't get any closer to him."

Chloe glanced over her shoulder. "I won't, officer. Promise." Then she looked back at Morgan. "Do you have any idea what you've done?"

He wasn't dead. That truth had penetrated the drug euphoria around him. And if he wasn't dead...

"You trusted the wrong man. You don't usually make mistakes like that. I suppose you thought...what...the enemy of your enemy could be your new best friend? Did the two of you first connect when you were down in New Orleans the first time?" She didn't wait for his answer but shook her head. "Paul never intended to help you disappear. He just wanted you to be his fall guy."

"I...didn't want to disappear...not without you." Didn't Chloe get it? He'd come back, for her. She was the only one who'd ever understood him. She was the only one who knew what it was like to feel the darkness inside and to know it wanted *out*.

"I realize you tailed Stephen to the cemetery. You killed him. Not because of anything he planned to do to me, but because you wanted to do it. Then, you and Paul sealed me inside the vault with Stephen. After that, you ran the whole elaborate play where you attempted to run down Paul outside the cemetery. Clever. That made him look as if he had no involvement with you."

"I clipped him...for fun. That had not been part...of the original plan." Not a hard enough clip to do permanent damage, but enough so that Paul would realize Morgan wasn't one of his experiments.

"The original plan. Right."

"You are so f-fucking gorgeous. I have missed—"

"Morgan, you put me in a grave with a dead body. I read the autopsy report that Ruben prepared. He thinks Stephen Wakefield was actually alive when you sealed us up. He died in the vault with me. His blood was all around me. On me."

Morgan started to smile.

"You knew I hate blood. And you still put me through that nightmare."

"W-wanted you to see...nothing to fear."

Her eyebrows climbed. "You think you made me face my greatest fear? Oh, no, not even close. That's not what I fear the most."

It...wasn't?

"You also thought you'd make Joel leave. You tried scaring him away before, but it didn't work. This time, I supposed you believed that by threatening me, you could get him to walk away?"

Yes, he had. Morgan's greatest wish...was that he could have killed Joel Landry.

"It won't happen." Chloe stared straight into his eyes. Made him almost think she could somehow read his mind. "You will never hurt him. You won't even see him. Not ever again."

Oh, she shouldn't be so sure of that. He was a fantastic criminal defense attorney. He wasn't sure what all Chloe might think the cops had on him, but—

"Your DNA was beneath his ring. Stephen must have fought you when you attacked him. I gave his ring to Cedric, and he had it analyzed.

You're tied to Stephen by that ring. And Gordon Jennings will testify that *you* kidnapped him. That you threatened to kill him. As for Wendy Hyde—oh, she's quite beside herself now. She is begging for a deal."

Wendy Hyde. He should have killed her when he had the chance.

"She was involved with Paul. Feeding him all sorts of information. She knew what she was doing was wrong, but Wendy is claiming that love made her foolish."

"I...love you."

"No, you don't. You love the idea that there is someone out there who can match the darkness in you." Her smile was sad. "That's not me."

Anger beat at him. "If...I go down...I'll tell every—everyone about y-you..."

She looked over at the cop. Smiled. Then leaned in a little closer to Morgan. "What will you tell? That Reese isn't really my brother? I know you and Paul thought his fingerprints would be taken, and his real identity would turn up in the system. Yet another reason why you drugged Reese and left him in Lucia's bed." She shook her head. "Silly Morgan. I fixed that years ago."

"Y-you killed..."

"I killed my brother? How could I have done that?" Now her voice was louder as she leaned back. "Reese is alive and well here with me in New Orleans."

He grabbed for her. The IV burned in his arm, and the cuffs yanked him back.

"Settle down," the cop barked.

"He'll settle when I leave," Chloe promised. Her gaze drifted over Morgan's face. "You won't get out."

"The hell I won't. I am the best damn criminal defense attorney—"

"I'm going hunting soon. Joel and I are taking a trip to your hometown. I figure we'll see what shakes loose up there. This might surprise you to know, but I am actually pretty good at discovering where bodies have been buried."

The machines around him were humming and beeping faster and louder.

"Like I said, you won't get out." Chloe's gaze swept over him once more. Then she turned away. She took two steps forward. "Oh...by the way..." Chloe looked back. "While you do not know my greatest fear, I know yours."

"Chloe..."

"You wanted the easy way out. You liked the big houses. The fancy cars. The power you got in the courtroom—and the power you took when you played God with people's lives."

"*I love you.*"

"In your way, maybe, but if love involves locking me in a tomb, that's the kind of love I don't want. Thanks, but no thanks." Her gaze seemed so cold. "The cell will seem big enough, at first. But with each day, it will get smaller and smaller. Dare I say it will be tomb-like?"

"I'm not afraid of being confined."

"It's not the confinement that will get you. It's the loss of control. You don't have any power, Morgan. It's all gone. I know that is what you fear the most. Being weak. You fear it so much you would rather die than become someone else's prisoner."

"No, no, that's not it! I didn't want to hurt you!" The machines were doing a near-constant beep. "Chloe!"

She was walking to the door. Patting the officer on his shoulder. Leaving.

"*Chloe! Come back to me! You belong with me! Come back—*"

The door shut.

The machines beeped.

"Hate to break it to you," the officer drawled. "But that woman ain't coming back." He didn't sound the least bit sorry.

"Screw off," Morgan snarled.

He laughed. "Oh, man, those guys in prison are gonna have so much fun with *you*."

***

Joel pushed away from the wall when Chloe stepped out of the hospital room. "Everything okay?"

"Everything is exceptional. Thank you." She inclined her head toward him. "But if it's all the same to you, I would really prefer to leave now." She looped her arm with his, and they began heading down the corridor. "I don't actually enjoy hospitals," Chloe admitted. "They're too cold for me. And all the pages that blast on the intercoms just distract me. It's hard to focus when the pages are constantly sounding."

"I hate for you to be distracted."

She slanted a glance his way. "Still not interested in going back to surgery?"

"No. I have a new career path that keeps me quite busy."

"Um."

He wasn't sure what to make of her response. But he didn't question her again. Not until they were outside, and the sun was beating down on them. "Chloe? Are we good?"

"Good?" Chloe seemed to taste the word.

Joel tensed. Chloe mattered to him more than anything else, and the idea of losing her, of something happening to this relationship that had come to matter so much—

"We aren't good."

His heart squeezed in his chest.

"I think...we are better than that." A nod. "Something quite special, in fact. Something that I never, ever want to lose."

Relief flooded through him, and Joel pulled her closer. "So we're still partners?"

"Yes. And I hope we always will be."

If he had his way, damn straight, they would be.

Joel's mouth lowered to claim hers.

***

When Chloe woke, he wasn't in bed with her. It was still night. Chloe could see the glitter of stars above the bed—and she quite appreciated that view. Especially after everything that had happened to her.

Chloe slid from the bed. She was naked, so she picked up her silk robe and slid it around her body. After belting the robe, Chloe went in search of Joel. The search wasn't overly hard. Knowing him as she did, it was easy to predict where he might have gone.

When she found him swimming laps in the pool, Chloe paused a moment to admire the sheer beauty and power of his body. Joel probably wouldn't appreciate being called a thing of beauty, but she thought he was.

Beauty and strength.

She sat on the edge of the pool. Dangled her legs in the water, but made certain her robe didn't get wet. It was a good thing the robe only fell to mid-thigh.

She enjoyed the view as she waited for him to come to her. When Joel needed to work off stress, when the past clawed up at him, he often went swimming.

Soon enough, he turned her way. Closed in. He broke the surface near her, and he shoved his dark hair back from his forehead. "I woke you up."

"You not being in bed was what woke me. I missed you."

Water glistened on his face and shoulders. The moon shone down on him, and the blue lights from the pool reflected from beneath the water.

His hand curled around the edge of the pool on either side of her body. She didn't feel trapped, though. Quite the opposite. With Joel, she always felt...safe.

He might not understand how very important that feeling was to her. After a life where she'd never really felt safe—he'd changed everything for her.

"Do you know what I fear most?" Chloe asked.

"I don't think you're afraid of anything." His thumb brushed over the side of her thigh.

"Oh, you would be wrong about that. I don't let fear stop me, but there are many things I fear." Not being able save the people she cared about. Letting innocent victims die. Turning into a monster herself. Those three were pretty high on her long list.

"What do you fear?" Joel asked in his deep, dark voice.

Her hand lifted and pressed to his cheek. Stubble covered his hard jaw. Sexy. "The thing I fear most is losing you." She was going to be completely honest with him. She kept secrets from nearly everyone else, even her closest friends, because that was second nature to her. With Joel, for Joel, she had to be different. "With you, I can be happy. I can love. I can see more than just the dark parts of the world."

His head turned. His lips brushed against her palm. His eyes never left hers.

Chloe could feel the fierce pounding of her heart. "I held back on telling you the truth about the man in Dallas—the man you discovered with that shovel—because I feared losing you." She didn't say *the man you killed with that shovel* because Joel had too much guilt already. He'd defended himself, and if Joel hadn't, she knew he *would* be dead. "I hadn't told you everything from the beginning, and when you learned what I had been holding back, I was afraid you'd leave."

"And I did—because I was a fucking idiot. But I wasn't gone long, Chloe. I can't be gone from you. Maybe it sounds like bullshit, but I swear, I feel like you are part of me. When I'm not with you, I'm not whole. I love you. I need you. You don't have to be afraid of losing me because that shit will not happen." A vow.

She believed him.

"But at the same time..."

His words had her stiffening.

"I don't know that you should be with me. I don't want to let you go. But maybe there is something about me...something that is too dark. Paul picked me for a reason, Chloe. He thought he could—"

"No." She jumped off the pool's edge and into the water with him. The water splashed around them. Her hands curled around his shoulders. "He didn't pick you because you are weak. That wasn't the reason."

His hands wrapped around her waist.

"I've been digging."

"Of course, you have," he murmured.

"Paul was stationed in Dallas a few months before your attack. You worked on one of the FBI agents in his group. You saved the man's life, Joel. You were a hero."

He shook his head—

"You *are* a hero. That's why he targeted you. He wanted to take something good and break it, but you were his greatest failure."

Joel gazed at her.

"He couldn't break you. If he had, you would have carved out Morgan's heart with that scalpel when you had the chance."

"Don't think I wasn't tempted."

"Good doesn't mean perfect. No one is perfect. But you are as far from weak or evil as it is possible to be." That was why she was so drawn to him. Her own father had been weak. He'd been so in love with her mother that he'd overlooked all of the terrible things she'd done.

Joel wasn't like that. He didn't bring out the worst in her. He helped her to be her best.

Her legs rose and wrapped around his hips. "Any other questions?"

"Yeah, I can think of one or two." Gruff.

She smiled. "Like what?"

"Like...will you marry me?"

Her breath caught. Chloe stared at him, completely lost.

Joel laughed. "Damn. I think I just did it. Made a move that you didn't anticipate."

He—he...yes. He had.

"I love you, Chloe Hastings. Now and always. You are the only partner I want in my life." He brushed his lips tenderly over hers. "Will you marry me?"

Chloe really didn't have to consider the question. She didn't need to weigh it for pro or con merits. Because there was only one possible answer. "Yes."

"Yes?"

"*Yes.*"

This time, his kiss wasn't so tender. It was hot and wild and happiness was exploding inside of

Chloe. She kissed him with a desperate, euphoric intensity even as her body pressed greedily to his. Joel was hers. Her lover. Her partner.

Hers.

Just as she was his.

Her robe was floating around her in the water, so she fought the silk and pushed it away.

Joel eased back and exhaled in appreciation. "You were naked beneath the robe."

"It saves time being that way."

He was wearing swim trunks. Rather cute that he'd bothered, but they were in the way. She could feel the thick, heavy length of his cock pushing against her. She didn't just want him *against* her. She wanted him in her.

Filling her completely. Driving them both into oblivion.

Her hands slid between them, and she pushed the trunks out of the way. Her hand curled around his heavy length and guided him toward her—

"Chloe, you have to be ready—"

Oh, she was. Ready for the next chapter with him. Ready for a life with him.

Joel's cock brushed at the entrance to her body. He caught her hand and moved it back, then his long, strong fingers were stroking over her clit. Driving her need ever higher until she was arching and twisting against him. "Joel!"

"Now, baby. Now you are ready."

His cock sank inside of her. His mouth was on her neck. Licking. Sucking. His fingers strummed her nipples, and her whole body went bow tight.

He plunged in and out of her, and Chloe was lost. Just as lost as she knew he was. Her nails raked over his arms, and her inner muscles clamped fiercely around him right before the pleasure slammed through every part of her body.

She might have screamed his name. She wasn't really too worried about keeping quiet.

He thrust into her again and again. Her legs were around his hips, holding so tightly. And her mouth moved to *his* neck now. She licked. Kissed, and when she felt his cock swell even more within her, Chloe nipped him.

His whole body jerked as he came. Joel held her in an unbreakable grip.

"I love you," he whispered.

With no hesitation, with the past not chaining her, Chloe said, "I love you, too."

***

A sharp knock sounded at his door.

Reese groaned as he pulled the pillow closer to his ears. "I know! I heard her. It is so embarrassing, but what would you have me do?"

Another knock. Harder. *Fine.* He shoved the pillow aside and stomped for the door. He wrenched it open. "Look, Marie, you go and tell them to take that shit inside—"

Marie stepped forward. Her arms snaked up behind his neck, and she pulled his head down toward her. While he was gaping, she put her mouth against his.

Stunned, Reese could not move. Not a single muscle.

Marie jerked back. "I-I—" She shook her head. "You're not doing anything."

He should speak.

"Mistake. I don't know what I was thinking." She spun on her heel. "This was such a stupid—"

He pounced on her before she could get away. Reese scooped her into his arms and whirled her back to face him. "You need to cut a guy some slack."

"What?"

"When the woman he wants most in the whole world comes to his room and kisses him...it can stun a man."

She licked her lower lip. "So you were...not rejecting me?"

Rejecting her? "Do I look insane?"

Her head tilted as she seemed to ponder—

"Let's try again," Reese growled. *Not* the time for the whole sanity versus insanity discussion. "Hell, let's try all night long."

She started to smile.

And he kissed her.

THE END

A NOTE FROM THE AUTHOR

Thank you for reading SAVE ME FROM THE DARK! I hope you enjoyed visiting with Chloe and Joel again. Their story was so big that I just had to give them a second book. And I certainly couldn't just leave Joel's attacker on the loose!

I've got lots more stories coming your way. More characters. More romance. More suspense. And, of course, more happy endings.

If you'd like to stay updated on my releases and sales, please join my newsletter list.

https://cynthiaeden.com/newsletter/

Again, thank you for reading SAVE ME FROM THE DARK.

Best,
Cynthia Eden
cynthiaeden.com

ABOUT THE AUTHOR

Cynthia Eden is a *New York Times*, *USA Today*, *Digital Book World*, and *IndieReader* best-seller.

Cynthia writes sexy tales of contemporary romance, romantic suspense, and paranormal romance. Since she began writing full-time in 2005, Cynthia has written over one hundred novels and novellas.

Cynthia lives along the Alabama Gulf Coast. She loves romance novels, horror movies, and chocolate.

For More Information
- *cynthiaeden.com*
- *facebook.com/cynthiaedenfanpage*

HER OTHER WORKS

Death and Moonlight Mystery

- Step Into My Web (Book 1)
- Save Me From The Dark (Book 2)

Wilde Ways

- Protecting Piper (Book 1)
- Guarding Gwen (Book 2)
- Before Ben (Book 3)
- The Heart You Break (Book 4)
- Fighting For Her (Book 5)
- Ghost Of A Chance (Book 6)
- Crossing The Line (Book 7)
- Counting On Cole (Book 8)
- Chase After Me (Book 9)
- Say I Do (Book 10)
- Roman Will Fall (Book 11)
- The One Who Got Away (Book 12)

Dark Sins

- Don't Trust A Killer (Book 1)
- Don't Love A Liar (Book 2)

Lazarus Rising

- Never Let Go (Book One)
- Keep Me Close (Book Two)
- Stay With Me (Book Three)

- Run To Me (Book Four)
- Lie Close To Me (Book Five)
- Hold On Tight (Book Six)
- Lazarus Rising Volume One (Books 1 to 3)
- Lazarus Rising Volume Two (Books 4 to 6)

Dark Obsession Series

- Watch Me (Book 1)
- Want Me (Book 2)
- Need Me (Book 3)
- Beware Of Me (Book 4)
- Only For Me (Books 1 to 4)

Mine Series

- Mine To Take (Book 1)
- Mine To Keep (Book 2)
- Mine To Hold (Book 3)
- Mine To Crave (Book 4)
- Mine To Have (Book 5)
- Mine To Protect (Book 6)
- Mine Box Set Volume 1 (Books 1-3)
- Mine Box Set Volume 2 (Books 4-6)

Bad Things

- The Devil In Disguise (Book 1)
- On The Prowl (Book 2)
- Undead Or Alive (Book 3)
- Broken Angel (Book 4)
- Heart Of Stone (Book 5)
- Tempted By Fate (Book 6)
- Wicked And Wild (Book 7)
- Saint Or Sinner (Book 8)

- Bad Things Volume One (Books 1 to 3)
- Bad Things Volume Two (Books 4 to 6)
- Bad Things Deluxe Box Set (Books 1 to 6)

Bite Series

- Forbidden Bite (Bite Book 1)
- Mating Bite (Bite Book 2)

Blood and Moonlight Series

- Bite The Dust (Book 1)
- Better Off Undead (Book 2)
- Bitter Blood (Book 3)
- Blood and Moonlight (The Complete Series)

Purgatory Series

- The Wolf Within (Book 1)
- Marked By The Vampire (Book 2)
- Charming The Beast (Book 3)
- Deal with the Devil (Book 4)
- The Beasts Inside (Books 1 to 4)

Bound Series

- Bound By Blood (Book 1)
- Bound In Darkness (Book 2)
- Bound In Sin (Book 3)
- Bound By The Night (Book 4)
- Bound in Death (Book 5)
- Forever Bound (Books 1 to 4)

Stand-Alone Romantic Suspense

- Never Gonna Happen
- One Hot Holiday

- Secret Admirer
- First Taste of Darkness
- Sinful Secrets
- Until Death
- Christmas With A Spy